The Forgotten SEAL

The Forgotten SEAL

THE REAL SEAL
BOOK 1

RACHEL ROBINSON

The Forgotten SEAL
Paperback Edition
Copyright © 2025 by Rachel Robinson

Love N. Books Press
An Imprint of Wolfpack Publishing
1707 E. Diana Street
Tampa, FL 33610

www.lovenbookspress.com

This book is a work of fiction. References to historical events, real people, or real places are used fictitiously. Any similarity to real persons, living or dead, is purely coincidental and not intended by the author.

All brand names and product names used in this book are trademarks, registered trademarks, or trade names of their respective holders. Wolfpack Publishing is not associated with any product or vendor in this book.

Cover design by Allison Martin
Edited by My Brother's Editor

The Forgotten SEAL was originally self-published as Black and White Flowers in 2016 by Rachel Robinson.

Paperback ISBN 979-8-89567-130-6
Ebook ISBN 979-8-89567-129-0
LCCN 2025942029

For anyone who has risen above their past.

The Forgotten SEAL

CHAPTER ONE

Carina

TEN YEARS OLD

THE LINES and imperfections in the wood surrounding me are my closest companions. There's a big black swirl directly over my head—right in the center of the roof. It's a long oval and solid black, with tiny lines that splinter away from it. The shape reminds me of a screaming mouth. I've told that mark since I was five years old that screaming doesn't work. We'll never escape. Not until he's ready to release us. I've dreamed about it, though— fleeing, running, finding something new outside of these all too familiar wooden walls.

The shed is nice compared to the dilapidated shed my friend Jenna has in her backyard. My stepfather, Greg, says I should be thankful. He's made it nice for me. He locks me in here when I'm bad, or so he says. I was a good girl today, but he still dragged me out of the warm house, through the yard, and sealed me in my *playhouse*. I asked for another cookie. One is always my limit when I'm lucky, but the house smelled so good, like sugar and chocolate, and my mouth was watering. I wanted one more small taste. My mother hushed me, but Greg still heard.

"She's fine, Greg. Leave her be. No need to bring her out there," Mama says, slurring. She takes a sip out of the straw dangling out of her Big Gulp cup. She won't say anything else to Greg. That's her fourth cup this afternoon.

I start to cry, wrapping my arms around my body.

He doesn't say anything while he leads me out the back door. The long grass is still wet, and it gets the ruffles on my white socks damp. My tears don't stop, and my quiet sobs make me hiccup and lose my breath. It's uncomfortable. I wish I had my teddy bear to hug.

"Shut your sniveling pie hole, Carina. Maybe next time you'll be happy with one cookie. You're such a disgraceful, disobedient child. It's no wonder your mother is so depressed. She has you as her daughter. I'm so sick of your shit. You're just like your deadbeat father." He tosses me in using one arm.

I try not to think about the words he says. I try to think about how it will be better once he leaves. Who will stop Mama from filling her cup again if I'm not there?

"Please!" I beg. Greg's smile is cruel. "I'll be good. I want Mama. Please. Let me be inside. I won't talk for the rest of the day. I'll stay out of your way. I'll be good. I'm good. Please. I'm sorry." I hug my knees against me. The pretty dress I picked out this morning will have black grease on the back. It has tiny pink and yellow flowers and green leaves. My grandma sewed it for me when I visited last summer. I went with her to the shop and picked the fabric out myself. It barely fits now. The arms are tight and the hem is a touch too short, but it's my favorite.

Greg shifts his weight from one foot to the other and

shakes his head. I pray he doesn't come in here with me. I can tell he's thinking about it. Not again. I've been a good girl. I back myself into the corner next to the bucket that I use for my bathroom. It smells, but I won't ask him to empty it. Greg will get upset. Like last time.

I pull my dress down as far as it will go, tucking it under my legs. I look down at the pretty pattern on the fabric, and a tear falls against one of the round pink flowers. It turns it a different shade of pink. A hot pink—like my Barbie doll's dress. I wish I had her right now. I could braid her hair and tell her a story.

I hear Greg's breathing. He's still standing on the step. He's not inside my playhouse.

Moving my head to the left a tiny bit, I let another tear fall off my nose onto a yellow flower. The wetness doesn't change the color as much as it did the pink. *Please*, I think. *Just leave me. Leave me. Please.* All of the muscles in my body stiffen, and I can't count my heartbeats anymore. It's beating too fast.

With a sigh, he slams the door, and I hear him lock it. He keeps the key in his pocket. I breathe out a big, long sigh and let a few more tears fall. Happy tears, though. It's over now. I lick my finger because it still shines from the oily cookie, and I hum when the sugar hits my tongue.

Crawling over to the loose wooden floorboard, I pull out my book. I could read it when I was six, so it's meant for children younger than I am, but it's the only one I've been able to sneak in. It's about a dirty, white kitten that no one wants. He lives in a beautiful candy shop. All of his siblings get adopted, but not him. One day, a sad girl enters the shop, and the candy man gives the dirty, white kitten to her. It cheers her up. You know what happens when she takes the kitten home? Her mama accidentally

3

dyes his hair blue! It washes out, of course, but that kitten is the talk of the town. The girl isn't sad anymore, and the white kitten looks beautiful.

Ever since I read the story, I've wanted my very own white kitten. A kitten no one loves. I would love that kitten more than any kitten on the planet.

The edges of the book are folded, and the pages are turning brown from being in here. I try to smooth the bends down and place it back in its hiding spot. Greg would be angry if he knew it was in here. He says I don't deserve anything. I guess I am a bad girl.

This is the part I hate the most. I don't have anyone to talk to. All my toys are inside.

There's a tiny window in the corner of my playhouse. I slide a wooden apple crate over and stand on my tiptoes to see outside. I watch and watch. There's an oversized gardenia bush that covers half of the rectangular window. If I press my nose close to the glass, I can almost smell the sweet flowers. Sometimes I'll pretend I'm a florist and my specialty is gardenias. I spread them around the wooden playhouse, and the scent fills the air. My bathroom doesn't smell bad when I play that game.

I'm not scared when the sun goes down. I know what to expect. He never comes back at nighttime. He'll fall asleep in the living room, on his reclining chair, a cigarette in between his fingers and a brown bottle between his legs. He won't come back until morning, and Mama will be happy then. Her Big Gulp cup will still be in the dishwasher. No fills yet.

I smile at the white flowers scraping against my window as the world darkens. The back of my dress isn't too dirty. I scrub some of the black off of my dress using spit. I'm clean. The lines and swirls in the natural wood change now. They turn into different characters. I can stay up as late as I want, talking to them. I lie right in the center of the floor, folding the dark gray sheet in half twice so it's thick enough to keep me warm. I like to wait for the world to turn black and white before finally closing my eyes.

Black and white is safe.

CHAPTER TWO
Smith

"BABY GIRL, I told you I had training this weekend. It's not a surprise. We wrote it on the calendar together. Remember that?"

I grab Megan's soft hand in mine. Her nails are always manicured perfectly. White tips and a soft pink base on the bottom. She doesn't call it a French manicure, though. She calls it a *classy, natural mani* because *trashy* women get French nails. Everything about Megan is sophisticated. She's a southern stunner—Miss Georgia back in her day, and as sweet as a juicy, ripe peach. Her drawl is equal parts sexy and charming. She's a catch by any man's standards. I don't care who you are.

Her blue eyes turn down in the corner as she brushes wayward hair off my forehead. "I'm not sure you're ready for trips and real-life stuff yet, sugar," she says. I take her other hand in mine. She clutches me tightly, and I see her bottom lip tremble. "You're not ready yet. They should give you more time."

I've had almost two years off. Slowly but surely, I've worked my way back into the teams. Proving my worth was more difficult than Hell Week and initial training combined. After my accident, I lost everything to a hospital bed. Lying there for days and months on end while my body caught up to my mind. The blast that killed one of my comrades spared my life. I lived when someone else did not, and I plan to make sure the second life I was granted makes a difference. "I am a Navy SEAL, Megs. This is my job. You knew I would eventually go back to it. I'm fully recovered." I flex my bicep and flash her a grin.

Leaning over, she kisses the muscle I'm showing her. "It feels rushed," she replies.

Taking her chin in my hand, I bring her gaze to mine. Her perfection never ceases to amaze me. She doesn't have pores on her skin or a mean bone in her body. I'm still not sure how I got this lucky. I'll never be sure, honestly. "Nothing is going to happen to me, Megs. God isn't going to punish me twice. I think I have a better chance of being struck by lightning or winning the lottery than dying on a training trip."

A tear rolls down her face, cutting a path through her powdered makeup. "I lost you once, Smith." She did. So completely and utterly that it should be labeled as death. Sometimes in my dreams I write my own eulogy and say goodbye to the man I was before the mortar careened into my sleeping quarters on a base in Iraq.

I fold my arms around her tiny frame and pull her into me as she cries. I pretend less and less every single day. I love Megan. She is my fiancée. I've loved her my entire adult life. I cheered her on when she won Miss Georgia. I held her hand as we walked into a candlelit bed and breakfast to make love. I took her virginity, and she stole my entire heart. Megan is the woman who spreads a blanket on the hood of her car and stargazes, picking out the constellations with one pretty-tipped finger.

I lie next to her, and we drink sweet wine out of red

Dixie cups. I danced with Megan at our senior prom. I kissed her for the first time at the fifty-yard line on the high school football field. She wore a red cheerleading uniform, and I was sweaty and victorious after the football game. Megan and Smith are a real-life fairy tale. Or so she's told me.

She wears strawberry body spray. She's always worn it, but I don't like the scent. It reminds me of children, but I'd never tell her that.

I suck in a breath by her ear. "Calm down, baby. I'll be gone for a week. Then when I get back, you'll see I'm perfectly okay. I'll always come back to you. You're my Ophiuchus." A rare constellation.

Megan smiles and presses her glossed lips against mine. Pulling away, she says, "Your mama agrees with me. She thinks you need more time."

I loathe and love that she's so close to my family.

I clear my throat. "More time to do what? Wish I were the man I was before? I'm healed. I want to get back to my life. I'm ready. I am. I've never been more ready."

But my scars remain. They mar sixty percent of my face. I have one good eye and one good ear. My hair is still patchy on one side of my head, but it's coming in fuller every day since Megan took me to a doctor that specializes in hair implants. My arms shouldered most of the damage. The scars ripple up and down both; some of the lines are smooth, others are jagged, sinking deep into my biceps and forearms.

My hands have had the most work to ensure they work just as well as they did before. They'll never look the same. I used to have nice fingers. Straight, tan, with square fingernails. You overlook so many things when you're perfect. I don't mean perfect in the literal sense. I mean perfect as in whole. Oddly enough, my feet weren't damaged, and looking at them now, I realize how wonderfully made they are. It's true what they say: you don't know what you have until it's gone. "This is my life," I say. Sometimes she forgets I don't need to be doted on or taken care of anymore.

She closes down when she sees she's upsetting me. Drying her tears with her fingertips, she then folds her hands in her lap. "Sometimes I don't understand why you want to do this. Again. What happens when we have a family, Smith? I'll have to worry about you *and* the kids constantly. Do you want that for me? Is that fair?" It's not fair at all. This is the first time she's brought it up.

"You knew this would be the outcome. Being a SEAL is important to me—the only thing I've wanted to do my entire life." I'm sure of this. It's a sentiment that rings true deep inside my bones. Smith Eppington was born to be a Navy SEAL. The rest of his life falls around it. "This career is what makes me happy."

"Are you sure? It's also what kills you," Megan sneers.

Folding her arms across her chest, she looks to the side, and I study her profile. I do it a lot to try to see the things I should know by heart. Her nose is small. It curves up the slightest bit at the tip. I think this is the reason she resonates as cute instead of stunningly beautiful. Her black lashes are long, and she has this perfect chin that pushes out when she's upset or when she laughs. Right now she's crying. I can tell she does this when she wants my attention. It comes easy to her. Most things come easy to her.

Sighing, I stand up and stretch my arms over my head. "Let's not argue anymore. It's a week of skydiving. Just a ho-hum trip to Arizona. You have nothing to worry about. Did you still want to go see the movie?" It would be just like her to make us late to something that was initially her idea.

She stands in one fluid movement, the fruity scent wafting in my face. "You just don't get it, Smith. You don't. I'll get my purse. Go start the truck."

I take her orders. Sitting in the driver's seat with my red hands on the steering wheel, I wait for her. She appears, jaunting down the front steps of our house, a smile on her face. She's forgiven me. The way she always does. This is why I love Megan. Not because of the million other reasons I'm supposed to.

She bubbles on about her plans with her friend as we make our way to the theater. I nod at the appropriate times. She grabs my hand and sets it on her thigh. "I like doing that," she says.

Sometimes, but not often, I wonder if she's trying to turn me into the man she wants me to be, not the man I was. I usually shut down that line of thought because Megan is not vindictive. She's not capable of it. Still, it doesn't stop my mind from wandering.

Balancing the man I am and the man I was is an everyday battle, and Megan is the only one who can guide me in the right direction. The only thing I know how to be without her is a Navy SEAL, and I'm sure that's the reason she's fearful of me returning to work.

I squeeze her thigh, and she laughs. The sound forces my mouth to curve up.

The theater is dark and busy. The smell of popcorn makes my mouth water. Megan buys the tickets, and I stand in line for the buttery goodness. People bump into me, and teenagers gawk at my face. I'm not self-conscious anymore. Not since I started working out and found my muscles again. Let people stare. This is me. I'm a survivor.

"I knew it would be busy for the new Marvel movie, but this is insane," she whispers as we make our way to a pair of empty seats high up in the theater. The screen is playing some advertisement about not drinking and driving. We sit down next to another couple. Megan apologizes for bumping into someone's knees, and I sit down, taking up more space with my mass than is probably okay. Once we're settled, I hand her the popcorn.

After a few bites, she leans over and asks for a napkin. "I'll be right back, baby," I say. She squeaks an annoyed noise and makes a show of her buttery fingers by placing them right in my face. Maneuvering as carefully as I can with my girth, I work my way out of the full aisle and down to the side exit.

I'm rounding the corner, hurrying because the previews just started, when I run directly into a woman. Her oversized purse hits the floor, and the contents spill, rolling everywhere by our feet.

"I am so sorry, ma'am," I say, immediately stooping down to help her. I grab a bright neon pink pen and hand it to her. The woman mutters under her breath. Her shoulders are shaking, and she seems visibly upset. She makes a reach to grab the pen from me, but I see the moment she sees my scarred hand. Even in the dimly lit hallway, it's obvious I'm not normal.

She pauses, her unpainted nails hovering inches from her writing device, and then flicks her eyes to my face. "Thank you," she says, her voice whisper soft, yet clear. "I'm so clumsy." After she studies my face for a couple of seconds, she swallows and quickly looks away.

"Hey, it's okay. There was this one time when I tripped and ended up getting blown to bits. You can't possibly be as clumsy as I am," I tease. The woman is shaking harder now. She offers a small, false smile as she catches a tube of lip balm before it rolls farther. I reach for a notebook that's lying open and close it. Her name is imprinted on the front. Carina. Check. "It's just a purse.

No need to be upset. We're two tampons away from having the mess cleaned up anyway."

I put the tampons in her hand and wrap my hand around hers. It gets her attention.

She stops. I stop. She stands. I follow suit, leaving our hands sandwiching the feminine products. She doesn't make a move to pull away, so I don't either. Carina has brown eyes. They're huge. She doesn't need makeup to enhance her face. I noted this at first glance.

Her bottom lip quivers. "I'm so sorry. I told him it was a bad idea to come here on opening night. It's a madhouse. There are just too many people," she says as she hugs her bag to her body, finally taking her hand away from mine. "I'm so stupid for coming here. I'm sorry again. You're so kind to help me." She makes a move to walk away, and I let her. Her fear is palpable.

Smiling wide, I follow her back out into the lobby. It's quieter out here. "Carina."

She turns, takes a deep breath, and closes her eyes.

"It helps if you talk to someone." Anxiety was my friend when I first woke. I worried about everything. Mostly, that I would never get to do my job again. "Do you want me to go get your...husband?"

Shaking her head, she pulls the bag around herself. The large leather satchel is like a child's security blanket. "He'll be upset. I'll send him a text and let him know I'll wait for him out here. Thank you again...sir. How did you know my name?"

What kind of man would be upset? My hackles are up.

"Name's Smith. Well, Carina, it was printed on your very full notebook. Are you a writer?"

Her eyes widen, and the fear is replaced by confusion. My distraction is working. She nods again, her mousy brown bangs covering one eye. She tucks it back behind her ear. "I am. Novels mostly, but I've branched out recently to write freelance articles, too."

Self-consciously, I slide my hands into my jeans pockets. I watch her eyes follow them until they aren't visible anymore. A year ago I wouldn't have spoken to a stranger. Fear ruled my world. This woman, Carina, she's scared. I hear myself in her voice. She speaks about her job, and I can't help but smile at her passion. I ask if I can buy her books at the bookstore. She says I can, but she writes under a pen name.

"Well, are you going to tell me what that is? Carina the writer?"

Swallowing, she looks away bashfully.

"You wouldn't want to read what I write," Carina says.

My cell phone chimes. Megan.

Licking my lips, I glance Carina's way. She's already looking at me, her eyes tracing my scars. For a tiny moment I wish she were looking at my exterior before the accident. I don't have time to ask why, though. I need to get napkins.

"You should go. I'll be fine. Thank you. My real-life Marvel hero." She's joking, but the words hit hard. At one time I was a real-life hero.

Taking out her notebook, she slides a business card out of a pocket and flips it into my hand. My heart rate accelerates, and a warm feeling hits me square in the chest. My phone buzzes again. Megan. I let go of the balloon and sink back onto earth. "Thanks," I say, tapping the card on my opposite hand.

"My pen name is on there. My website, too." Carina tucks her hair behind her ear one more time and walks away.

I look down at the card. Greenleigh Ivers. Flowers dance around her name. I think how ironic it is that she uses a pen name. Essentially my life these days is lived under a pen name as the accident stole my memory. Well, parts and pieces of it, anyway. It stole my love for Megan and my childhood dog. It took from me slices of a beautiful life. It also took away pain and sorrow. The accident stole things of importance—because memories and experiences are what shape a person. I'm not who I was before it. I have the same name, but I'm a stranger in my own skin.

I watch Carina's retreating back for as long as I'm able to—intrigued, sad, excited, so many emotions vibrating in my mind. The volatility of the unknown draws me in.

"Smith, did you fall into the toilet? I was worried about you!" Megan screeches at my back. As smoothly as I can, I sneak the card into my back pocket. I'm not sure why I hide it from Megan. I'm not sure of anything these days, but I do know, for the time being, I want to keep the strange, beautiful, married woman a secret.

CHAPTER THREE

Carina

I'LL NEVER COVER this black eye. It's in that stage where it looks worse than it feels—all purple and dark black with hints of yellow. I pat some more makeup onto my left eye and glance at my sleeping fiancé in the reflection of my vanity mirror. The birds chirp outside my window, the dryer buzzes, and the coffee pot percolates. I've been up for hours already. It's when I write. It's unsuspecting—the beginning of the day. There's so much promise in the morning. There's hope for change. Hope for love. There's significance in a sun rising.

My fiancé, Roarke, brought a flask to the movie theater and was piss drunk when the movie ended. I waited for him on a bench outside, away from everyone else. I wrote in my notebook about a strange, beautiful, kind stranger. I lost track of time, honestly, and hoped to see Smith leaving. Not to talk to him, just to gaze upon his kind eyes and his muscular body. He's nothing like Roarke. Nothing.

As soon as we got back here, Roarke showed me exactly how upset he was that I didn't *act like an adult* and watch the movie with him. That was three days ago. Honestly, I deserved it this time. Something needs to fix me. Why shouldn't it be his fist? Claustrophobia controls more aspects of my life than I'm willing to admit. Fear cripples me.

"You're going to be late, honey," I say loudly.

Roarke moans, pulls the blankets up, and rolls over. If I let him sleep any longer, he'll be a vapid shade of angry. Instead, I pour him a huge cup of coffee, fix it how he likes, and set it on his nightstand.

"Roarke. Honey, it's time to get up."

Finally, he wakes. It's the coffee, not because of my voice. "Jesus, Carina, why did you let me sleep so long?" It's one minute past the time he usually wakes.

"Sorry. It's my fault. I was caught up with my work," I lie. "I'm headed to the café to work some more this morning. If you don't need anything else?"

Swallowing, I try to make eye contact without seeming frightened by him, and I smile. This tactic worked for me as a child. Abusive men are like mean dogs. Don't make eye contact. Seem happy. Smile. It makes them less likely to lash out. My stepfather was an awful man, though he's paying his penance now that my mom passed away from colon cancer—in hell. A drunk driver mowed him down while he was riding his motorcycle about a year after Mom died.

Thinking about my childhood gives me hives. Literally. I try not to dwell in the past or think of my mother. When I grew up and left the house, the face she would make when I left after a visit was embedded into my nightmares for days after. A visit to the house of horrors was never worth it. Although the house was left to me, I don't want anything to do with it or the backyard. I haven't returned since she died. A property management company keeps up on the yard maintenance and checks in from time to time to make sure everything is okay. I can't even fathom renters in there, so it sits cold and empty—a haunting reminder of the truth in my nightmares.

Roarke isn't nearly as bad as Greg was.

"I need a lot of things. None of which you ever give me. I don't know why I stick around here. Look at you. Do you even try anymore? Are you so comfortable that this is what I'm expected to be happy to have?"

Sucking in a deep breath, I taste my words before they exit my mouth. It's time for prudence, time to select just the right thing to say to avoid his wrath.

I look down at my jeans and T-shirt. "I was planning on putting on a sweater. The nice one your mom gave me last Christmas. Would that look better?"

Scoffing, he takes a sip of coffee and hums in delight. "A face transplant would look better, Carina. Go work. Make money. I'm sick of being the only one to pay the bills. Your royalty checks don't cover the electricity."

My royalty checks don't go anywhere near our joint accounts. A paltry fraction of my pay does. The rest is safely hidden in accounts my agent controls. I let Roarke believe whatever he wants. Usually it's best not to respond when he's in a mood.

I grab the pastel pink sweater that I hate out of the closet, kiss Roarke on the forehead, and grab my laptop bag on my way out of our house. It's a nice, beautiful house. Roarke owns, or inherited, better yet, his father's home-building company. He takes care of me. Even though he's cruel sometimes, I know he loves me—he needs me. I'm lucky to have him in my life.

I start the oversized SUV he forces me to drive and make my way to my coffee shop.

After I check my email, I make a list of the work that needs to be done. I have two articles to write. I should be able to finish that in an hour or two and then focus my attention on my current passion: a nonfiction piece on military soldiers and the effects of war on the psyche. Roarke doesn't know I'm working on this. No one does, actually. It's a personal project. I want to shine light on something important that I'm uneducated about. I want to help people.

I put out a request for interviews on my website a couple weeks ago, and I've called around. No one wants to talk to me. Stalking the web and Facebook for stories and information isn't helping at all. Who wants to spill sordid details of their life to a complete stranger? I understand. It's still upsetting to not have any leads.

I'm texting Roarke to ask him what he wants me to bring him for lunch, when my email pings with a new message.

To: writerpaint@memail.com
From: Eppydawg@memail.com
Subject: Interview me

I saw the ad you posted online looking to interview military members for your work article. Are you still interested? I have multiple years of experience, and like the ad states, I definitely have a story to tell. I'm active duty now as well. Would you like to meet for coffee?

Your ad did promise free coffee along with anonymity. 😊

In your service,
Eppington

Throwing a hand over my mouth, I let out a small squeal. Finally. And he's active duty, so he'll have recent stories that will be relatable to those seeking help right now. I can barely type a response with the excitement reverberating in my bones. Novels are fun to write and articles make money, but this will be something that may help someone. It could save a life.

To: Eppydawg@memail.com
From: writerpaint@memail.com
Subject: RE: Interview me

Thank you so much for getting back to me, Mr. Eppington. I would love to interview you at your earliest convenience. It may take several sessions to get the information I need for my piece. Is that okay? I understand if not. I'm sure you're a very busy man. I'd like to meet in a public place. There will definitely be coffee in it for you. (I'm sure you can appreciate my reservations about meeting someone after only communicating online.) And my undying, unyielding gratitude for the rest of time.

Café on 6th? You pick a time. I'm flexible Monday-Friday.

Best,
Carina

After I blow through the articles that needed to be written, I close my laptop with a smile on my face. I pick up Roarke's lunch from his favorite deli, let him know I'm on my way, and head for his Southern California office, careful to watch my time lest I be late. Or early. My phone chimes. It's already a reply email from my military man.

To: writerpaint@memail.com
From: Eppydawg@memail.com
Subject: RE: RE: Interview me

How are you so sure I'm a Mr. Eppington?
Looking for a date along with an interview, are you?

I can meet you tomorrow at 5:30 p.m. Does that work?

Eppington (Mr.)

My stomach flutters. I'm not sure what reason forces my hand, but I delete the emails off my phone. Roarke would never go through my personal emails, but if he did, it would be bad. I'm not supposed to keep things from him. He likes to know *everything* even though he cares about nothing. Then realization hits me. How am I going to get away with a late-afternoon meeting? Roarke will come home from work and expect dinner and a drink—a la' Betty Draper style. I never leave in the afternoons.

The mere thought of lying to him makes me sweaty. My sweater sticks to me as I exit my vehicle and make my way into his office. The very pretty secretary, who I'm sure never does anything wrong, greets me with a cheery smile and a wave.

"Carina. You look beautiful today! So good to see you. I'll let him know you're here with lunch. Wait here a sec, please?"

I nod and run my fingers through my hair. I hope he's not embarrassed by how I look. I'll be mortified if he is. He'll never get mad at me in public, but when we get home, it's even worse.

I was distracted by the email, so I didn't check my face in the mirror. The one good thing about black eyes and living in San Diego is that I can always hide my face with large sunglasses. No one questions it. Not even now, standing in the lobby of the expansive office. There's so much sunlight pouring in that it requires shades.

The secretary returns moments later with a frown

perched on her face. "He left a note for you to leave his lunch and go. He just left for an inspection."

Panicked, I look at my watch. I'm on time. Perfectly so. "I'll head back then," I murmur. I try to keep my shoulders back and head high. It's how confident people walk. I remember to smile and look approachable. I close his office door behind me and take in a deep breath.

I scribble a note for Roarke, leave his lunch in the mini fridge in the corner, and take a quick visual sweep of his desk. He has a framed photo of me. I look happy, but I'm not. My smile is wide and white. My cheekbones carve a subtle line in the sides of my face. An attribute my father passed down to me, or so my grandma explained. I'm wearing makeup, and my appearance is blessedly free of kisses from his fist. It was taken at his work Christmas party last year. I'm always *on* at his work functions. The image makes my head feel light.

How long will I feign happiness? When will true contentment with Roarke commence? I just need more time. Something is fundamentally wrong with me, I know. Any woman would be lucky to have my life. A tear forms in the corner of my eye, under my sunglasses. I leave it there for fear of wiping away the precious cover-up.

I'm happy. I am.

I open a side drawer in his desk, looking for a small pack of tissues. He keeps a package in his desk at home, but I find three loose condoms instead. Closing the drawer with a loud bang, I leave Roarke's office. I shouldn't have snooped in his things. It's my fault. A couple of years ago I caught him cheating on me with his partner's wife. No one knows except me. Since then he's promised that he's been faithful. Sometimes a woman has to deal with certain things in life. This is my penance. We have never used condoms. At least he's being safe.

I'm happy.

I wave at the blond, bubbly secretary on my way out the door. She calls out a goodbye at my back, but I don't respond. I'm too upset. Plus, I can't confirm she's not the one he's cheating with. What a fool I must look like.

Climbing into my car, I turn it on and grab my cell phone. I email back the military man and confirm the date and time. I'll do whatever I have to do to make it work out. Talking to a stranger is something I need for my mental health.

I hold little to no control over my life. I'm flailing, drowning in an ocean of pain and grief. Something has to change. It needs to, because the more time that passes, the stronger my outlook on the world gets.

It's better off without me in it.

CHAPTER FOUR

Smith

"YOU'RE FUCKING STRONG, DUDE," Moose says.

Weights clank, and the heavy metal music blasting through the speakers fades into another softer song. Sweat is pouring off my body as I bench the weight. It's a new PR for me. Moose is spotting me from behind as I lie on the bench and put the weight up on the rack. Done.

I'm out of breath, and my arms feel like Jell-O when I sit up. Bending over, I put my forearms on my knees and attempt to catch my breath. "I've been trying to get that bitch up for a week now. Thanks, man," I reply through jagged breaths. "Fuck, it feels good to be back." Moving out of his way, I grab my water bottle and let him adjust the weight for his turn.

"It's good to have you back, man. I'm sure Miss America doesn't feel the same," he says, waggling his eyebrows.

I merely shake my head. Megan's pageant days are behind her. She teaches fourth grade now. I'd guess she's probably the hottest teacher that ever entered an elementary school. I cringed when she mentioned going back to school to teach high school students. Teenage boys. The guys at work will always only see her as a pageant queen, and that's bad enough.

I pull my arms over my head to stretch them out. "She's upset I'm joining in this work-up. We've been fighting about it. We've been fighting a lot, actually." A work-up is all of the training trips and the readying for a deployment. In other words, months and months of ignoring home life.

Moose throws some plates around and gets his weight on the bar. "Everything okay?"

"You know women, man. You never really know until it's too late." I laugh. He chuckles as he lies down and adjusts his lifting gloves. "I forgot you wear your little lady gloves. Have to keep your hands soft. Jacking off isn't the same with calluses. Right?" I grin down at him.

He smirks. "Keep your eyes on my lady gloves. Watch them beat your PR. Spot me," Moose says.

One of these days I'll beat him. Today won't be that day.

Typically I avoid looking at the floor-to-ceiling mirrors that cage us into the gym on our base, but today, I'm feeling okay—excited actually. I give myself silent praise as I let my gaze flick over the muscles that I built from nothing. Again. I keep Moose in my peripheral vision as he grunts and groans. "You got this. You're looking stronger than last week," I say. He is. He loads the bars with more weight and gets the massive amount up and down with little struggle.

Moose Perry is an all-around good guy. The size of his muscles is comparable to the size of his brain. He's handsome, like I used to be, and cocky because he is one of America's elite, but he's also funny and old-fashioned. He doesn't sleep around. Moose is on the proverbial hunt for Mrs. Right. Dating in this century caused him to lose faith in humanity, or so he tells me any chance he gets. I'm pretty sure the only person he lets set him up is his mother or his Aunt Ethel. Which should be illegal. I'm told on a semi-regular basis how lucky I am to have a woman like Megan. I guess if you hear it enough, you start to believe it.

I high-five his lady glove after he finishes, and we make our way to our cages. The cages are in a huge, dark, warehouse-like room. Each SEAL has his own cage with a lock to store our gear in. It doesn't house a quarter of our shit, though. Most of mine is stacked in bins piled in my garage and in every spare closet in our house. Megan doesn't complain, but I know most wives and girlfriends do. One even requested a house with an additional bedroom so boxes of survival gear and cold-weather clothing wouldn't litter the rest of her house.

Moose is in his cage right next to mine. We share a wall. "I have to tell you something. You can't repeat it," I say, peeking behind a jacket hanging in front of my face.

Moose moves his head so he can see me through the bars that separate us. His eyes widen. "Oh shit. What?"

My mouth curves upward. "It's not always something awful when I want to talk."

"It's not usually good, bro. The suspense is killing me. Out with it."

"I met this woman," I say.

He plugs his ears. "Do not tell me anything else, Smith. Don't breathe another fucking word."

"Oh, come on. She's a writer, and she wants to inter-view me. Anonymously," I explain. I leave out that she's beautiful and intriguing and sad. How my curiosity about her piqued the moment our gazes locked.

He sighs. "Why didn't you start with that? Don't you

even think about screwing up what you have with Megan. You don't realize how lucky you have it, man. She's stuck by you through everything." He shakes his head, eyes closed. "Megan is the needle in the haystack."

I feel sorry for him that he's still wading in the haystack, because no one deserves a great woman more than he does. If I didn't remember my friendship with Moose, I'd think he carries a flaming torch for Megan.

"It's truly just an interview?" he asks. Moose draws his eyebrows in as he surveys me, trying to peg a lie.

"Yes. I'm not lying. You don't have to watch me like that. Remember I took that course too. I'm reading you reading me. What do you think? It's a good idea to talk about it, right? She is writing a book or an article or something." I feel guilty because I don't have more information. I didn't ask.

Moose stares at me, his blue eyes unblinking for several odd seconds. "Maybe."

"Maybe? Who are you? Confucius? A lot has happened since the accident. Sure, I've talked to the Navy psychologists, but this is different. I'll be able to talk about the details. Stuff I haven't wanted to share before now. I'm healed. I'm on the other side now. Not that I look back with fond memories to the day that turned me into a gargoyle, but I still can't remember anything, Moose. Not anything outside of my military career and my parents. And you. You motherfucker."

He runs a hand through his hair. "Still? The docs made it sound like you were making improvements. You still don't remember Megan?"

I swallow the lump in my throat. I need to talk about this. It's obvious. "Made improvements in pretending to be the man I was before, yes. If that's what you mean. No. I still don't remember her. I probably won't at this point.

The doctors aren't sure because selective amnesia is such a rarity. I don't want to do psychotherapy. Megan respects that. She makes it a point to remind me of everything to do with our former relationship. Whether I ask her to or not." I pause to take a deep breath. Hearing the words spoken out loud makes my palms sweaty.

Moose looks at the floor. "Go talk to her then. The author, that is. It could help you remember. I'm sorry. I had no idea."

Because I haven't told anyone. Why would I? I don't want pity. Especially from my friends. It's hard enough to believe I'm their equal looking the way I do. My selective amnesia is something I need to distance myself from.

We say our goodbyes, and I head for the showers alone with my muddled thoughts.

I knew right away something was off when I woke from the coma. There's a certain face people use. It's an expectant face. You know immediately they expect something from you. It's a subtle human cue that most take for granted. Megan had that face about her when I woke and gazed into her unfamiliar eyes. Of course, now I know why the expectant look was tangling her features. I had no clue who she was, of course, and she assumed I would. Megan expected me to wake up and cry with happiness upon seeing her. She expected Smith. She expected love.

Selective amnesia is bitter that way. You tend to forget hobbies and relationships. I was happy to realize I knew my parents and all the memories that went along with them. I was even happier when my skills as a SEAL were deemed fully intact and functioning. Out of all the things I could have lost, Megan came with the least casualty. Is that because I don't remember our relationship, though? I'll probably never know.

I think about these things frequently. More than I let on to anyone. It's my cross to bear. I think of Megan with her boxes of photographs and photo albums she's put together in chronological order, all the hours she spends focusing on the life we used to have together. The guilt is enough to crush even the strongest man. So I pretend to remember. I laugh at the memories with her. I get wistful when I read that sentiment on her face. I laugh when I'm supposed to. I go gooey-eyed when it's prudent, because it's not her fault. Not at all. She doesn't deserve this any more than I did.

The lump in my throat is the size of Texas by the time I park in the café parking lot and fist my car keys in my palm. My house key pokes the sensitive skin that will never be the same on my hands. I'd compare it to a baby's ass. It's red and always raw. The skin grafts to get me to this point were painful. Everything about this experience is painful. That brings me to the present. Walking through the door to meet a woman I'm merely curious about. Guiltily so. I should be curious about the seventy-five photo albums that hold photos from my past with Megan.

I'm not.

I look both left and right when I enter. I'm able to pick out Carina immediately. She's sitting in a corner booth, her laptop open, a pair of thick black glasses perched on her face, typing away. Pausing, she brushes her bangs out of her face and then continues the tirade on her keyboard. I make my way to her slowly. She looks up the second I get in her line of sight and startles.

A funny thing happens. I swallow down the state of Texas, and an unfamiliar calm overtakes my body. I smile. "You must be the famous author I'm supposed to meet?" Taking a few more steps in her direction, I extend my hand.

Removing her glasses, she stands, takes my hand lightly, and shakes it. "Carina Painter. I'm trying to figure out how it's you, but then I remember I gave you my card. Smith, right?"

I nod and make a joke about giving information to strangers. She doesn't laugh. I slide into the booth opposite her.

Gently she closes her laptop and folds her arms on top of it. "Thank you for agreeing to meet with me. I appreciate it."

I eye her closely. She's hiding a shiner with several layers of makeup. Most probably wouldn't notice, but she knows the second I do. She slides the thick-rimmed glasses back onto her face to help cover it. Goose bumps prickle my skin, even though it's warm in here. It would be rude to bring it up.

She clears her throat. The tan skin on her neck draws my gaze.

"I have so many questions. I'm not sure how long it would take to interview you in person, so I thought maybe if you're comfortable answering some through email correspondence, it may go quicker?"

I tell her I'm not in any rush. That I want to stay here with her and answer every single question that crosses her mind. No one will give her black eyes if she's sitting in front of me, in my proximity. I order a large coffee and a sandwich when the waitress comes by and asks if we want anything.

Carina declines. "I'll have dinner with my...I'll have to eat at home tonight after we finish here."

I sigh. Her explanation is brimming with unease. "Fair enough. Where should we begin?"

Carina's eyes light up. "I'll start at the beginning. I want to write a piece, an article, maybe even a novel, depending on how inspired I get."

I hold my hand up. "What if I'm not inspiring at all?" I laugh.

She grins, a half smile pulling one cheek. "Then I'll have to cast my net again. It took months to get you here, so I'm really hoping you can be as inspiring as possible." Her gaze, for the first time, dips to my hands. I fold them in front of me. "Tell me about your military career. Just a brief overview to start. I'll fine-tune the questions after that. If you don't mind, that is. Everything will be confidential. Your name won't be associated with anything, and if this turns into a novel, it will even be deemed fiction. Fiction that may help someone, though." Carina glows when she speaks of her writing.

"As I am still active duty, I'd appreciate the fictionalized version. Anonymity will work out well for a nonfiction piece as well. Well, as I'm not in the habit of talking about myself or my military career, I'm afraid you're going to have to try a little harder than that," I joke.

Her small mouth pops open. "Oh. Of course. What branch of the military?"

"Navy. I enlisted straight out of high school."

My coffee arrives. Wincing when I grab the hot mug, I set it back down again. Something merely warm feels like scalding water to me. I blow on the black liquid instead. Carina scribbles down notes in a black-and-white spiral notebook. Like the kind you'd carry in high school. The white paper tabs get everywhere when you have to tear a sheet from it.

"I have a question for you," I say. "It comes off a little personal. If I'm telling you personal things, perhaps we can trade one for one?" It's a bold move. One I'm sure she'll shy away from.

With her head still down, she lets just her gaze flick up to meet mine. "Okay. What is your question?"

"Who gave you the black eye?" I ask, wrapping my hand back around the mug, owning the burn.

She raises her eyebrows. "The dresser. I tripped. I believe we met because my own feet got in my way. Remember?" Her smile is weak. She lies about this a lot. It makes me sick. I swallow a sip of coffee, my throat matching the temperature of my stinging hand. Carina doesn't look at my hand, though. Her gaze is locked on my eyes. She's sizing me up, figuring out what I really want. I see a shrewd knowledge about her. "My turn to ask a question now?"

I nod. She knows damn well I didn't take her answer at face value. "What do you do in the Navy, and how long have you been in?" In essence, she wants to know my age. I've already told her since high school. She has no way of knowing that I read people better than most in the world.

A quick glance around assures me we're out of earshot of café patrons. "I'm twenty-eight, and I'm a SEAL, Carina."

"Wow. I've read about your kind before. This is going to be awesome," she says, her eyes wide. Scribbling more notes, I watch her long fingers and unpainted nails as they move. "I know you don't want vague questions, but some are going to be open as it's the best way to get information. Can you tell me a little about your experience in that position?" She lets her gaze dart around the room. She'll be just as cautious and subtle as I will. Amazing.

"It's my turn to ask a question."

She sighs. "This is going to take a long time if this is how you want to play it." Carina tilts her head to the side and looks down at my coffee.

"What's the dresser's name?" I ask, my tone just as quiet.

She swallows, fidgets with the collar of her shirt, and avoids my gaze completely. "I'm really not comfortable talking about this with a stranger," Carina replies.

I nod, a smirk stretching across my face. Perhaps she'll understand. "Let me tell you the personal details about my life now," I deadpan. "One for one, I thought?"

She blows out a breath, and I can't help but focus on her lips and then the rest of her face. She doesn't wear a lot of makeup. In fact, I don't think she has much on. Maybe a little mascara, but her skin looks flawless but for her black eye and where she tried in vain to cover it up. "If I tell you my fiancé hit me, it doesn't just speak about him, it also says a lot about me. Sometimes you want to hide from facts, Smith. Is that the case with you and your military career? If so, we can cut the meeting off right now and pretend this never happened." She makes a grab for her bag sitting next to her in the booth.

I don't grab her, but leaning over, I gently touch her arm still on the table. "Whoa, whoa, whoa, no one said anything about hiding from facts. You shouldn't hide from anything. I'm here. I want to do this interview. I want to know who did that to you so I can do it to them. Marring perfection is a felony in all fifty states, Carina." I smile lightly, although every muscle in my body is coiled and ready to strike out. A man, a man who is supposed to love her for the rest of her life, beats her. She stays with him. The dynamics are confounding and infuriating, yet I don't know her. Now, it's almost mandatory I do.

"I'll answer anything else. Just please don't go there." She adjusts her glasses. I grit my teeth when I see the bluish bruise under her eye appear and disappear under the black frames. "Okay?" Finally she looks up. Her long lashes almost brush against the lenses of her glasses. They're dark and thick, and her brown eyes have swirls of green and gray in this lighting.

I pull my arm back to my side slowly. "What's your favorite TV show?" I ask.

She smirks. "Sort of an inconsequential question for a writer, don't you think?" Her face transforms with a tiny grin.

I swallow. "Sorry. I didn't bring my A game today. What's your favorite book?"

The smile widens into something more stunning, something I'm not sure is ever shared with anyone else. Perhaps this smile is just for me. It's the first time since the accident that I've had to remind myself I'm taken— that I have no right to own any of her smiles.

Tilting her head to the side, she says, "I don't have one favorite. At the moment I have one hundred and thirty. Wait, no, one hundred and thirty-one favorites." She taps one finger on the table to punctuate her sentence. It's cute. "*Crazy Good*. I finished that one last night. It's officially on the favorite list."

"Quite the list. I'd like to see it sometime."

She shrugs. "Sure. Your turn."

My answer is interrupted by the shrill sound of her phone ringing in her bag. Her sweet smile transforms into a terrified grimace.

"I have to take this," she says, avoiding my gaze.

I nod, take a bite of my food, and pull out my own cell phone. I open my email and start scrolling aimlessly. That's what you do when you're playing at ambivalence.

Carina answers with a clipped "hello" and wanders a few feet from our table, turning her back toward me. "We're just finishing up. Yes. Jasmine says hello," she says, her voice hushed. My hearing is still top-notch. "Sales are great. I'm pitching her my newest novel."

I clear my throat and delete a junk email with a left swipe. Megan tells me I should just unsubscribe, but that seems like too much effort. I left swipe another and another one.

"Uh, no, she's in the restroom right now. I'm making some notes. I'll be home soon."

I wish I couldn't hear this. As if sensing my wayward thoughts, Megan sends me a text asking when I'll be home. I hear Carina tell him she's at a diner several blocks from where we are. Another lie that doesn't come easily for her—a fact that makes my stomach pang with helplessness. She's a stranger, a complete and utter foreign body in my world, and I find myself caring about her well-being.

Honestly, I'm not sure, but it sounds as if my interview today will be cut short, so I text back "soon" and a smiley face. Megan sends back a weird emoji, and I'm not sure what it means.

Carina sits back down in front of me. With shaking hands, she places her cell phone face down on the table. "I'll have to get going shortly."

"Of course. Me too. I'll walk you to your car."

"That's very kind of you. You're a stranger, Mr. Eppington. I can walk myself out to my car." She switches her reading glasses for her oversized sunglasses.

I hold back the urge to point out to her what the man she loves and knows well does to her. "I was going to tell you a little bit about the day everything changed for me. In my career, that is." I hold my hands up. "It's not a conversation I'd have in here." Glancing around, I realize we're mostly alone in here anyway. "Let me give you something to work with until the next time we meet."

She smiles. "You're right. I didn't get anything yet. I'd appreciate that. Walk me out, please."

I pay the check against her wishes and hold the door for her. Her posture is nervous as she glances left and right when we exit into the parking lot.

I follow close to her side as she makes her way to her large, dark SUV. She unlocks the door with a fob, puts her bag and laptop case on her seat, then turns to me with a tape recorder in hand.

She looks me up and down unabashedly. Carina isn't judging. She's appraising. "Tell me, Mr. Eppington. Tell me about the day everything changed."

My skin prickles. My chest aches. I begin.

CHAPTER FIVE
Carina

SMITH'S FACE CHANGES. His soulful eyes glaze over, and then he speaks words that will haunt me for the rest of time.

"The day everything changed felt like any other day. I didn't wake up and have any bad feelings. Some people have those, you know? A friend told me he knew he was going to get shot. A prophet of death appeared in the form of a light breeze, and his reality shifted. He told me he was extra cautious that day while on the mission. That caution is what ultimately led him to take a bullet in his left shoulder. He was half a second too slow. Thank the stars it wasn't a full second, you know?"

I let out the breath I've held since he began speaking. "I don't know, but I know about intuition and sensing things," I manage to squeak out.

Smith nods, then looks away. "In retrospect, I'm glad I didn't know that mortar was coming—glad I didn't sense the impending destruction. Glad I didn't know my best friend was about to die. I would have treated him differently, behaved in an untrue way. I would have looked at my hands one last time. I would have cried. For a past I would never remember and a future that was unsure.

Mostly I would have cried for him. For his wife and newborn baby, for a friendship so solid not even selective amnesia could steal it away."

My words lodge in my throat. I have to try to speak twice. "Where were you?"

He grimaces. "In my quarters on a base in Iraq. I wasn't on any important mission, or saving lives that night. I was getting ready to go to bed, bullshitting with my friend Henry." Smith turns his eyes skyward. What is he searching for? A memory? "I've never told anyone this. So you know. It's hard."

My hand that holds the recorder visibly shakes. "I appreciate this, your kindness, very much," I say. I feel like a bully in this moment. I didn't ask for this specific information, though it will more than likely end up being my main focus. "You lived and your friend died. That's what happened to your—"

Leaning against the hood of my car, he says, "Yes. That's what did this to me." He lifts his free arm up in the air. It's hardly noticeable unless you're really looking for it, honestly. His face is still gorgeous in a roguish sort of way, and his smile more than steals all my focus anyway. It's a genuine smile. I respect it even more now.

"You have amnesia?" I ask.

"Selective," he says, smiling, finally meeting my gaze. "I forgot how to juggle and who my fiancée was." He laughs. "I mean, you have to admit it's kind of funny the extremes of it."

I don't laugh. "You're still with her?" I ask, my voice low. "And you don't remember her at all?"

Smith nods. "Of course I'm with her. It's a learning curve, for sure. I owe it to her to start over regardless of whether or not I ever remember our past."

This has little to do with his military experience, but I

want to know more. I want to know everything about this unimaginably tragic story.

I swallow. How can I ask follow-up questions after that? Standing out here in a parking lot while he bares his soul for my tape recorder. "I'm sorry. That's so sad."

He stands, straightening his shoulders. "Did you think interviewing a veteran would be happy, Carina? Or should I call you Greenleigh? You are wearing your author hat right now." He's not being rude. Not at all. He's truly curious. It is my pen name.

Clearing my throat, I say, "I guess I wasn't sure what to expect with the interview. I'm curious, that's all. I want to make a difference. You could have started with training or why you wanted to join the military. I didn't expect you to launch into a dreadful love story with death and destruction." I regret my honest word choice.

He laughs. "You didn't expect that, did you? I guess I've wanted to tell someone that story for a while now. The fact that you're a stranger makes it a little easier. Hand me your phone," he says, eyes twinkling. "Come on. You have to get going, right?"

Narrowing my eyes, I turn to rummage through my oversized purse for my iPhone and hand it to him. He shakes his head when he realizes it's not locked. Then he launches into a two-minute lecture about how I need to have an alphanumeric passcode on my cell phone to protect my personal information. He programs his cell phone number into my phone as he goes, glancing up at me every few seconds to make sure I'm listening.

Crossing my right foot over the left, I tuck a foot behind the other. I'm brutally aware of my self-conscious posture yet can do nothing to remedy it. "Did you ever think there might be a reason why I keep it unlocked?" I ask. *Because Roarke demands it*, I think. Even though I would never cheat on him. His phone is always locked. If that makes any sense whatsoever.

My cell buzzes in his hand, and he looks down at it. "Roarke says you have fifteen minutes to get home. Or else." He hands me back the lit phone. I tap a quick message to let him know I'm on my way now. Smith sighs. "Or else what? I can't, in good conscience, send you back to a man who did that to you. That makes me just as bad as he is." He lifts my sunglasses and brushes my bruise with the side of his thumb.

Although the gesture has no meaning behind it, I can't help but blush. I blush out of embarrassment and desire. This man is a stranger, but somehow hearing a tiny snippet of his life's story brings him closer. What will I feel when I know more? Why am I so anxious for that moment to come to fruition?

I don't desire any one thing more than another. I desire Roarke to be as dedicated to me as Smith is to a woman he doesn't even remember. What must a love like that feel like? "Don't be silly. I'll be fine. He's just joking. I promise. I really can't thank you enough, Mr. Eppington. For your time and for being so...open with me."

Smith brings his thumb across his lip and shakes his head. "Let me know when you want to meet again. Call me...I mean, call Sansa if you need anything. Okay?"

Clearing my throat, I smile and wave. I hoist myself into the driver's seat and take in a deep breath when the door closes behind me. I watch his broad back as he makes his way across the parking lot to his truck. I start my own vehicle but follow that blue pickup in my rearview until it disappears.

I call Jasmine on my way back to the house, telling her everything that just happened. She's my best friend first, but she's also my literary agent. Jasmine sold my first fiction novel for an awesome six-figure deal. She supports me as much as she can in all ways. She also pretends she doesn't know the extent of my relationship issues with Roarke, but it's impossible to keep things from friends as close as she is. I wouldn't say she turns a blind eye, but perhaps she wants to believe my lies.

Jasmine prompts me for more. "He even agreed to meet with me again. The material he gave today. It was amazing, Jaz. I mean, his story is better than fiction and just as sad as a Nicholas Sparks novel. I'm telling you. I think I can make this into something spectacular!"

"I've never heard you this excited before, Carina. Like, you're seriously mad-dog excited about this. Is it the prospect of the story, or is it something more?" Her voice echoes through the Bluetooth speakers in the cab of my car. I'm speeding to get home to Roarke as quickly as possible. *Or else.* Somehow having Smith privy to his cruel words disenchants me further from Roarke after today's condom discovery.

I'm not sure how to answer her question. "I think it's a little of both. He's so interesting. He has obvious scars from the trauma he's been through. I'm thinking he's going to leak his internal scars all over my laptop keyboard. He hasn't told his story before. Do you realize what I have here?"

She laughs. "You have your next bestseller."

"Don't be so money hungry," I tease. "This guy, this guy is one in a million. More than that, I think his story is one in a billion." I'm vibrating with excitement when I think about my tape recorder. I get to listen to it a thousand times if I want.

Jasmine and I bounce several story ideas around, and then I pull into my driveway. The dining room light is a beacon, signaling Roarke is home and waiting for me. "Hey, if Roarke calls, which I'm sure he won't, our meeting tonight was in person. At our usual café."

She swallows audibly. "Sure, babe. Call me later. Stay safe." She clicks off the line, and I make my way into the house. Passing my office, I reach in to hang my bag on the coat rack hook and make my way into the kitchen. Seeing Roarke makes me visibly ill. I smooth down my sweater, directly over my stomach.

"How was your meeting? Took long enough," he spits. A lowball with ice rattles in his left hand as he hunches over the dining table. "Thank you for lunch." An insult followed by a courtesy. It's always his way.

The mention of lunch brings me back to earlier rummaging in his condom-filled drawers. I could never bring it up. Not right now, at least. "My meeting went great. We polished some of the finer details for my next project. Did you eat yet?" I spy a bag of potato chips on the granite countertop.

"I'm not hungry," he says, standing from his chair. Roarke stalks forward. "You look hot right now, Care. Get undressed. I want to fuck you tonight."

I take in a deep breath. I'm getting off easy. He'll forget everything about my absence tonight. In between the alcohol and sex, my misdemeanor in his eyes will fade to black. "I love you too," I say back, teasingly. "I think you always look hot. Shall we mix hotness in the bedroom then?"

He laughs, but his smile doesn't reach his eyes—not like Smith's does. This is as close to the old Roarke as I'll get. I savor it. Roarke hasn't always hit me, although he's always shown violent tendencies. After we became engaged, his monsters arrived and made their appearance as a broken nose on *my* face. It's still a little crooked.

I take him by the hand and lead him to our bedroom. When the door is closed, I start my slow assault on his clothing. He loves when I take charge in the bedroom. It's the only time he accepts a power exchange. I don't care that he's using me. I only care about getting him off so he will pass out for the night.

Then I'll get to spend the rest of the evening in my office with my laptop and the tape recorder. Right now, I'll do whatever it takes to get back to my happiness more quickly. The cold hard facts are staring me in the face. I connected to a damaged, confused stranger in one hour, more intensely than I've ever connected to Roarke—the man I'm engaged to be married to.

As he kisses my neck, I realize this is it. This is what I've been waiting for. My awakening. The reason I am where I am. Where purpose meets something remarkable. I smile to myself, my thoughts bringing a newfound clarity.

CHAPTER SIX

Smith

I'M NOT DOING anything wrong, but I can't shake the feeling Megan might feel differently. I've yet to tell her about my meeting with Carina. I haven't even told her the full story of what happened the day of my accident. It's for selfless reasons. I don't want to burden her with anything more than she's already endured. Megan feels so much. My pain is her pain. It reflects in her eyes so delicately that it twists a knife in my heart. I got back from my skydiving training trip, and she cried the second she saw me walk through the door. She'd been waiting by the window. I think they were tears of relief, but I'm never sure anymore. She's distraught more than she's happy. I'm confused more than I'm moving forward.

I keep things from her in an effort to protect our paper-thin bond. Carina is on her way over to my house right now. We're going to continue the interview in a less public venue. It was her idea to meet at my place, and I wasn't in any position to tell her no. Megan is in Georgia visiting her parents this weekend, and essentially, I'm chomping at the bit to see Carina—to talk to her more.

When the doorbell rings, I jump out of my skin. As

Carina walks in, shoulders slumped and head down, I try not to look at her in any other way but friendly.

"We have an hour," she says matter-of-factly, smiling weakly as she turns back to face me. "If you have any monumental stories like last time, we should get to them first."

I can't help but return the grin. She's straight to business. A fact that should please me given our circumstances.

Carina starts unloading her leather bag.

"I started with the bombshell—literally, in our first meeting. Hopefully everything that follows will be breezy," I say.

She nods in return. She's hoping for more.

My nightmares returned the night after I recounted my story. I've been told most people have false bad dreams—scenarios of an awful caliber that would never happen in real life. My nightmares, bless them, are the actual night the mortar launched into our world, destroying it completely. Henry's smiling face as he joked about something he had for lunch. The green, watercolor screensaver on my open laptop; my hands, my scar-free hands clutching the rail of the top bunk as the whistle of the mortar pierced our senses. Reality forms my nightmares, and it's always too much to bear. I wake up in a cold sweat, praying for my amnesia to take something else. It never does.

As I close the front door, I catch sight of my neighbor across the street. Damn Mrs. Waters. She waves at me stiffly, her unruly gray curls peeking out of the bottom of her huge gardening hat. I put my palm up quickly and shut the door. She thinks the worst, and I can't blame her. Mrs. Waters, like most women her age, lives for the daily gossip. I'll have to tell Megan about the meetings. It's not a conversation that will be easy, nor one she'll understand, but my neighbor just made it mandatory.

Carina is perched on my sofa, eyeing one of the dozens of photo albums Megan leaves out to *help me remember*. It's Megan trying to forget. "Go ahead. Take a look. It's part of my 'therapy.'" I air quote the last word. Gently, Carina slides the album closer and opens it up. "My fiancée is a photo aficionado," I explain. "I think she documented every single moment since we first started dating." I laugh. Mostly because it doesn't make one damn bit of difference. The photos could be of strangers for all that they mean to me.

She looks up at me confused. "The photos are all in black and white."

"Ah. Yes." I swallow down the lump in my throat. It lodges there for several reasons.

"Why?" Carina asks.

I sit down next to her. "Can I offer you something to drink?"

"Sure, water. Please. I'll still want to know why, though. Are all of these albums in black and white?"

I glance at the photo she's examining. It's me carrying Megan in my arms. Running away from the camera into the ocean. Her blond hair cascades down over one of my arms. The caption explains it's a vacation cruise stop.

Heading for the kitchen, I nod, knowing she can see me. "Black and white lasts forever, Carina." I chuckle under my breath. "It's more permanent in some finite way, I suppose. That's how Megan explained it anyway. My memories are gone, but they're still there. On those pages. Color fades, sort of like memories. Black and white, though?"

"Is forever," she finishes for me.

I laugh once more.

"That's not funny. It's actually quite romantic," Carina

says, closing the thick book. Folding her hands in her lap, she fumbles with her tape recorder and scratches a few lines down in her notebook.

I scratch the side of my head. "Is it really that romantic, though?" I hand her the water with my question. I tap the linen cover of another album sitting on a side table. "These books don't contain my love story. Not anymore."

She unscrews the cap and takes a long sip, her almond eyes focused on my face. "When you put it that way, I guess it's tragic. I understand why she does it, but as a woman, I think deep down these photos are more for her. At this point, anyway."

I grin. "You stole my thoughts. I humor her. She's a beautiful, kind woman. I love her in a different way now. I respect her."

"I can tell," Carina says, tabling the water and leaning back into the sofa. It's a light brown leather that Megan and I chose a few years back. I don't like it any longer. "She's a very lucky woman."

I sit in a chair opposite her and lean back, folding my arms behind my head. "Some would argue that, but thank you."

Her gaze draws to my forearms. That's all it takes to get the conversation back on track.

Carina presses the record button. "Okay, Smith. Tell me why you joined the military. Make it good."

I laugh, and it brings a beautiful smile to her face. She shakes her head as her gaze darts down to her hands. Her black eye is healed. Her olive complexion is even and smooth. The way it should always be. She has the type of skin that doesn't blush, but it scars easily. That I'm sure of. "I was eighteen, and I wanted to kill Bin Laden," I say.

Carina tilts her head shyly. "I think that's why most our age got into the military."

I sigh. "It is and it isn't. I wanted to make a difference. In what way can a solitary man make a difference in the kind of world we live in? Truly, though. I went through many options when I was deciding how best my one human soul could affect the world the greatest. When I realized there's no way for me to cure cancer in one lifetime or solve the world's greatest problems in one lifetime, the answer was easy. Join the Navy. Become a Navy SEAL. Make a difference with my brothers beside me. Try to rid the world of bad, one bad guy at a time. It's a daunting concept if you really think of it."

Carina's eyes are wide and enrapt. I smirk. She swallows. "Daunting how?" she asks, voice small.

"Trying to make a difference by chipping away at a huge stone with a toothpick. I know I won't live to see the end of this conflict. Knowing that and having that knowledge is overwhelming. I wish I could do more." I open my arms to the side and clasp my hands between my knees. "I want to save the world." *I want to save you.*

"What a philanthropic heart you have, fine sir." Carina crosses her legs at the ankle and shifts on the sofa. My gaze draws down, but I quickly look away.

I lean forward, placing my elbows on my knees. "It's actually quite self-absorbed at the root of it. I want to die making a difference. A big difference, actually. I want to change something. Be someone worth remembering."

"I like that," Carina says. "That's a fantastic tag line. I think you label it as self-absorption, but it's not. Not really. You aren't what I was expecting. Especially for a Navy SEAL." She takes another sip of her water.

"I can't help the stereotypes they place on us, and yes, I may subscribe to a few."

She smiles widely. "You have the frog tattoo?" she asks, her voice more brazen.

I nod, eyes closed. "I do. You did your research?"

Carina laughs. "But you're obviously not a womanizer," she says.

I smirk. "Are you asking? Or is that an invitation?"

Carina's mouth pops open. "No, of course not."

I hold up a hand. "I was joking. Using some of that inappropriate humor we're stereotyped for, you know?" I laugh. "I'm not a womanizer. I've only been with Megan. Or so I've been told." I flash her a megawatt smile.

She shrinks back into herself a little more. "Noted." My sexual non-promiscuity is a little embarrassing, but at least it's an honest answer. Even now, with Megan, our sexual encounters are scripted and dull. I haven't steeled enough nerve to ask if our sex life has always been this leaden or if it's because she's afraid to break me more.

"I was just lightening the mood a little. This is going to get heavy otherwise. Can I ask you something personal?" I want to start our one-for-one game again.

She hits the pause button on her recorder. "I can take a joke. I'm not used to your humor. That's all. It depends on what that personal question is." She runs a hand through her ponytail, and I watch as another photo album catches her eye.

Standing from my chair, I pick up the offender in question and open the album on the table in front of her. It's a recent one from before I deployed and got blasted into smithereens.

"I'm giving you all of me here. I want to get to know you—the person who sells tall tales for a living, the person who hides behind a false name and big sunglasses. You have to know how intriguing you are to others." I sit on the coffee table next to the album. I'm close enough to touch her, but I won't. I'm thinking about sex with Megan and how lucky I am to have her.

She shifts again, and her skirt rides up a hint. I don't look. I'm merely made aware in my peripheral vision.

"There's not much to know about me. I was born and raised in a small town north of here. My mom is dead. My biological father, whom I've never met, lives somewhere in this city, and my stepfather, who was a monster, is also dead. I don't have any siblings. I've always used my writing as an escape from reality, although I mostly write sad stories, which doesn't make much sense."

I pick up on it right away. "Why doesn't it make much sense?"

"I write to escape sadness, but it trickles into my writing anyway."

"Why are you still with Roarke?" I remember his name from her cell phone. It's an awful-sounding name. It makes a guttural noise in my throat. I searched his name and found a company photo of him. All white, fake veneers, and bad hair transplants. The portrait of a wife beater. My skin prickles at the memory. I almost broke my iPad while I read his biography. From a well-to-do family, with a penchant for sailing and bourbon tasting. I wonder how much bourbon he had in him when he gave her the black eye.

She sighs. "That's the one place I won't go. Please. Don't ask. He's a good man. He really is. I have a lovely home and a nice life because of him. It's not fair to talk about him when he's not here to defend himself."

There would be no defending. I'd kill him outright.

"You couldn't have those things without him? I think you could. A good man would never hit a woman. You don't have to be afraid of him, you know? You could leave and never look back."

This is what I've learned about domestic violence. Women tend to blanket themselves with fear and never come up for air. It's a crippling, mind-numbing, reality-altering terror.

She smiles sweetly. "That's very kind of you to say. I

better be going now, Smith. Thank you ever so much for today. Shall we meet again soon?" Carina isn't ready to come up for air. She's not denying the abuse either. That, perhaps, is the best thing of all.

She stands. I stand. The black-and-white photo peeking up at me is Megan kissing my neck. My eyes are closed with a blissful smile arching my face. It makes my stomach hurt. I'll never feel that again. Not with Megan. And I'll have to pretend. Carina catches me staring. "You're very lucky, Smith. Very lucky indeed," she whispers.

I shake my head. "Luck never has anything to do with it. Be well. And, Carina? I want you to know something."

Gathering her things, she heads for the door. I open it wide. Mrs. Waters is gone. "What's that? I could guess, but you're surprising in that way. I can't predict what you might say next. With regards to me, it's very much a mystery. Tell me. What do you want me to know?" Carina's voice seems emboldened.

"That I'm not hiding from you, so you shouldn't hide from me either. I'm here for you. In whatever capacity makes you most comfortable. If we're going to continue this, which I hope we will because it seems therapeutic for me, then we should be friends. Give and take. Okay? Let me be there for you."

Her big eyes turn down in the corners. "Oh, Smith. You can't save everyone." She lays her smooth palm on the side of my face. The bad side of my face, the one that is hard to look at. Carina sees well past the surface into the uncomfortable, ignored zone of my psyche. And with such ease. Bringing my hand up, I grasp her wrist. She leaves her hand on my scars.

"I can try," I say, smiling.

"You can," she returns.

And so I will.

CHAPTER SEVEN
Carina

SOMETIMES STRENGTH IS DISPLAYED in unfamiliar ways. It doesn't look like the ass-kicking heroine in the latest blockbuster. She doesn't use a gun or have a sharp tongue. Sometimes a woman's strength comes from enduring. Going on—waking up and doing the same thing over and over again.

Since I began meeting with Smith, thoughts of leaving Roarke creep in more and more. Instead of enduring, I'm envisioning a life without him and his controlling dictatorship. These thoughts always end with me shaking with terror. I made a plan to leave him after he manhandled me last night. Luckily, this time, it wasn't my face.

I didn't sleep all night. I lay awake with fear picking my plan apart piece by piece. When it was time to wake up, I knew I needed my friend to take my mind off everything.

Jasmine sips her tea. "How many meetings have you had with Deep-Smith-hot-body?" She giggles. I love the sound.

We walk together through the farmers' market, shoulders touching. I turn my face up so warm sunshine kisses my face. "Four. Four amazing interviews where I question things about myself because of the stories he tells." I sigh and glance at her. "If I'm not with him listening to his stories, I'm thinking of them. This project is eating me alive."

She grimaces and shakes her head. Her black hair, cut into a sleek bob, bounces back and forth. "That doesn't sound good. So dramatic," Jasmine jokes. "Why are authors so dramatic?"

I smile. "Feast or famine. You know that better than anyone. This is feast. I'm feasting, Jasmine. Be happy for me." I wish I could take off my cardigan and tie it around my waist. It's a beautiful San Diego day. Roarke made sure that wouldn't happen.

She loops her arm through mine, causing me to wince. "I'm so happy for you. For us. Let's get crepes," she exclaims, leading me to our favorite food vendor cart. The sweet scents of sugar and butter seep into my awareness and lighten my mood even further. "I'm glad you called me this morning. I was slugging through my inbox on a Sunday morning. How depressing is that? Work on a Sunday."

She orders for both of us, and we take our paper-wrapped crepes and sit on the curb to devour the confections. In between bites I say, "I'm going to leave him, Jaz. I'm going to leave him, and I might need your help. In fact, I know I will."

She chokes on a bite and bangs on her chest in an exaggerated gesture. "Jesus, Carina. A little warning would be nice. Of course, though. Of course. What happened?"

Using my very best what-do-you-think-happened face, I raise both brows. She cocks her head to the side in confusion. I slip my sweater down my shoulder until the huge purple bruise on my bicep is exposed.

"I can't take it anymore. He's getting worse. There's no talking to him in a rational manner. I'm afraid what will happen if I stay, but I'm even more terrified of what he will do if I leave," I say, readjusting my cardigan back on my shoulder. "I'll need access to my account. I'm going to start depositing all of my money from our joint account into that one a little at a time so he won't notice. We've kept half of all of my advance money in that account, right?" Deep down I knew it would come to this. I didn't think I'd ever be brave enough to follow through.

Using one arm, she pulls me against her side and tilts her head on top of mine. I collapse into her gentle hug. "Oh, honey. I'm so happy you're doing this. We can do this. My brother will help out. Don't worry about anything. You can stay with me. Yes. The money is in there, and your account is safe." She exhales a huge pent-up breath. I imagine it's from years of watching her best friend go through torment and not being able to do anything about it. Her brother, Sean, is a police officer. He's always been kind to me.

"I'm so relieved," I admit. I take a cleansing breath. I'm okay right now.

She sighs and pulls away to face me. "You're doing the right thing. The best thing. Say the word. Whatever you need from me, you have it. You could have counted on me in the past—left him sooner. You know that, right?"

I absorb her words. "I wasn't ready in the past. Not like I am now."

My sunshine vanishes into shadow. "Greenleigh Ivers, may I have your autograph?" he says, his voice a perfected, low timbre.

Smith stands tall in front of me, a beautiful woman, Megan, by his side. "Why, hello. I think you've mistaken me for someone else," I reply.

Jasmine laughs, and we both stand.

Megan smiles. "Smith has told me so much about you. I'm a little starstruck right now, to be honest. I loved, and I mean absolutely loved, your first novel, *Pinion Lane*. I cried for days," she says, eyes wide.

Turning my face down, I shake my head. "I'm so bad with this." I meet her eyes. "I'm glad you loved it. You have made my month. Public relations aren't my strong suit." I laugh. She still looks a little stymied. As am I. Smith told her about our meetings, and he didn't tell me. I let my gaze flit to Smith. He's grinning.

Jasmine breaks the awkward silence I so eloquently created. "That book was my demise. I knew I needed it for my own as soon as I read chapter one," she gushes and extends her hand. "I'm Jasmine Chen. The business behind her creative." Jasmine bows like a lady-in-waiting. "I got lucky we live in the same city because she's also my best friend."

"Today she isn't my agent," I say. "Today we eat crepes without tallying caloric intake."

Megan giggles. "Look, Smith, she chose your favorite flavor." She motions to my hand. It's a simple cinnamon sugar crepe. I like it because I can taste the actual dough.

Smith quirks a brow. "Really? My favorite? Guess that one slipped the goalie, too."

Megan's smile fades. "Oh," she whispers. Her pain seeps into the air surrounding us, and he wrapswraps an arm around her waist.

I look over Megan's shoulder at the stall of fruit behind them. "You guys enjoy your day. Let's go grab our fruit, Jaz," I prompt. "We were going to make that pie. I bet they have some great berries."

Jasmine pops the last bite of crepe in her mouth and dusts the powdered sugar off on her khaki shorts.

"You're so right. It was wonderful meeting you both. Stay tuned for Carina's next masterpiece."

I elbow my friend. "It was great meeting you, Megan. Smith has told me so much about you. You're just as lovely as he described," I say, shaking her hand.

Megan gushes about my novel one more time, and we exchange brisk pleasantries.

Taking a small, strengthening breath, I let my gaze slide to Smith. "It was great running into you. Take care, okay?"

Smith bites his lower lip and raises his brows. The one on the left side of his face doesn't rise as high as the right brow. He smiles. It's the beautiful smile—the one that melts away anything negative. I'm too cynical to say that a smile fixes anything, but his might. "You take care, Carina. I'll see you soon?" Smith says, his eyes pushing for a firm date. The intensity in them forces me to turn my head down, and I nod.

Once again, Jasmine links her arm in mine and steers me into a crowded group of flamboyant men talking about wine. "What was that?" she asks. "Oh my god, Carina. That man. That man."

I furrow my brow. "That man what? What was what?"

Jasmine is known for turning a molehill into a mountain.

When we've separated ourselves from Smith and Megan, she spins on me. "You were all nervous in that I-think-you're-hot I love you way. Don't say I'm overexaggerating. I saw it all. Including Megan's face." Jasmine shakes her head, eyes wide. "He was looking at you the same way. I wouldn't think it was possible to gauge a look so thoroughly, but it just happened. Gaze sex. Put that in your next book. You were just gaze fucking."

I clear my throat as my heart starts hammering. What did Megan's face look like? Oh, god. My stomach sinks. "He was a perfect gentleman, Jaz. You're imagining things. He loves her more than…anything else. Trust me. I'm not certain about a lot of things, but this is one thing I know is a fact. Smith loves Megan."

"I know what I saw."

"You saw two friends exchanging a harmless glance." I felt more than that. How could I not? Even with Megan by his side, every nerve ending in my body was aware of his proximity and how elated it made me feel. I glance in the direction we left. Smith and Megan are waiting in the line to get crepes. His back is wide and his biceps look strong as they pull Megan's tiny body against his side.

Jasmine runs her hands down her sides. "Fine. You win." She holds her hands up in front of her in defeat. That says something because she never gives in. Not in any aspect of her life. I remember sweating bullets when we sold *Pinion Lane*. She was holding out for a larger advance, and I was scared the publisher was going to tell her to stuff it and take the book elsewhere. She got what she wanted, and now I don't question any of her business decisions. Her defeat in this moment says more than words can. She's right, and she's not going to argue anymore. I should be offended, but I'm scared of what that means.

We talk about nothing except fruit and pies all the way back to the car after we collect our supplies. Once we're safely tucked in the cab of my SUV, I know no subject is off-limits.

Jasmine clears her throat. "Please tell me that man isn't why you're leaving Roarke. I mean, in one sense I'm happy because it gets you away from him, but on the other hand, he's a taken man. A very, very taken man."

"You know very is a meaningless filler word. Don't

use it twice, Jaz," I say, avoiding her realization. There it is. Jasmine's accusing look I was waiting for.

"I don't know," I reply honestly. "I think partly. Not because I think I can have him, but maybe it's possible to have a good man *like* him." Saying it out loud forces reality to creep back in. Roarke. He'll never let me go without a fight. "And I need to leave him before it happens again. Regardless of the reason." I rub the side of my face. The place that still aches even though the visible wounds have long since healed.

I zone out as I drive, imagining different scenarios. All of how leaving Roarke is a bad, most definitely horrible, idea. Jasmine makes a phone call, and I'm vaguely aware that it's her brother because she says his name every so often. My name comes up a lot, but I've switched on autopilot. My stepfather's face looming over me flashes in my mind. His front teeth overlap. The right over the left. You don't notice it when he smiles. Only when he's sneering. His face morphs into Roarke's. Then the insults ricochet. I'll never be good enough. I'm lucky to have Roarke. Why would I leave him? This is what I deserve.

I pull into my driveway and put the SUV in park. My fiancé's European sports car is in the drive. He'll be watching the game, probably half-drunk already.

Jasmine grabs my hand. "We're going to get your stuff right now, Carina. Sean is on his way here with reinforcements. You will stay with me until we find you a place of your own. You have plenty of money. Plenty. Don't worry about that, okay?"

My skin crawls. I put my face in my hands. "No. I'm not ready yet. He's home. We can do it another time when he's away at work. He can't be home." I feel cold and hot at the same time. Sweat beads on my forehead, and my fingertips are ice cold. "I need to do this the right way. This isn't it. I told you out of confidence, Jaz. You can't do this to me." I'm panicking at the thought. My breaths turn shallow and erratic. I feel her hands on my back, rubbing.

"You don't have to go in. I'll get everything. He needs to see the show of force to know you're serious. Sean says sneaking away will only anger him further. This is closure, Carina. This is you standing up for yourself, telling him you want out. This is happening right now because I can't lie awake and wonder about your well-being another night. More so because you deserve to get out of this now. It's your life on the line. Your life."

I nod. She's right, but I'm so scared.

She asks if the SUV is in my name, and I nod again. Several other pertinent questions are raised in my direction that I answer with shakes and nods while we wait for the police. I give her details—gory facts of my life that I hide from everyone. Jasmine winces but nods firmly, her matter-of-fact business persona arriving to conquer. I show her the photos I took of the last time he mutilated my face. Photos I'm so disconnected from that it looks like another woman. Because, surely a strong woman such as myself wouldn't allow a man to do this to her. Self-perspective is skewed when you're living in horror.

I'm crying, mascara streaking down my face, when Sean and several other cruisers pull up to my beautiful home in my affluent suburb. The rest happens in a blur. Roarke comes out the front door in a pair of shorts and no shirt. His gaze finds me immediately. I don't have the courage to get out of the car. I can't. The car is my shield.

He starts yelling because he isn't half-drunk, he's full-on piss drunk at two p.m. Sean is trying to calm him down, and Jasmine enters my house, completely unperturbed by Roarke's presence. It's like she doesn't know what he's capable of, but she does.

A police officer knocks on my window, and I roll it down.

"Ma'am, we're going to detain him in one of our vehicles. You're free to go in to get your things. His words are enough for us to corroborate what we assumed and what you told us." He means what Jasmine relayed to him.

Roarke's gaze spits fire as he passes in front of my SUV on the way to a cruiser. It says he's going to make me pay for this.

On shaking feet, I hop down and walk into my house like a zombie. It looks like such an artifice. It's a stunning home where ruses are made. Stories of fiction and lies of love. Love never lived here. Not the real kind, anyway. This gives me the bravery I need to tackle the task at hand. I call out for Jasmine, and she calls back from my bedroom. I grab as many suitcases and duffel bags as I can carry from the hallway closet and drag them into our bedroom.

"Pile it in. We'll sort through it when we get home," Jasmine says as she dumps the contents of my underwear drawer into an open bag.

I wipe several tears from underneath my eyes. A text pings from my back pocket. I take it out and see that it's from Smith.

Tomorrow?

The timing is horrible and perfect. Will I be ready tomorrow? Nothing will help me cope better.

Yes. Usual spot.

Officers tell me about the restraining order and my rights and his lack thereof. They tell me comforting things, they tell me facts. Sean offers his protection while I stay at Jasmine's house. Everyone reassures me that I'll be safe from harm, but they don't know Roarke like I do. I push those thoughts to the back of my mind because at the moment, I am indeed safe.

Taking a deep breath, we finish packing the contents of my world in fifteen minutes flat. It didn't take enough time to erase me completely from this world. Fifteen minutes is what it takes for Carina Painter to vanish.

I'm terrified of the unknown. I've also never felt stronger in my life.

CHAPTER EIGHT

Smith

THE SUN IS SLANTING through the blinds in our bedroom, and half of Megan's face is covered by a streaking, black shadow. She's been upset since meeting Carina. A day has passed, and she's still talking about it. We just had morning sex, and it's still the main subject in our world. Sex did nothing to assure her that she shouldn't have any fears with regard to my loyalties. "I love you, Meg. You," I say, cradling her face.

She shakes her head, tossing her blond hair around. "I was upset when you told me about the interviews. You know that, but when you combine the fact that you're telling her things you're not comfortable telling me, and the way you look at her...I can't handle it," she says, pulling my hand down. "The way you looked at her. That look."

I clear my throat. It's a solitary look she's dissecting. It's unbelievable. "How did I look at her?" I clutch the sheets in my hand. "Since you're obviously a master in reading people and body language now." I am. She knows that.

Megan pulls the sheets up to cover her bare chest. "That's the horrible thing. I don't have to be an expert,

Smith. It was so glaringly obvious." She sits up, and the shadow encompasses her whole face. "I'm a master at reading you," she says. "That's what is important to note."

There is truth in her words. A poignant sentiment I can't deny no matter how I spin it. Isn't that why I'm with her? Because she knows me and us so well? "I don't want to argue about this anymore. I'm here. In our bed. With you."

A tiny sob escapes her mouth. She's a pretty crier. A fact that breaks my heart. I usually avoid saying anything that invokes it. It bothers me that much. "That look, Smith. It's the one that used to be reserved for me. I haven't seen it since the accident." Megan stands from the bed, her naked back exposed. She perches her hands on her hips. "It was so innocent, too. You had no idea you were even doing it. It was effortless."

I blow out a long breath and run my fingers through my hair. "You can't be sure. It was mere seconds, Meg. Please," I beg. "Come back to bed."

She told me I was insatiable before. Hopefully this show of my old self can straighten this argument out for good.

Slowly, she spins. My mind plays tricks on me as the angular shadows cut across her body. "I need you to be honest with me. You owe me honesty. I deserve it." Standing there, she looks so stunning, I'd agree to anything she wanted.

Her beauty overtakes my fear, and I respond, "Of course."

"I've given this my all—trying desperately to show you what we had," she says, shaking her head. "It would be selfish of me to even be upset about it, I guess. But you're not going to remember us, are you?"

I scoot closer to her by sliding to her side of the bed.

"You know I can't answer that. I promised we could start over and try to incorporate old memories with the new. That's what I can say as truth. That doctors don't know if I'll ever remember."

"You're a different man now. I'm trying to stay in love with the man from my past. That's not you, and if I'm being brutally honest, I know you don't love me. Not like you used to. Seeing you look at Carina reminded me of that." The look that destroyed everything. "The fact is you don't see me like that anymore, Smith. It's time we both move on. I can't settle for this." She waves her arm in my direction. "And you deserve to have happiness. I won't be the reason you don't."

It's twisted. Megan has been my sole reason for happiness during my recovery. On my darkest days, when I thought my arms had turned to fire and would never heal, she brought me my favorite meal—and then fed it to me. She told me jokes and did everything in her power to help me forget about my pain. That was all I could do at that point. Forget. Even more than I already had.

This is a huge mistake. I can't accept it, no matter how I *look* at Carina. Megan is my safe place. I make a move to stop her, but she cuts me off with a look and a wave of her hand. "I'm a lady, Smith. Please let this happen on my terms. I was there for you. I'm glad I could be there for you, but I think it's best if we go our separate ways now. I have nothing left to give you." She wraps her arms around her middle as tears cut a path down her face. I approach her slowly, making sure she'll accept me.

In between sobs, I wrap her in my arms. "This is what you want?" I ask. It's rhetoric, mostly. I know it's not what she wants, but it's what she's going to do regardless, because that's the type of woman she is.

She pulls away from the hug to look me in the eyes.

"This isn't what you want," she corrects. "I'm tired of fighting for something that doesn't exist anymore."

My pulse picks up, hammering a symphony against my neck. Uncontrollable nerves and anxiety overtake my body. This wasn't supposed to happen. I don't think I want this to happen, but a funny thing occurs. I don't try to fix it. When I open my mouth to speak, she kisses me, her hands pressing the sides of my face.

"Let me have this. Don't say anything, please. My dignity is on the line," she whispers.

I nod, holding her fingers in my hand. I look down and see her beautiful nails and thin fingers shake in my grasp. She leaves the room, closing the door behind her as she goes. This wasn't make-up sex, this was breakup sex. I blow out a huge pent-up breath.

I realize something monumental has happened. Something that changes everything. And if all she's told me is factual, this will be the first time in my adult life I will live without Megan. I sink back into the bed in shock. Reaching for my cell, I dial Moose because I can't call the first person that came to mind. Not yet. That wouldn't be fair to Megan.

And I'm not quite sure what that means.

I have three large suitcases and six seabags in the back of my truck when I pull into the parking lot of Balboa Park. Megan left the house before I got out of the shower, leaving a note that said I should be out of the house by tonight. It's the oddest sensation to be free and clear, without a clue of what comes next. I have another training trip in a few days and then a six-month deployment looming. If I concentrate on that, perhaps it will be an easy transition into forced bachelorhood. Am I upset? Both yes and no. I mourn our recent memories, but I know I don't feel the grief that she must. A decade of memories being obliterated by my accident. As if I didn't have enough to feel guilty about.

I find Carina's huge SUV and park next to it. I almost canceled the meeting, but I had to get out of the house, and Moose isn't home yet, so I can't head over there for a few more hours. She looks over from the driver's seat of her vehicle when I hop out and open her door for her.

Grabbing her bag, she slips out and looks both left and right, searching for him. That's nothing new. "Hey, how are you?" I ask and then notice her hair. "Made a big change, huh?"

Mindlessly she runs a hand through her freshly dyed locks. "Oh, yeah. They were able to squeeze me in early this morning. It's different, I know." She slings her bag over one shoulder and hands me the blanket to spread on the ground. I tell her it's a good different, that it reminds me of the sand at an exotic location, and she smiles bashfully.

We walk down the sidewalk, heading for the large banyan tree in the corner. The roots are exposed, but there's a section of flat ground for seating. More importantly, it's away from people and has the perfect amount of shade and sun.

Carina walks a few steps in front of me. Her hair isn't dark anymore. It's shades of blond with light browns, and it fades gradually from root to tip. She looks completely different—more confident, less of a wallflower. Not that she was ever unattractive. Quite the opposite, actually. Now, more people will notice her. I don't like that.

With a huff, she sits down on the blanket, crosses her ankles, and leans back on her elbows. She makes no motion to grab her tape recorder or her notebook. A fact I notice first and foremost. She's usually straight to business. "Sit," she says, patting the seat next to her. "I have some news for you." She smiles, her cheeks rounding and her eyes narrowing.

"I have some news, too," I reply, making myself comfortable.

With a sigh, she says, "Let me get mine out of the way first." Carina closes her eyes. "I left Roarke and filed a restraining order against him. I'm staying with Jasmine while I look for a place." Her new hair makes more sense. This is the best possible news I could receive today.

"All since yesterday? You've been busy," I remark. My own smile eases when I see that she's visibly upset. Gently, I place my hand on her shoulder. "You did the right thing. Of course you did the right thing."

She groans. "You know when you look in the mirror and you see the person you used to be? Sometimes you don't recognize who you are? Maybe other days you see a stranger—someone who can't possibly be you because the person staring back at you has none of the redeeming qualities that respectable people have? It sounds foolish, doesn't it? To view yourself one way when in reality you're the opposite."

A lump forms in my throat. Running my hand up my arm, I rub the back of my neck. "I know the feeling all too well. If you want to talk glass half full, realizing this is the first step to becoming who you want to be," I explain.

Carina looks off over my shoulder, her amber eyes filled with an emotion I can't quite pinpoint. Her eyes are so beautiful. They shine with so much, but sometimes I don't think she uses them to *see*. She uses them to hide from everything that resides behind.

"I want to be the person I thought I was. It's hard, though, because I'm terrified. Not because I'm fearful of him. I'm fearful of what he'll do to any progress I make. I'm afraid to start making a new life if he's going to take it away again. I'm not sure I'll be able to come out on the other side of that. Not again," Carina says. Her gaze flits to mine and holds. She grins. "I'm sorry for talking your ear off. Didn't you have news? Probably better than mine."

"This is way more important than my news, Carina. I'm happy for you." I pick up a strand of her lighter hair that lies on her shoulder. She keeps her grin as she watches my hand. "Nothing is going to happen. He's not going to hurt you again."

"What if I'm not strong enough, though?"

"Strong enough to what? You left him. That's the hardest part."

Carina sighs and takes my hand in hers. Her gaze stays on the red, scarred skin of my hand. "What if I'm not strong enough to stay away from him? I know he's going to try to get me back. I don't know if I'm strong enough to tell him no. Isn't that sick?" With her thumb, she rubs the skin between my thumb and forefinger.

I capture her thumb with my thumb. "I see the woman who you think you aren't. You're more than capable of handling this with ease and strength. You have support, you have a plan. You are strong enough."

She coughs, removes her hand from my grasp, and folds her hands in her lap. "I hope you're right, Smith. God, I hope you're right."

Giving her my biggest smile, I say, "I'm almost always right, Carina."

She presses her lips to the side. "Somehow, I believe that," Carina says, folding her hair from one side to the other. "Thank you for listening to this mess. I know that's not in your job description. You're a good friend to me."

Somewhere in between email exchanges and interviews, we became friends. The kind that you can tell anything to. The kind that lasts a lifetime. I'm sure of it.

"You're writing my story. I have to be good to you. What if you kill me off?"

She laughs, and a genuine smile graces me with its presence. I can't help but laugh in return. The fact that true happiness exists in this day is confusing.

A small dog runs over to pick up a red ball that's landed at our feet. "I want a cat," Carina says.

"Because you saw a dog?" I ask with a chuckle.

She smiles and waves at the owner, who is several yards away calling for the little fuzzball. "No, I've always wanted a cat, but Roarke is allergic."

Of course he is. That fucker is allergic to life. "You can have seven cats now. If you want."

"Ha. Ha," she says, a sarcastic grin pulling her lips. "The writer with seven cats. You're trying to bury me early, aren't you?"

I don't respond. I just watch her in this peaceful moment. It helps ease the Megan pain buried in my chest. It's like even my heart knows what my mind has forgotten.

Carina leans her head back when a stray sunbeam finds its way through the tree branches. It lights her face beautifully. She hums. "I was thinking last night when I obviously couldn't sleep. With the pace of my thoughts, it was never going to happen, and I realized something. You know how in horror novels, sometimes right in the middle, there's this really great, warm chapter to break up the gore?"

I grunt in agreement even though I don't read horror novels. I watch her pink lips as she opens to speak again.

Her head falls to the side, and she looks at me. "You're my warm, fuzzy middle chapter."

The sentiment steals my breath.

"In the most proper, platonic, friendly way, that is," she tacks on the end.

I want to tell her that it doesn't have to be that way anymore, that even Megan knows how I feel, but somehow bringing my feelings into this conversation seems dirty and wrong. I don't want to sully this moment with anything. Carina is opening herself to me, and in response, my entire heart is grateful. That's enough for now.

I laugh. "Of course. In that proper horror novel way," I reply.

She shakes her head.

"I should tell you a story. I'll tell you my news another day."

She sits up straight, excited. "That's a great idea. I've written a couple chapters already. I couldn't hold back any longer. Greenleigh is in the building. Whenever you're ready."

She doesn't take out her tape recorder this time, just a small notebook and a hot pink pen. She presses it between her lips as she waits for me to begin. I decide on a funny story about my very first deployment as a SEAL. It's when Moose and Henry became my best friends—when the brotherhood everyone talked about was defined. It involves cigars, sunburns, a wrecked four-wheeler, and a video camera.

I tell her about the surreal quality that lingered around me during those months. I was finally doing what I'd dreamed of doing my whole life—of what men across the world die to do. Everyday motions seemed that much more important because I was contributing to an effort bigger than anything I could think of. All of those months of trials and training—Hell Week, SEAL Qualification Training (SQT)—were being put to use. I was prepared for anything. I can't describe the feeling of pride that happens when preparedness meets talent, knowing the caliber of men surrounding me. All of it was surreal perfection, albeit dangerous.

Carina scribbles down her notes furiously as I keep talking. She asks so many questions. They aren't superficial questions, either. She wants to know what I was thinking when so-and-so happened and why I made a certain choice. She forces me into this introspective atmosphere that stings with reality. Her whole demeanor changes when we talk. Gone is the meek, mild-tempered woman. She's replaced with a voracious, hungry woman. She's sharp-tongued and holds nothing back. Carina isn't scared when we're talking. She's merely herself.

"You remember all of those details from that long ago? It's so strange. Your amnesia," Carina remarks.

I'm thankful for the memories I've kept, but a lot of times they're just a reminder of everything I've forgotten. Megan. My stomach flips. I have an honest-to-goodness bout of dizziness.

Sighing, I hang my head down to regain my wiles. "I'm lucky to be alive. That's the fact we need to focus on." I blink several times to clear my head. "Do you believe in a higher power, Carina?"

She seems taken aback by my question. "Of course," Carina replies, waving her hand to the side. "Look at this." She lays a hand on her chest. "And this," she says, gently laying her fingers on my exposed forearm. "Why do you ask?"

"I have to believe the things I've forgotten were meant to stay that way. When I think about it, I feel guilty, so I've come to blame someone else. I may never remember, or I could wake up tomorrow and have every single memory come flooding back. I chose to believe I have no control in that. Someone or something larger than life has a hand in that choice. I'm okay with it. So, yes. I remember those details because I was supposed to."

Carina shakes her head and slides her notebook back into her bag. "I don't know if I believe in it that much. I understand why you do, though." She sits up straight, tucks her golden locks behind one ear, and narrows her eyes. "It's easy to blame anyone other than yourself."

With one sentence, she's torn a hole in my defense. I can't blame myself because I can't remember. But I should be to blame. For pushing Megan away inadvertently. For trying to get our old relationship back for too long. For spending more time rehabbing my career instead of my engagement. I am to blame, and I've realized all of that is okay. I take her hand in mine. "Thank you."

She smiles and looks away. "I have no idea what you're thanking me for, but you're welcome. I should be the one thanking you. You gave me enough to write into the wee hours of the morning." I release her hand, but she doesn't move it away from me. I do see her quick gaze dart around us every once in a while. Her gaze flicks back to the little dog. She smiles.

"Don't be afraid, Carina. You're safe. I'm proud of you. I'm here for you." I also tell her that there's no way he would recognize her with her new hair.

She doesn't think the joke is funny, but she does tell me she's shopping for a new car this afternoon with Jasmine. She is trying to disappear without disappearing.

"You can't be there for me," she says, stopping midsentence. Carina closes her mouth and looks away. "You can't."

"Of course I can," I return.

She sighs. "You don't live with me, Smith. No one can keep me completely safe twenty-four hours a day. There's vulnerability in merely living. I'm sure it will get better with time," she says, swallowing. "But right now the last thing I feel is safe."

I nod. With a hammering heart, I say the first thing that comes to mind. "I'll live with you."

"What?" Carina asks, voice loud.

I shrug. "I'm not allergic to cats."

CHAPTER NINE
Carina

SWEAT IS POURING down my body. "And then he said, 'I'll live with you,'" I say, dotting my brow with my workout towel. My workout capris and tank are soaked through. "Just like that. Tell me what that sounds like to you."

"He didn't say anything else?" Jasmine asks.

Our other friend, Teala, the one I usually just see at our boot camp class, looks at me with confusion. "That seems really weird. Like he asked to move in with you? Or you to move in with him? Confusion isn't strange in this instance, honey."

I shake my head, still breathing heavily from the intense cardio. We're unable to talk during the ferocious hour we're getting our butts handed to us by the trainer, so it all spills out as we make our way into the street to find our cars. "He got a phone call from Moose and had to leave after that. I didn't have a chance to probe. God, I should have. It makes no sense whatsoever. He texted me this morning and wants to meet for dinner tonight."

"Dinner?" Teala asks. "Not an interview, but dinner?" She knows our story, so she's able to keep up for the most part.

Raising my sweaty brows, I nod. "Dinner. At my favorite tapas place in Gaslamp." I wipe in between my boobs with the towel and then tuck it into the back of my pants. The Gaslamp District is downtown San Diego. They have the best restaurants and bars. It's eclectic and vibrant, full of museums and historic apartment buildings. It's a place where you can *feel* everything. "That isn't a place where we'd ever do an interview. It's loud."

"It's a date," Teala says. "You said yes, right?"

If my heart wasn't hammering from my workout, it would be now. Someone else saying the word I've been thinking makes it real. Smith asked me on a date. I can't be the other girl in this twisted relationship. Megan is the woman he should be with. The photos I saw of them confirm that. He loved her. Everything about her, Smith loved. He cherished her smile, worshipped the ground she walked on. But then again, I catch myself thinking in the past tense. He loved her in those photos from their past. Everything changed after he lost Henry. After he lost pieces of himself.

"I said yes. He's my friend," I reply.

"Moose. That's a real name, Care?" Jasmine asks, detouring our conversation to something that may benefit her.

Tossing my hands up, I say, "That's what you're worried about in all of this? Smith's best friend is named Moose. Yes. I don't know if it's short for something. They all have weird nicknames, so I'd assume so, but they're goddamn Navy SEALs, so Moose fits. It's part of the culture. Or so I've gathered from talking to him." Smith wants me to meet Moose. Our schedules haven't jived yet.

Both Jasmine and Teala laugh. I shake my head. Try as I might, I was unable to write anything last night. Visions of Smith clouded my thoughts. One would think that's what I would desire to gain focus to write a novel about his life, but it was so distracting. The way he touched me and looked at me seemed so intimate. I wanted him all to myself. More than I've wanted anything else in my entire life, I wanted him to see me like he sees Megan. And he did. I believe he really did.

Teala downs the rest of the water in her bottle. "I need to find a friend who looks like that, too. Can you make that happen? Write me in as the love interest!" she exclaims.

A wave of mild annoyance washes over me. In my mind the love interest has always been Megan, but perhaps, just maybe, another woman enters the picture. My stomach sinks and flips at the same time. If I write it, it's fiction, but I could live in the place I so desperately desire to be.

I unlock my car door. It's a brand-new German-engineered sedan. The windows are tinted, and I ordered new tags. It gives me another layer of security against my past.

I haven't seen or heard from Roarke. His mother called me twice to "talk." What she really wanted was reasons. For the first time in the history of knowing Roarke's creator, I told her everything. The reason we spoke twice is because it took two hour-long phone calls for me to get the whole story out in between her sobs. She told me she suspected something was amiss in our relationship but never would have guessed how dubious her son was behaving. She apologized for him several hundred times. It made no difference. If anything, it solidified my decision.

I wave a quick goodbye to Teala, tell Jasmine I'll see her at home, and excuse myself to write. And write I do. I plot and outline and add quotes to the large marker board that covers half my wall. I'm a mad woman—a woman on a mission. I don't change out of my workout gear. The sweat on my clothing and my hair eventually dries, and I'm sitting in the middle of my bedroom at Jasmine's house, staring at the last blank, white bubble at the right side of my board.

"The ending," I whisper. "How does it end?" Love triangles aren't my strong suit, or any suit if I'm being honest. This is two love stories streaming at the same time. One from a forgotten time and one present—now. One that is wildly alive and thriving. The choice should be easy, but I see no easy choice for my characters. I close my eyes and think of the photo albums. I let my mind replace Megan with me. The images flit through one by one until, when I open my eyes, tears are pouring down my face.

Jasmine pokes her head in my room after knocking softly. "You have an hour before dinner. Smith called the house to remind you. I told him you were zoning." She closes the door after widening her eyes at the mess of my multicolored marker board. She never asks questions about my process.

I don't stop thinking about the blank bubble while I shower or blow-dry my hair, nor when I have a meltdown trying to decide what to wear. "A date? Not a date?" I ask myself as I toil between a skirt and blouse or a low-cut dress. Jasmine made the executive decision for me. When I open the front door to greet Smith, I'm wearing a dress covered in sloths. The neckline dips down low enough to reveal the swell of my breasts. *This is a date*, I think when I see Smith.

"You're early," I say in greeting. "Sorry, I was busy when you called." Planning our future without you realizing it.

"No apologies needed. Especially when you appear like this," he says, turning his hands palms up and motioning to my body. "And on time, too, might I add. Wearing sloths. You should join me on my planet. I think you'd enjoy the weather there."

Shaking my head, I giggle. "Come in," I say, flustered. His hair is coiffed like I've never seen before. The smile he wears is mine, and everything inside of my being is drawn to him. I have to repeat her name in my head. Megan. It's my mantra. What is he doing to me? When he walks past, I smell his soap, and I swallow down a lump of desire.

"You have a beautiful place, Jasmine," Smith says.

Jasmine acts bashful, turning her face down. He's fucking with everyone. It's pheromones. It has to be. And I have to spend a whole dinner pretending to not be affected. Jasmine finally thanks him and retreats to the kitchen to continue making soup.

Smith licks his lips and turns his gaze my way. "Are you going to show me your room?"

I panic. The marker board. He can't see that. Oh my god. What was I thinking? It's a book about his life. He will read it. In my frenzy, I failed to remember the most important part of this. Smith and his feelings.

"Aren't we going to be late? It's a mess right now. Plus, I have so many questions. I'm pretty confused, Smith. Should I grab my notebook?" Finally something intelligent comes out of my mouth. "You look like that. I'm wearing my sloth dress. I don't know what that means."

Laughing, he lays a hand on my bare shoulder. It's warm and dry. I shiver anyway. I don't shrink away from his touch like I did with Roarke. Smith's hands have never done anything to betray me. There's nothing sinister in his actions—only honesty and sincerity.

"It's dinner, Carina," he says. His explanation does nothing to quell my nerves. "We're going to eat at your favorite place. I showered, if that's why you're wondering why I look like this. I'm clean. Also, I'm assuming the sloth dress is only reserved for special occasions. I'm honored to meet you, sloth dress," Smith says, running a finger underneath the strap on my shoulder. No cardigan is needed tonight.

My breath catches in my throat. "Smith. What is this?"

"Whatever it wants to be, Carina."

I blow out a large breath through both my nose and mouth. Before I put my foot in my mouth, I ask, "Explain, please." I keep my voice low and hold up one finger when he parts his lips to speak. I know Jasmine is listening to every word, so I usher Smith out the front door into the warm, breezy air. "Now explain." My hand burns where it lies against the outside of his shirt. It makes me wonder what it would feel like to touch his bare skin on the other side of the shirt.

Looking up at the sky, he pauses a few beats. My pulse hammers against my neck, and I rock from one foot to the other, thanking Jasmine for choosing a pair of ballet flats instead of heels. She told me sexy heels don't belong with my sloth dress. It was a fair point. Smith's gaze flicks down to meet mine. He's determined something in those few seconds of silence. I see the steely reserve reflected in his dreamy eyes.

"We broke up. Megan and I are no longer together. I wanted to tell you the other day, but you left him, and I was so happy for you that I didn't want to ruin that news with my news." He works to swallow. "It's over."

Relief hits me square in the chest, but it's quickly replaced by sadness. She's not only a real live person. She's also one of my beloved characters. "You broke up with her," I say.

Sighing, he clasps his hands behind his head. "She

initiated it, but I agreed with it. It's for the best. It's not fair to either of us. There are no hard feelings."

Of course there aren't. She's perfect. Megan wouldn't be catty or cruel to this man. He's perfect. He wouldn't make this harder on her than it has to be. I cough. "It's tragic," I whisper, hiding my face with both hands.

He shakes his head. "A second ago you would have been happy about it. I see the way you look at me." My eyes widen. "I know there's more between us than either of us will admit. You asked what this is," he says, motioning between our bodies. "We can finally find out." This is why he spoke of living with me. It's a real option now. When I stay silent, he continues. "You're going through a lot," he says.

I interrupt. "We're standing on my best friend's deck because I had to leave my abusive fiancé. A lot doesn't define what I'm mucking through right now, Smith."

"Nothing has to happen between us. This means I can be at ease looking at you."

I scrunch up my nose. "Looking at me?"

He nods, asks if I still plan on eating dinner with him, and then leads me down the steps. Next, he opens the passenger-side door of his blue truck. The same one I had fantasies of riding away in the day I met him. When he's in the driver's seat, his hands on the steering wheel, he looks over. "If there's one thing you should know about me, it's that I honor my commitments. I can look at you and not feel guilty, Carina. I can let my mind wander to places I didn't let it before. I don't have to wonder what if, because I can live it if we choose to. We have freedom of choice. Friendship? Of course. More? Who knows." His words comfort me in a sense, but I can't imagine how Megan must be feeling. "So, yes. Look at you." Pointedly, he lets his gaze roam from my neck down to my waist and back up.

He leaves his hand on the seat between us, the pink scars visible against the beige leather. Accepting the subtle invitation, I place my hand in his. "If I'm to blame, even in the least, I hope you know I won't be able to sleep at night ever again. I would never wish ill will on anyone. Especially her." My voice cracks on the last word.

He squeezes my fingers. "That's something you don't have to tell me. I know you're a good person. You're not to blame at all. Circumstances are. Ones that are out of our control. My relationship with Megan after the accident was tedious at best."

Sure, but for her it was more than that. Smith leaves me no choice but to remove myself from their breakup equation. It's not my fault. It's not. It can't be. I didn't do anything wrong. I have to believe their demise happened organically. A fading away that happens gradually when one person loves another person more. I'm well versed in that arena.

Smith drives, and I think. Never in all of my years have I felt such a serene calm. There's no fear about what tomorrow brings or how I'm going to survive another day. It's the first time I've felt this carefree since I was a child. Before my stepfather, Greg, came along and changed me down to the cellular level.

"The photo albums, Smith. All that love. As a romance author, I can't in good conscience let that go by the wayside. You had a timeless love. Amnesia isn't something that stopped that. It can't. It's inside you."

Smith clears his throat. "Not all romances have happy endings. You know that," he says. For a second I think of all of my favorite books. About half of them have a happy ending. The others end poetically sad in that literary way that serves the story well.

At the reminder of stories, I think of my current work in progress and my marker board of shame. I can't write myself into the story if Megan isn't in the picture any longer. It's cheating. It's fiction. I can do whatever I want. In *Pinion Lane* there were so many truths about my childhood, and the love story was contrived of my hopes and dreams for a life with Roarke. I twisted everything to my liking. I'll do it again.

We arrive at the restaurant, place our drink and dinner orders, and make small talk over the live band in the corner of the restaurant. Sipping my mojito, I try to steer the conversation away from our personal lives. I end up asking him questions about his career, which frustrates me because I don't have anything to write with, and I know I'll forget important details.

"I told Moose to stop by and say hi. I hope that's okay," Smith says during a lull. "He was next door at the pub with a few of our friends." He motions with his thumb to the wall to the left.

I've heard so many stories about Moose that I'm literally bouncing with excitement. "Yes. That's fine. I've wanted to meet him for a while," I reply.

Smith scratches the side of his head. "You can't grill him like you grill me. Don't get too excited." Smith smirks, waves to someone over my shoulder, and stands. His stance is tall and regal.

I make a show of crossing my arms under my chest. "Who do you think I am?" I ask. "I'm not going to grill him. Too hard." I smile.

Standing, I turn to see Moose heading our way. The restaurant is full, but there's no question who Smith's best friend is. He's a lumbering man with broad shoulders, a don't-mess-with-me attitude, and a smirk that is probably famous all across the world.

Smith shakes his friend's hand and motions to me. "Carina, I'd like you to meet Moose. Moose, this is my friend Carina."

Moose smiles. It's genuine and kind—it seems displaced on a man of his magnitude. He extends his hand, and my own gets enveloped in the sheer size.

"A pleasure," I say, smiling in his direction. Smith's gaze is locked on my face. From the corner of my eye, I see his smile the second I smile.

"Is all mine," Moose replies, tilting his chin down and to the side. A perfect gentleman. I'm waiting for him to curtsy. Moose releases his grip and turns his focus on Smith. Smith doesn't notice. He's still staring at me.

"I probably won't hear the end of it, so I have to ask. Why Moose?" I ask, laughing to break the odd pause. My friends will be happy with this information. "I mean, I understand for the most part." I motion to his figure that seems to be well over six feet, then motion with my hand side to side.

Smith tells me it's a long story and suggests we sit down. I take a sip of my mojito and swirl the drink with the long cane of sugar. Smith orders a few more orders of tapas and a drink for Moose and then launches into a story about how Moose can actually make a true-blue moose sound. Both of the men laugh, and I see a new side of Smith. It's eye-opening to see how carefree and unencumbered his personality is when he's living inside his friend's grace.

Moose turns to me with mirth reflecting in his eyes. "I'm from upstate New York. When I was twelve, I was attacked by a moose," he explains, gesturing with his hands.

Smith coughs. "And he won."

I let my eyes widen. "No way. That can't be a real story."

Moose nods. "I was large even as a child. From that day forward, I was Moose."

"The nickname has nothing to do with the weird

SEAL thing then?" I ask, lowering my voice. The small amount of alcohol has already hit my bloodstream, but I know enough to make an effort to be quiet when I speak of their profession. "I find that hard to believe."

Smith laughs. "I knew you wouldn't be able to hold back," he says, shaking his head. "He learned the moose call to try to befriend the beasts. The joke is that the animals mistake him for their kindred because of his size. All he's missing is antlers and fur."

"I have to hear it. You know that, right?" I deadpan. I've been in Southern California my whole life. The fact he's seen a moose is enough to impress me. He might as well be a host on an animal television show. That's how versed I am with any sort of wildlife that isn't a coyote.

Moose looks left and right. "I'm afraid I haven't had enough to drink tonight, but I'll give you a moose call rain check. So, Smith has told me so much about you. How's the book coming along?" Subject change status: expert. His eyes narrow. Like any good friend, he's concerned. I wonder if he knows about his breakup and how much of my drama he's privy to.

Swallowing another large gulp of my drink, I tell him the truth. "It's the single most meaningful thing I've written. It's coming along very well, thank you. Smith," I say, looking at Smith.

His eyes crinkle as he flashes me his very best smile. The scars on one side of his face pull his skin oddly. I rarely notice his scars. Sitting in front of both of the men, one whole and one dismantled, it's easy to understand Smith Eppington's life a little better than I did before.

Without breaking eye contact, I finish. "Is a great man. I didn't know men like him existed. His story is sensational, actually. It's better than fiction. As his best friend, you already know that. Between his stories and my imagination, there's no telling where this thing will land." I take a beat to gauge Moose's reaction to my words. He's satisfied. Wiping the sweat off my glass with my finger, I smile widely. It falls a little when I remember the blank circle on my marker board back home.

"She's good for my self-esteem at the very least," Smith jokes. "Carina is too kind." His molten gaze meets mine, and heat rises up my neck.

I pop a stuffed olive in my mouth. "I'm not good at stroking egos. It's all truth," I reply. It's a lie. Stroking egos is something I'm actually masterful at because of Roarke. I'm not stroking egos now. It is truth.

Moose shakes his head. "I don't know how you do it, man."

"Do what?" Smith asks his friend, eyes narrowed.

"Nothing," Moose says, clapping Smith on the back. "I'm starving. Do they have burgers here?"

Smith quirks a brow at his friend but lets him change the subject without another word. I think they have the kind of friendship that's beyond conversation. I imagine them telepathically finishing their dialogue to keep me out of their business.

I push a few trays of tapas in front of him. "Eat seven trays, and it's equivalent to a burger," I explain.

Moose smiles and begins eating. After he swallows a mouthful, he says, "You know, I have better stories than he does." He jerks a thumb to his right. "Sure, he's all scarred and decorated, but I'm pretty sensational, too."

Smith coughs, laughing. "She's booked. Sorry, Moosey. No interviews for you."

I laugh. Moose grunts.

"Another perspective might be good for the story," I say, fishing for a reaction from Smith. In actuality I have more from Smith already that I'm not sure I'll be able to fit it in one story. I meet Smith's gaze and smile. It's fierce, protective—not happy with my suggestion. It tells me all

I want to know. "Just joking," I say, letting my lips pull to the side.

Smith tells me my joke was funny, and Moose laughs at his friend's response.

Moose is happy and polite. Truly, I can't help myself. Or, I'd kick myself. "Rumor has it you're single."

Moose tilts his head to the side, chews with his mouth closed, and furrows his brow.

"I have someone I want you to meet." My girlfriend Teala will be ecstatic if I can snag her a date.

Smith scoots his chair back and holds his large arms out to the sides. "Come on, man. Carina has better taste than Aunt Ethel. Ol' Eth still thinks you like blonds with small dogs in purses."

I cover my mouth to stifle a giggle.

Moose sighs, looks me up and down once, and says, "For some reason, I trust you." After he agrees, he makes himself scarce, disappearing into the bar next door, leaving me alone with Smith on our date.

CHAPTER TEN
Smith

CARINA IS TALKING about a funny short story she wrote in high school. While I do hear her words, all I can focus on is her lips. They're so full and pink, and she licks them every so often, causing a riot of emotions. She has foreign lips. I've never tasted them. I want to. Badly.

Moose loved her. She loved Moose. Their meeting was almost too easy. I expected some hesitance on Moose's part because he's a huge Megan fan. He did tell me he had to respect our decision to part ways because of our extenuating circumstances. On some level I'm sure Moose thinks I'm an idiot for letting Megan go. I had to—it's more of a need at this point.

All my thoughts of anything else are eviscerated now that the possibility of *more* with Carina has risen. When her mouth stops moving, I alternate my gaze from her lips to her eyes, and she smiles.

"Did you hear anything I just said?" Carina asks. She runs her hand through her hair and tucks her bangs behind one ear. It's a self-conscious gesture she hasn't banished since her ex destroyed every shred of normal confidence from her body.

"You're so beautiful," I say.

She turns her eyes down.

"Don't do that."

Carina meets my eyes, her molten chocolate gaze questioning. "It's me. I can't control it," she explains. "Thank you. You're a pretty fine specimen yourself." She has to be joking. Maybe a few years ago, but not now. Perhaps I can turn heads with my sheer size and presence.

I ignore her compliment completely. "Moose really liked you."

"Did you think he wouldn't?" Carina puts her chin in both hands and leans on the table in front of her. "Are you baiting me?" She quirks one arched brow while looking at me up and down.

I bite my bottom lip. "Baiting you how?" Mirroring her, I lean my chin into both hands on the table in front of me. A gesture that clearly isn't as endearing as when she does it. I've never been this close to her before. The flecks of amber that reside in her eyes glow brighter. I smell her shampoo and her perfume as it mixes with the scent of her skin. Subtly, when I breathe in through my mouth, I taste her on my tongue.

For a short moment I think she's going to back away, retreat into her personal space, and I'll have to respect that. She doesn't make a move to lean away. She studies me as intently as I study her. "Baiting me to say that I really liked Moose too. And then the string of questions that comes when I tell you I like your best friend." Carina smiles. It's all white teeth and genuine amusement. "I saw your face. You thought I would think him more interesting." Tilting her head to the side, she dips her gaze down to my forearms.

"Who do you take me for?" I say, focusing on her mouth. When a person is physically attracted to another person, they focus on the triangle while listening to them speak. Eyes, nose, and mouth. I find myself lost in her triangle anytime she speaks. Even subliminally, I want Carina to be mine.

She leans away, taking her smile and eyes entirely too far away. I let my eyes close and open in a slow blink. "I take you for a tired man," she replies.

It's true. I'm exhausted. Moose's couch isn't an expensive mattress. I walked away from Megan and left her everything we accumulated together. "Indeed." I flex my fists on the table in front of me. "I need to get a place of my own."

Carina's eyes flare wide. "That's right. This changes things. If we lived together, it would probably complicate things. Now that, well…" Carina trails off.

If I let her know how much I want her in my space, I'd frighten her away. Playing it cool is my best bet.

"Now that we are going on dates," she finishes, tucking a strand of hair behind her ear.

A waitress brushes my shoulder as she walks past our table. When I glance to the side, she winks at me. I turn quickly, hoping Carina didn't see the exchange. Megan tends to get jealous when anything like that happens.

Carina laughs and shakes her head, tossing her styled hair over one shoulder. "You're completely unaware of your wiles. It's both endearing and infuriating, Smith."

"We can still live together. That's up to you and what you're comfortable with," I say, ignoring her honesty. Holding up one finger, I stop her from interrupting. "I leave for a six-month deployment in a few months. I'll need a house sitter then anyway."

Moose alerted me to that fact when he was attempting to convince me to stay with him. As a perma-bachelor, he thinks of circumstances I've never had to worry over. My own space is something I need.

"Just think about it," I say when I see hesitation cross

her features. Now that I've mentioned it, thoughts of cohabiting with her run through my mind. Cooking meals together, getting to see her when she first wakes up...in whatever she wears to sleep. Late-night movies, being able to look at her anytime I want. Does she wrap her hair in a towel when she exits the shower? Does she snore? How does she go about her morning routine? I know how she takes her coffee and her favorite foods. Excitement reverberates in my bones. I want this badly.

She closes her mouth and nods. Carina finishes her drink, and I clean up the rest of the tapas plates. I pay for our check, against her wishes, and we make our way out of the restaurant. There's still the tiniest bit of burnt orange light reflecting in the warm San Diego sky. She's backlit against it—a mere silhouette of perfection.

She turns, her profile now dark and visible in contrast. "When do you deploy, Smith?"

I swallow down my emotions and catch my breath. Her beauty is something to behold. It's more than skin-deep. It's soul deep, and it's calling out to me like my favorite song. "Three months from tomorrow, actually. If we lived together, it could be a nonstop interview. Think of the possibilities. You'd finish that book in no time," I tease. I know it takes her about a year to write a novel from start to finish.

She stops dead in her tracks and faces me when we get to my truck. "Where are you going when you deploy?" It's then that I hear the underlying fear in her words. My safety. She's worried. The sentiment is touching and fearsome at the same time. The feelings are already there. I was right. Not only will she agree to *more* in our relationship, it already exists on its own.

"Iraq," I reply simply.

She nods, lets me open the passenger-side door, and remains silent in thought—questions whirring quicker than her mouth can process, I'm sure. When I park myself in the driver's seat, I make a move to place my hand on her bare thigh.

First she looks at where I'm touching and then directs her gaze to my face, her eyes heavy with desire. "You're persuasive when you're trying to change the subject." She thinks I don't want to talk about Iraq. I don't care about that, though. I want the conversation back to what matters tonight. Us.

"I'm an honorable man. I'll always do what's right. When I want something, I merely figure out the most honorable way to obtain it," I explain. I start the truck and reluctantly pull my hand away from her smooth, warm thigh. From the corner of my eye, I see her rubbing the spot where my hand just was. I smile.

Carina shifts in her seat. "That seems a little dishonorable if you ask me. If plotting is involved to get something you want, perhaps it shouldn't be obtained in the first place. Shouldn't it be effortless?"

I nod, driving slower than the speed limit down a back road heading to Jasmine's house. "Nothing worth having is easily obtained. Or so I've learned in my experiences in life. Some things are seemingly effortless, though. I agree with that."

"Can I quote that?" Carina asks, smiling. She's so endearing—growing into a more confident woman. I joke that she can't quote me and ask if she's hidden a tape recorder. She taps me on the arm lightly, horsing around.

As I drive, I keep my hands on the steering wheel. Regardless of what I was told in the past, I prefer both hands on the wheel—the control all mine. Carina alternates pulling the hem of her dress, tousling her hair, and looking out the window. She's shifty and nervous. I know why, and it makes me uneasy. There are expectations even though there is no need for them.

This—this energy and our emotional connection happened organically, in a way this Tinder-obsessed culture can only dream of. "We didn't talk about work tonight at all, did we?" I ask, grinning. I want to break this pregnant silence. Her questions and unburying past horrors are preferable to this.

Carina looks over. "Are you disappointed? I have several questions ready to go if you are."

I clear my throat. How best should I approach this? "No, no. It was a date after all, right?"

I pull up to a red light and fist my hands around the steering wheel. The scarred skin on my hands tightens uncomfortably.

Carina swallows audibly. "Suppose it was. Does that make us bad people? We've hidden behind interviews for our entire relationship. This is new, and I'm not sure if it's wrong." This isn't wrong. No, everything before this was wrong. This is my right. It makes sense, it's the most visceral, real circumstance since my accident.

"It's not wrong. Don't think that for a second." After several long talks on the phone with my mother, she gets it. She still talks to Megan, so I think my gracious ex-fiancée has a hand in her acceptance. Margaret Eppington loves Megan as much as I used to. Or so I've surmised. On the last call, she told me she knows about Carina and the novel. "No one thinks anything is wrong about us," I say.

Carina sighs but nods. Pulling into Jasmine's drive-way, I pull the gearshift up to put my truck into park. She shivers as I wrap my arm around her small shoulders and guide her to the front door. I stroke her bare, tan skin with one finger just to see if goose bumps will rise. They do.

She spins out of my grasp and faces me head-on. "I'm only me, Smith." She's confusing yet perfectly clear at the same time. Only is a dangerous word, though. It's used as an excuse. *If only I had more time. I'm only insert self-deprecating adjective here. I'm only me.*

I take her cheeks in my hands. The flawless, smooth skin on her face makes the skin on my own hands look atrocious. "That's a good thing because you're the only person I want."

She places her hand over mine to hold it in place. Carina shakes her head, but her eyes tell me that I'm the person she wants regardless of what she thinks of herself or of my past with Megan. I'm overwhelmed by the urge to hold her—to kiss her—to claim her as my own in this new, most desirable way.

"This seems so complicated. Or am I overanalyzing?" she asks, her eyes closing in a slow, lazy blink but meeting mine directly after.

"Are you happy?" I ask. It's such a loaded question. She's been through so much with Roarke that asking for her happiness now seems selfish and rushed, but I'm asking anyway. I don't need validation in my job, because I know I'm good—the best even. With Carina, it's different. I don't have a rule book. I don't know what comes next. She surprises me and keeps me on my toes.

A strand of hair blows across her face, and I catch it between my fingertips. She smiles. "I am. If I put everything else aside and think about you and me, I'm happy. Yes."

My heart pounds, and the blood rushes to my head. Pure elation. "I think it's simple. Happiness is what it comes down to. If I make you happy and our arrangement makes you happy, then let's forget about the rest. Let's do this, Carina."

"Very honorable indeed. I see what you mean about taking the moral high ground," Carina smarts. She rubs her hands down my biceps and stops when she's holding my forearms in her hands. "Okay."

It was easy. It was effortless. "You'll move in with me?"

She slides her hands down a little more and holds both of mine in hers. "Mainly to finish my book. And to house-sit."

I bite my bottom lip to hold back laughter. "Of course," I say. I squeeze her hands to make sure this moment is real. "We'll start looking tomorrow then. If your schedule allows, of course."

Carina frowns and tilts her head down.

"What is it?" I ask, confused.

"Nothing. Nothing," she says, fixing a smile. "Tomorrow will work perfectly."

I grunt. "I know better than that. What's wrong?"

"I was just thinking about my story," Carina replies. She tucks her hair behind her ears. "I just remembered I have some plot holes to patch up."

"Can I be of any help?" I ask. With one thumb, I cradle her face and draw the finger across her lower lip. My tongue slides out of its own accord to wet my own lips. I never really want for many things in life. I don't remember wanting anything more than I want Carina Painter's lips on mine. I lean down and feel my breath stick in my chest.

She sighs through parted lips, and I feel her warm breath on my finger. Oh god, to taste her sweet lips would be the ultimate satisfaction, but I can't. Not yet, at least.

"Are you going to kiss me?" she asks, her voice low and husky.

I use honesty as my weapon. "I want to kiss you badly. I want to taste you. Your lips haunt my dreams. Maybe I could finally match my dreams with reality if I did it, if I leaned forward a few more inches and claimed you," I say, leaning down toward her even more, until her lips are a breath away from my own. A tiny puff of a sigh exits her mouth. It's anticipation. It's desire in spades. It's fire.

"And," she edges.

"But I want all of you more," I say. Leaning away is painful for numerous reasons. My cock, bless it, is already at full attention at her mere proximity, and every nerve ending in my godforsaken body wants Carina all over me. Not just her lips. Her skin. Her hair. Every particle that forms this woman calls to every part of me. "As badly as I want your lips, I'm not going to rush this. It's going to be perfect."

She lets out a pent-up breath. When I see her lips pull into a tight, frustrated line, I grin. She reaches up, locks her hands around my neck, and pulls herself to my body for an embrace. "There is such a thing as being too honorable," Carina mutters in my ear.

I chuckle and pull her tighter.

I know she feels me hard against her. I know my heart is hammering against her body in a very noticeable way. I'm aware that in every light touch, I'm falling deeper and deeper, sliding sideways, skidding to a place where I've never been. Not as this version of Smith Eppington, at least. Her delicate curves coexist with my own hard, flat planes in perfect harmony.

My breath comes quickly, and I know I must break free of this moment if there's any hope of leaving her here on this doorstep. "Perfection is honorable," I say, separating her from me, keeping my hands on her waist.

"It is, isn't it? Good night, Smith. I had a wonderful time tonight. Thank you for dinner and the fascinating conversation."

I close my eyes for a quick beat to regain some control

over my thoughts and the dirty turn they've taken. She seems to know what I'm feeling.

Carina crosses one foot over the other and lays one hand on the door handle. "I'm sure Jasmine's watching us on the security camera right now, by the way." She waves at the small black ball in the corner behind my head. "Call me tomorrow and let me know what time you want to look at places."

I can't help but smile. "You make me so happy. Sleep well," I say. I lean down, like I'm going to kiss her, but turn at the last minute and touch my open mouth to the side of her cheek. "Next time we'll give her something worth being creepy for then," I whisper in her ear.

Goose bumps rise on the side of her body where my lips touch. "I've waited so long for your touch. You said it. I'm holding you to that," Carina whispers.

I put my palm over my rapidly beating heart. "On my honor," I say.

CHAPTER ELEVEN

Carina

IT'S BEAUTIFUL. The bungalow house is tiny by most people's standards, but for a true-blue SoCal girl like me, it's idealistic. A quick walk to the park, a short drive to the beach, and four walls that aren't shared with a neighbor. Our new house smells like fresh paint and hardwood polish. It's smaller and isn't as upgraded as the house Roarke built for us a few years ago, but for all it represents, it might as well be my own Buckingham Palace.

Smith is away on a training trip, so Jasmine is helping me set everything up. "You should have taken more when you left Roarke," Jasmine says. She's swearing under her breath as she cranks an Allen wrench. "Furniture that comes in boxes will be my ultimate demise." She flips the instructional page in one overexaggerated movement. "You're lucky I love you."

I readjust the headband holding back my bangs. "I don't need anything from Roarke. If it means I never have to look at him again, I'm happy to bear this burden. Well, I guess I should say I'm grateful you are tackling that burden," I say, laughing.

Even though I'm smiling, fear is coiling my insides. I'll be here alone. A lot, if I'm being honest with myself.

Smith is away much of the time, and that says nothing of the six solid months he'll be deployed.

I try not to think of Roarke often, but he seeps in during moments of weakness. I know I haven't seen the last of him regardless of what Smith promises. New cars and moving houses, haircuts and dye jobs only really lend a false sense of security. Men like Roarke always find a way. They're above the law.

"I know. I know. I'm sorry for mentioning his name. Sean's kept tabs on him here and there, and he's truly obeying the order," Jasmine says, standing with the long piece of wood that will eventually be a bed frame.

I swallow down the lump in my throat. "I didn't know he was watching him."

"I mean, it's not for his job. It's for you. Because I wanted to make sure you were safe with, uh, your new friend gone." Jasmine covers a laugh with a cough.

I toss a piece of Styrofoam at her head. It misses. She's able to help me today because she caught up with her other client's manuscript. Matthew Manning is a woman who writes romantic mysteries under a pseudonym. She's prolific. More so than I am. Jasmine reminds me of this whenever she passes by my marker boards leaning against the wall in the hallway. I haven't pieced together the ending, and she can't pitch the novel without it cemented.

Bending over, I resume circling my own Allen wrench to finish the bookshelf. "You think I've gone mad, don't you?" I ask, turning my gaze to Jasmine's face. "My life. This book. Everything."

She shrugs. "The way I look at it is that before Smith, you did nothing right in the relationship department. I understand your reasons for the most part, but he's different from Roarke. Totally and completely, but..." Jasmine trails off.

"But what?" I ask. Folding my arms over my chest, I raise one freshly waxed brow.

She stops her wrenching and sighs. "You're an artist to the core. Are you in love with him or the story about him, Carina?"

I scoff and readjust my paint-spattered overalls. "No one said anything about love," I hiss.

Jasmine rolls her eyes. "Answer the question. Replace love with like, if it makes you sleep better at night, but answer me." She draws her chin down, much like a scolding mother would look at her child. "You are living with him—his stuff and your stuff colliding in one dwelling. It's more than like. Maybe you're confused as to what exactly that means."

She's right. The thought is painful and terrifying because I know the answer. Do I love his story? Of course I do. It's becoming my story. I'm buried so deeply in this world that I feel like I've always been a part of Smith Eppington. I'm in love with him. I sit down on a plastic ghost chair behind me. Finally, after several long seconds, I answer her. "I'm in love with him, okay?"

Jasmine smiles widely, her eyes drawing up in the corners and almost disappearing completely. "That must have tasted like chalk coming out," she replies. "Have you talked to him about this yet?"

I stomp one foot on the floor. "What if he thinks the same thing? That it's the story I'm after. That it's not him. He's such a romantic, Jasmine. I'm never sure how to approach a conversation so blatantly tinged with love for fear of ultimatums or bringing up old feelings. I mean, my god, I've basically agreed to reside in the ghost of his love for Megan. What if his amnesia goes away? If he's cured? What will my love mean to him then?" It's hard to think of Megan without guilt, and I'm not sure how long it will take to go away. Even when I'm working on my novel, I wince when I write a scene between her and Smith. I've given her a new name and a new description, but she'll always, always be his first love.

Nodding in understanding, and knowing she can't help me out of this situation, Jasmine picks up the bottle of wine we've been working on and pours the rest of the contents into my red Solo cup. I take a long swallow and set the cup down on my new bookshelf and head for the kitchen, where my cell phone is vibrating on the Formica countertop. I leap forward quickly and jab the green button when I see the S name flashing on the screen.

"Sansa! It's you!" I say.

Smith chuckles, and the sound warms my stomach from the inside out. I haven't had the heart to change the name since he programmed his number in my phone.

"It's amazing to hear your voice." I mean it. The masculine timbre creates a pang of regret for being away from him. Never in my wildest dreams would I have envisioned myself in a relationship with the Navy—this feeling of longing warring with reality. We haven't even kissed yet, but the intimacy between us seems deeper in a way. I think that's why you need to have a relationship that flourishes under the pressures of separation. That's what I'm telling myself, anyway.

He clears his throat. "How is moving in going? I wish I could be there to help. I feel awful," Smith says. Hearing his voice again sends shivers down my spine.

I shake my head. "Do not feel bad. You're giving Jasmine an opportunity to participate in her favorite pastime. Furniture building," I say.

Jasmine yells from the bedroom some unintelligible threats in Mandarin.

"It was perfect timing for your trip. I'd think it was planned if I didn't know better. Moose dropped off several large tubs. Why isn't he with you?" I ask. Strong willpower has kept me from peeking in Smith's things. Honestly, I'm probably one glass of wine away from popping the top off.

Smith sighs. It's a long, drawn-out noise.

"What's wrong?" There's a flurry of background noise. Maybe they're in a restaurant? It is dinnertime.

"Nothing. It's nothing for you to worry about. Moose is leaving tomorrow for a different training trip. They split us up." There's a hint of anger in his tone. Silverware clanks against a plate. "Sorry about the noise. We're out. I wanted to check in and see how you were doing."

I walk into the empty living room and sit down in the middle. The sunlight has almost faded to black. The polish scent is strong in here, and the window that overlooks the street outside has been Windexed to death. There's not a smudge to be seen. Busying myself with mundane observations helps with the unease that Smith has created. "When you tell a person not to worry, it has the opposite effect. I'm vacillating between fear and straight panic right now."

"Hold on," he says. I think he mutes the phone because it goes silent for several seconds. "Are you there?" he asks, his voice now clearer. I confirm I am. "Moose has been speaking with Megan." I blow out a tiny, pent-up breath and fold my legs crisscross, finding a yoga pose. My friend Teala owns a yoga studio. She'd be proud. This isn't so bad.

"I may need a little more to go on. I don't see an issue," I reply.

The stubble on his chin rubs his cell phone, creating a scratching noise. "She's been calling me too. I'm not giving her the answers she wants, so she's resorted to trying to extort information from my best friend. At least I think that's what's going on. When I said it's nothing, I meant it. It's just irritating me right now. For the first time since the accident, I'm happy and I just want to move forward."

"I see. Well, if you think about it, Smith. You and Megan have been with each other longer than you've been without each other. You were teenagers. You may not remember, but she does. Something like what you had can't be easy to let go of. I hate to play the devil's advocate here, especially when it's in my interest to agree with you, but I can see why she's having a hard time with the recent events." I look at the rubber storage tubs emblazoned with "Eppy" written across them in black Sharpie marker. "And for the record, it sort of, kind of, is something I should worry about. What is she asking Moose?"

"He's always held a torch for Megan. I can't be sure what's going on, Carina. She wants to know about me. About you. About us."

I swallow down a ball of nerves. "I should talk to her." Part of me thinks I have no right to suggest it, but if things move forward as hastily as they have been, I owe it to her to give her my side of the story or at the very least listen to her and answer her questions firsthand. Moose wouldn't go there with Megan. I have to believe their friendship is stronger than that. "Moose would never do that to you. He's your friend." On the other hand, what if they could make each other happy?

"None of this matters, and I didn't want to concern you with it. I shouldn't have told you," Smith breathes. I can tell he's finished with this conversation. "Hearing your voice makes everything better. You should know that this doesn't make a difference to me. Moose called and left a vague voicemail and won't answer now. Where are you at right now?"

I know how to let something go. He doesn't want to talk about it, so I won't push. Right now, at least. Face-to-face is probably a better time to have a conversation such as this. "Fine. I trust you. Know that. You're allowed to be upset about Megan." Her name catches in my throat. "Why do you want to know where I am?" I ask, cradling the cell phone in the crook of my neck.

Jasmine swears in Mandarin from my bedroom. At least something I assume is a swear because of her angered tone.

"I want to know where you're at so I can start my list."

I smile. "List?" I ask. "A list of what?"

"The list of places in our house where I'll eventually make love to you." His voice is a low, rough timbre. Desire hits me in waves. It's shocking and immediate. My face flushes and my stomach flip-flops. "Every square inch, obviously. But I'm making a list with the order."

He's stolen my words and my breath. Something that's hard to do. "Oh," I reply.

"Where are you?" he asks again, his voice cutting straight to my core.

"The living room. Sitting right in the middle. Looking out the window," I explain. The sun sets completely, sheathing me in night.

Smith lets out a breath and audibly swallows. "That will be the first place," he says. "Make sure there isn't any furniture in that exact spot."

Licking my lips, I take note of my position and agree.

It takes a few moments of breathing. Feeling the oxygen enter and the carbon dioxide exit my body to clear my head. It's the first time we've spoken of sex. Not that it's not an undertone in every conversation we have, but it hasn't been allowed in the past, nor has it felt so right. This is our time now. I have to believe it is fate allowing a perfect circumstance. Nothing else explains the sheer coincidence of our predicament.

"I won't. I'll keep it clear," I reiterate.

If there is such a thing as hearing a grin, I do now. Smith is smiling, and this is a tiny victory in the middle of whatever he's dealing with in regard to Moose and Megan. "I wanted to ask you something," he whispers. It's still quiet. He's remained outside for our conversation.

"After our exchange, I'm pretty sure anything else will be icing on the cake," I joke.

He laughs, the turmoil from the beginning of our conversation extinct. "I'd like to bring you to meet my parents when I get home. It's my nephew's birthday, and they're having a little party for him. They want to meet you. I want you to meet them."

There are many things racing through my mind. *How can I follow Megan? What must they think about me? Do they think I'm to blame for the demise of the fairy-tale relationship? How will I respond if they do?* Most of all, I'm excited to take this step forward with him. As unorthodox as our relationship has been, this is a slice of normalcy I need—what I want. Roarke took away so many of my years. So, so many years of life that I now know could have been better spent without him. "Is that a good idea? I'm ready, of course, but is your family?"

"It's a ready-or-not type of thing. This is my life now. They accept that."

Picking at my nails restlessly, I imagine the scenario in my mind. My insecurities are many. Try as I might to overcome what I've dealt with, I'll carry the bothersome traits with me for the rest of my life. They disappear when I'm with Smith. When I'm writing. When I'm able to be myself truly and fully. "When?"

"Next weekend. They're only about an hour away."

The pit forms in my stomach. We talk for a few more minutes about his family, and I answer questions about the house and which tubs Moose dropped off. I tell him it basically gives me free rein to go through them. He laughs but agrees. I decide right then that I won't look. When Jasmine pops her head out of the door in the hallway wearing an irritated grimace, we say our good-byes. I stand, stretching my legs out in the first place where we will make love, and my head spins.

Deployment. Love. Endings.

CHAPTER TWELVE

Smith

I'M HUNGOVER. Hair of the dog isn't touching this mean headache. I shouldn't have had the fifth whiskey. We landed an hour ago, and Moose is hitting every pothole in the road as he drives me home. Home. To the place where I will live with Carina. She moved in while I was gone, so we haven't even spent a night together in our new house. We knew right away this was the place for us. The realtor opened the door, and it was right—every little flaw and corner seemed to fit us.

I belch and swallow down the bitter taste. "Who taught you to drive? Your little sister?" I grumble, holding my stomach in both hands like a pregnant woman.

Moose laughs, swerves unnecessarily around a wide corner, and replies, "Your mother."

"Ha. Ha. Are you going to tell me, in more detail, about your friendship with Megan?" I ask, glancing sideways at my friend. "You understand why I'm irritated," I finish.

Moose is a good man. Some of my SEAL brothers don't have the same strong morals as my friend here, so it bears asking the hard questions.

"If you want her, just say it."

He shakes his head, eyebrows furrowed. "I would never go there, as tempting as it may be. I'm being a friend to her. Remember, as long as you and I have been friends, Megan and I have been friends, too. You guys breaking up doesn't mean that I have to break up our friendship as well. Correct me if I'm wrong. Do I?" Moose asks.

My stomach rumbles, and my head pounds out a staccato in rhythm with my heartbeat. "Now isn't the best time for this conversation. If you're friends with her, then I believe you're friends with her and nothing more. I'm trying to keep Megan and Carina separated, but I'm finding it difficult."

Moose groans. "Megan is a wonderful woman. I thought you were the luckiest bastard alive. Carina is amazing. For you, lightning struck twice. Twice," he says, drawing out the last word. "If you want my sage advice, then move on and don't look back. Don't give Megan or her concerns a second thought. Move on with Carina. You've already made the choice."

I want to correct him and say that Megan made the choice for me, but I don't think it prudent in this moment, as he's obviously going to be in contact with her. The part of me that knows Megan wants to keep herself from harm or pain at all costs. It's an odd sensation because the other half of me only cares for Carina and how my feelings affect her.

We pull down my new street, and my heartbeat pounds out a warning. She's near, and she's finally mine without any barriers.

I just spent a week jumping out of airplanes. The land below me looked like a map with tiny dots—the blue sky expansive—swallowing a person whole. The falling sensation is that of ambivalence compared to what I feel right now. The anticipation of seeing Carina, of letting myself fall without reservation. Kissing her, touching the spot on the side of her stomach I've only seen when she leans over to retrieve something off the floor. Most of all, finally taking her lips—her body—and marking them as my own.

Moose pulls into the circular driveway. We end our conversation the way most men end conversations, with grunts of understanding and plans to meet at the gym. We've come to a silent agreement about Megan.

The house is shades of light brown and terracotta. Cacti and rocks litter the landscape. The ease of care was immediately a draw for both of us. Grass is an inconvenience that I don't want her to deal with while I'm away. In Southern California, grass isn't mandatory anyway. The large bay window in the front of the house is bare of curtains—I can see directly into our living room. There's a moment before she realizes I'm here that I appraise her. Carina's hair is in a ponytail, and she's wearing her black, thick-rimmed glasses. She was up writing all night. I want to be the reason she's up all night. She sees me approaching, smiles, and runs to open the door before I can reach the threshold.

Her brown eyes are pools of emotion, and her soft skin—this uncharted, perfect territory—glistens. I'm more familiar with the clouds wrapping my skin than I am of the expanse of Carina Painter's body. Her mind has been mine for quite some time. A fact that both makes me happy and hesitant at the same time. I know exactly what she's been through in her past and with her relationship with Roarke, and I'm hoping to erase every scar it produced.

Moose shouts a quick hello and farewell to Carina and rumbles away. During all of this, she hasn't taken her eyes off me.

"Welcome home, Smith," she says, smiling with her eyes.

My large duffel bag hits the ground the second her voice grazes my ears. I take her in my arms, pull her tight against my body, and tuck my head into the side of her neck. A few deep breaths later, I'm more delirious with lust than I was envisioning her naked. "I missed you," I whisper into her ear. The urge to lick her neck and kiss her war with my moral sensibility to wait for the perfect moment.

She pulls back, sliding her hands on either side of my face to look at me head-on. "It couldn't possibly be more than I missed you." She leans forward, a very subtle gesture, but I'm tuned into her at the micro level, so I notice. Her lips twitch. "I put together furniture. Remember? Of course I missed you more."

I smile, full and wide. "So you just missed my alpha male muscles and testosterone?" I sling my duffel back on my shoulder. Carina pulls me through the door and closes it behind me. The house smells like her—the light scent of perfume and freshly-washed clothing. I drop my bag and kick it to the side.

"I missed a lot more than that," she says. "I was teasing. I'm more than capable of doing testosterone-fueled jobs, but I missed your testosterone more than I probably should have. Just in a different way than you're implying."

My cock hardens in a swift jerk. I readjust it through my jeans, and her gaze dips down.

"I hope you agree with my choices."

"That's a tactic. Isn't it? Blindsiding me with lust in two sentences, and then asking a question? You can get anything you want that way. For future reference."

Ignoring every testosterone-driven response in my body is difficult, but I do. I need everything to be perfect before we delve into that passion-fueled place of no return.

Carina smiles, tugs on the bottom of her black workout shorts, and says, "Let me show you what I've done."

I nod. "Lead on," I tell her, extending an arm at the hall to the right of us. I want to look at her ass as she walks—something that won't help the current situation in my pants. "It smells like home already." I hate to compare, but this place, with Carina in it, is homier than the house I purchased with Megan. The house I lived in for years.

"Yeah? I'm glad it doesn't smell like fake wood and spray cleaner anymore," she says over her shoulder. Carina rambles on about how she wants me to put my touches on the rooms and says multiple times that I can change anything I want.

"I don't want to change anything. You've done an amazing job." And she has. The house looks lived in, minus my huge rubber storage tubs pushed against a wall in my bedroom. My room. We talked at length about living together and the challenges that may arise. We agreed that our friendship is the number one priority regardless of how taking things to the next level goes. I've told my family that Carina is my girlfriend. We're expected at my mom's house late this afternoon.

She turns completely when she's in front of one of the bedrooms at the end of the hall. "I set up my bed in here. I know we said we'd keep separate bedrooms until, well, you know, we established some sort of status we were both comfortable with, but you don't have a bed yet. And I won't have you sleep on the couch I put together. For fear for your life, of course. We can sleep in here together. If you're comfortable, that is." She's rambling, looking everywhere except at my eyes.

Glancing over one shoulder, I study her room and the four large marker boards covering a light gray wall. The scribbles and circles confuse me, but my name, always written in black marker, stands out. She backs in a few steps to provide room for me to enter. "Sleep with you, huh? Didn't you put together this bed as well? Who's to say this one is any safer than the sofa out there?" I hike my thumb behind me and flash her a grin.

She blushes. "Jasmine put the bed together," she says, sitting down on the edge of the king-sized mattress. It's covered in a soft purple duvet. "I told you it was a hidden talent of hers." Carina bites her bottom lip and pats the bed next to her. "See?"

With her seated, she's eye level to my dick. A fool would hesitate, so walking a couple more steps, I sit next to her and rest my hand on her knee. "You do realize we'll need to do more than sit to test her craftsmanship?" I turn in time to see her swallow deeply.

"Right now?" she asks. So few things are this simple anymore. We're both on the same page—we know exactly what we want. "You mentioned taking it slow when we had the relationship conversation before. Humping like sex-deprived rabbits five minutes after you walk through the door is scarcely slow." Before I can respond, she slides her hand over mine—the one on her knee—and guides it up her smooth thigh to rest at the hem of her shorts. The skin on my hands is sensitive to textures and temperatures, and gliding against hers is an extreme pleasure. "Say the word, Smith."

If I said the words fuck, sex, make love, bang, copulate, or tap, we wouldn't leave this room for months. Maybe years. I can't be sure.

Gently, I take her wrist in my free hand and pull her over to straddle my lap. Her face is so close that her nose is brushing my own, and her sweet breath makes me lightheaded. Carina's arms wind around my neck, and her fingers find their way to my hair. She pulls it softly while she catches her breath.

"While I'd love nothing more than to rip off your clothes and fuck you until I can't remember my name, we have to go to my parents' house soon. When, and notice I didn't say if, I said when, I finally take your body, I'll need days. First, days to plan exactly what I want to do with you, and then days to execute said plans." I brush my nose from her ear down her neck.

A tiny moan escapes her lips, and she lowers her hips to sink herself onto my hard-on. Every muscle in my body flexes in response. "What if I have my own plans?" Carina breathes, her voice a mask of longing. This is a new side of her. One I've only dreamed about.

My phone vibrates in my pocket, startling us. "It's divine intervention. Even my cell phone wants my plans to be successful."

With an exaggerated sigh, she leans to one side to afford me room to reach my cell. I'm not in a career where I can send a call to voicemail. At this point in my work-up, I have to be ready to deploy on a moment's notice. If I get the phone call, I have two hours to be on base and ready to pack out. It doesn't mean I have to answer gracefully. "Talk," I say, holding the phone up to my ear without checking the caller.

Carina leans over to my opposite ear and whispers. She tells me how she can help make my plan successful. I've never wanted anything else more. My mother, on the other end, telling me to pick up limes on our way is merely background noise.

She leans back, smiles, kisses me on the cheek, her lips barely brushing the corner of my mouth, and hops off my lap.

I reach out my hand as she goes. My balls are painful

reminders of what I almost had. "All right, Mom. She's excited too. Yep. Yeah. The house is great," I say, answering her mundane questions with as much patience as I can muster. I hear Carina in the bathroom. The water turns on, and I'm sure I hear the moment her clothing drops to the floor.

I run a hand through my hair and then press my palm down the front of my jeans. "No, there's nothing to worry about. Yes, I saw it as well. There's nothing to worry about. Turn off the news. Nothing good comes of it these days." It's both truth and fiction. She really shouldn't watch television anymore, but worry? Yeah, she should. Every day the news reports a new terrorist attack. Here on American soil. Each attack gets a little more organized, a little more threatening, and more innocent lives are taken. I hang up the phone after I console Mom one more time and lie back on Carina's bed.

I want to close my eyes for a few minutes to clear my head and rest my wiles. What feels like minutes later, Carina wakes me by tousling my hair and pressing a kiss to my temple.

"Time to go, sleepyhead." She's dressed in a soft pink dress. Her perfume is mouthwatering, and she looks stunning. "I let you sleep as long as I could."

I drank too much last night. This nap has to be my substitute for the hair of the dog.

I smile at her, letting myself appraise each one of her features thoroughly. "I think this bed will do quite fine," I remark. Standing, I take her chin in my hand and tilt her head to the side, exposing her neck. Inhaling deeply twice, I close my eyes.

She sighs. "I'm glad you approve."

CHAPTER THIRTEEN

Carina

IT REMINDS me of the Amityville house of horrors. The large wooden house is set back away from the street. It's a tall, sky-blue monster with an octagonal stained glass window at the highest peak in the center. I'm always amazed at how my surroundings change after a short drive. Smith's parents have a wooded property. We live close to the beach. And we're both considered SoCal residents.

Smith drove us in his truck and told me all about them on the way. His nephew is turning seven, and his younger sister is married to an accountant. They live a few houses down from his parents. "I wish I could take you to meet my parents," I say, violently twisting the chiffon dress in my hands. "You can never trust a person without any family." I smile, but it's wistful. There has to be some truth to that statement. The only person I considered true family, my grandmother, died when I was a teenager. "I'm a broken, orphaned woman." I'm only half joking.

After I split from Roarke, I spoke with a professional. Because some things shouldn't be bottled up inside, and although I know what's wrong with me, hearing it from someone who specializes in crazy is refreshing. He told me it could be why I create characters in my stories. It combats the loneliness and fills the void where loving parents are supposed to reside. He also told me it's one of the reasons I stayed with Roarke after he beat me both verbally and physically. There's nothing like clinging to attachments no matter how destructive they may be. Smith doesn't have my same concerns, but when we spoke about it, I think he understood.

"Show me the house you grew up in?" he asks. He knows every sordid detail about my past. When I interview him, he always asks questions in return. What's fair is fair and all of that. "He's gone now, Carina. It's just a house now." Smith knows not to use his name. We know each other well.

I shrug, sigh, and make a grab for his leg. The heated moment in my bedroom turned into a heated hour and a heated drive, and basically it's simmering in every pregnant pause and lull in our conversation. "We could drive by," I say. Thinking of the house I grew up in sets my teeth on edge regardless of my insane libido.

Smith pulls behind a large garage structure and puts the truck in park. He takes my hand in his but leaves mine on his leg. His need to touch me is as strong as mine to him. "No one is ever going to hurt you again," he promises. When he smiles and squeezes my hand, I believe him. He's the type of man who can protect me from anything that goes bump in the night. Smith has my trust implicitly.

"What about you?" I ask. "You have the means to destroy me. Destroying is kind of in your job description if you want to get technical."

His gorgeous eyes close, shielding me from his true

thoughts, and he exits the vehicle to reappear on the passenger side. He opens my door.

Taking my head and neck in his hands, he says, "I would never hurt you. You mean everything to me. You're like *my precious*. I've wanted you from the first moment I laid eyes on you." I wasn't the same person when he saw me in that theater.

I smile because the radiant truth I find in his eyes is too much. Also, the *Lord of the Rings* joke. "Does Gollum live in the basement? It looks a little bit..." I trail off, my gaze flickering to his childhood home.

"Scary?" he asks.

I nod, and he pulls me against his chest. I can breathe here. The monsters that follow me disappear. I'm not truly afraid of the house. Smith knows this. I'm afraid of everything that follows. The future. The unknown. Deployment. Tiptoeing in the new waters of our structurally unsound relationship. "Let's go. I know a little man who wants to eat cake. He is waiting for us. I'd be scared of him before anything else."

Smith leads me into the house, one hand securely on my waist. He is wearing a blue, long-sleeved button-up. I observe that he tries to cover his arms when we're in public, so I notice he's doing it now when we're visiting his parents. It says something. I'm not sure what quite yet. When a petite brunette rounds the corner with a stack of teetering, multicolored presents in her arms, Smith tightens his grip.

"Fiona," Smith says. The house is warm and smells of scented candles and pizza.

She peeks around the gifts. Her eyes light up as she sees her brother, then her face falls when she notices me. "It's so good to see your ugly mug," Fiona says, setting her son's loot down on an empty table and approaching her brother with arms wide. I step away so she can hug him properly. "And who might this lovely lady be?" She's polite, at least. I expected some magnitude of hostility because of our strange circumstances and because of Megan.

I extend my hand. "I'm Carina. It's so good to meet you. Smith has spoken so highly of his baby sister."

That garners a smile from her. She takes my hand, says the pleasure is all hers, and excuses herself to tend to the mob of children clamoring for cake. Brief, yet pleasant. If all of the interactions with his family are similar, I'll be free and clear.

Smith tells me he's going to help and says I should make myself at home. I wave him off and keep the lump in my throat under wraps. The foyer has childhood photos in every direction. I spot Smith in most of them. Watching him grow up from year to year makes me giggle and swoon at the same time. He went through the bowl cut, crooked teeth, and chubby bunny phases like most children who grew up in the '80s and '90s. I see the strapping man he would grow up to become when I get to the wall that houses their high school years. My heart drops when I come upon Megan in a glittering prom dress, and then again clutching his hand, sitting on the tail of a truck, and several more. I have to remind myself she's been the only one. She's his only one. From first kisses to bedroom acrobatics, it's been Megan.

"He was quite the handsome fellow back then, wasn't he?" a voice chimes from behind me. Smith's mother is beautiful. She's petite like Fiona but holds more authority. Her graying hair is swept up into a neat chignon, and her face is free of any deep wrinkles. She's aged well. Her smile, though? I see where Smith got his from. It dimples on one side, and her white, straight teeth are on full display.

I shake her hand. "Carina," I say. "He's quite the

handsome fellow now as well." I return her grin, and in an unexpected move, she wraps me in her arms, hugging me tightly. When she pulls back, her mascaraed eyes are brimming with tears. "I haven't seen him this happy in a long time, Carina. Thank you," she whispers, looking both left and right to make sure we're alone.

I clear my own throat. She's skipped all pleasantries. No weather, no work talk, just straight to the core of why I'm nervous to be standing here. "Please," I say, shaking my head. "Don't thank me. Smith is the most incredible man I've ever met, Mrs. Eppington."

"Margaret, please, dear. Call me Margaret," she corrects, waving one hand. "He is indeed incredible. We're lucky to have him with us. I remind myself of that daily."

I hear children chattering and Smith laughing in the kitchen. The sound reassures me that everything is okay. I'm safe here. He's safe.

"He wasn't this incredible after his accident, though." She smoothes her hair back on both sides even though it's already perfect, not a hair out of place. "The man you know is the best version. Hearing that excitement in his voice when he talks about you is something I feared I'd never hear again." She looks behind me at the photos of Smith and Megan. "Not even back then was he this smitten."

How is that possible? And what does she have to gain by telling me this tidbit? I know she loves Megan like a daughter. Smith has told me as much. I know she still speaks with her too. There isn't a woman in the world that would be this okay with her ex-fiancé moving on. And with such severity and haste. We're living together. If Megan is at peace with this situation, she's truly a better woman than I ever gave her credit for.

I resume twisting the sides of my dress.

"I find that hard to believe, but appreciate the sentiment nonetheless." I nod, trying as hard as I can to keep my posture straight and my chin up. Subconsciously, I always shrink into myself, warring with feelings of self-loathing.

"He is a good man. Perhaps a little confused right now, but he's a good man. I hope you realize what a treasure you have." It's very sweet. I hear the threat behind her words, though.

Crossing my arms, I let it roll off my back. This is what mothers do. They protect. Seeing it firsthand is odd and reassuring. There was one time when my own mother, God rest her soul, tried to save me from Greg. She snuck into my bedroom early in the morning and told me to run. She didn't stand up to him or shield my body with her own, she told me to get out of dodge because he was angry. I went to my friend Jenna's house for two whole days. When I returned, she was on a liquor run, and my stepfather was home, waiting for me. That was the first time he raped me. I always wonder what would have happened if we never went down that road —if I hadn't listened to my mother. If I'd stayed, perhaps Greg would have locked me in the shed for a few hours— maybe a night. He was upset I couldn't get the blood stain off his favorite button-up. The memory forces a shudder.

"I couldn't possibly hurt him, ma'am. I'm not that kind of woman." I open my mouth to tell her that I love him, but I can't. I haven't admitted my feelings to Smith yet. "He's important to me."

"Because his story is your next bestseller?" she asks, avoiding eye contact.

I shake my head. "Because he's the single most amazing man I've encountered in my life. He's a man with qualities I don't take lightly. Trust me that he's in good hands for as long as he'll keep me."

His mother smiles, and I force my own, my heart hammering in protest.

At the reminder of the book, my palms begin to sweat. It will be impossible to explain my pseudo-romance, nonfiction, fiction novel to his family. With the ending still up in the air, the mere thought of my book makes me cringe and wish I were in front of my laptop toiling.

Margaret pats my shoulder and excuses herself into the kitchen. I return to studying the photos on the wall, the ones with Megan and his high school friends. He wasn't as happy then, I remind myself. It's a small victory in the big picture, but a victory nonetheless.

Conversation is pleasant with his family. His father looks like an older, carbon copy of Smith, and he is very quiet and reserved. I get the feeling that when he does speak, everyone listens and appreciates it. He's a little less rough around the edges than Smith. As an introvert and people-watcher, I'm comfortable going out on a limb and assuming that Smith's career path was a shock to his family. Now that it's stolen parts and pieces of him, I'd fathom neither parent is as glamorized by his SEAL status as the rest of the world.

As we hang out, Smith always makes sure to touch me, or kiss the side of my head, or include me in conversation even when I'd be better left out. He says my name like a praise, passing his lips into a world I'm unfamiliar with. The way he talks about me is almost embarrassing. It's the first opportunity I've had to witness how highly he regards me. I blush. I fidget. Especially when he speaks of my novels and accolades.

"But no one will know it's about Smith?" Fiona asks after sipping coffee. The children are loud, sticky with sweet-smelling candy, and buzzing around with youthful fury. "Kids, outside!" she finishes, pointing a finger into the air.

The children go, their pounding feet resembling the noise of drunk cattle.

"No one will know," Smith answers when quiet settles.

I clear my throat. "I've changed everything. His facts are in there, but they're twisted in a way where his identity could never be uncovered. No matter how much someone sleuths," I say. Taking a sip of my own coffee, I let the heat burn my throat on the way down. "I truly think this novel will help someone. Not because I'm writing it, but because Smith's life is spectacular and relatable." Over the time that we've known each other, he's given so much of himself to me in his stories. It's helped me to open up too. It happened unexpectedly—he caught me off guard. At this point I've told him my darkest secrets, and he knows my life driven desires. In divulging his darkest nightmares, he's helped me heal my own demons.

"I can't wait to read it," Fiona says. "He never tells us anything." She smirks in Smith's direction. Smith balls up a napkin and tosses it at Fiona's face. She swats it away, laughing. The banter is light, unforced. It's like I've been sitting at this table with these people for a long time—not meeting them for the first time.

Margaret's cell phone rings. She raises one brow and takes the call in another room. Fiona looks uneasily at her mother's retreating back and continues talking to her husband about books.

"Want to go play a game of hide-and-seek with the kids?" Smith asks. He takes my hand and doesn't wait for a response. "I'm sure adult supervision is required after that much sugar."

I laugh. "It's the equivalent of an adult having four cocktails," I say. I'm trailing behind him as he guides me down the porch steps and around the house to the thin copse of trees the children are circling. "Why the hasty exit?"

Smith runs his free hand through his hair. I notice the scars on his hands as I admire his strong, large physique. "Megan called my mom."

I raise my brows. "I'm glad you see no need to lie," I reply. "I should be sad, but after listening to you sing my praises for the past hour, I'm confident nothing else matters." It stings. I can't erase his or his family's past. Megan has every right to call. To visit. To wonder how the birthday party is going on without her presence.

"Sad? I was afraid you'd get pissed." Smith yells at the kids to get ready for the best game of hide-and-seek the world has ever seen.

Furrowing my brow, I try to bring anger to the surface. Most women would be mad or self-conscious at the very least. "How could I possibly get angry?" On the contrary, most women haven't received a beating in their life. I know whom I should appreciate and trust. I squeeze his hand. Smith shrugs, shakes his head, and licks his lips. I smirk as the children disperse through the yard. "Turn around and close your eyes," I whisper into his ear.

When he chuckles, I peck his cheek and take off in the opposite direction, heading for several large trees that might conceal me. He calls out after me, but I don't stop my hurried pace. Echoes of laughter fill the air, and eventually I hear Smith's booming voice call out, "Ready or not, here I come!"

"That was not twenty seconds," I huff under my breath. I pin my lips together between my teeth, and as slowly and carefully as I'm able, I peek out from behind the tree. Smith is chasing a little boy, his pace indicating he's giving the child the benefit of a head start.

My heart thumps loudly as I watch him, the man I love, play. He looks so carefree, innocent, and unassuming. This isn't the war-torn soldier shouldering loss, tenuous responsibility, and memories that invoke the worst kind of nightmares. He's opening my eyes to a softer side. A side I've always known has been inside but hasn't had the opportunity to come to light. Flashes of a future I never dreamed of having start flickering in the part of my brain untainted by Roarke. It's like magic. Like healing. Like maybe sometimes miracles do happen.

I hear when his footsteps approach my hiding spot. They're quiet at first, and then almost silent when he realizes I'm near. Reaching behind me, I lay my palms against the rough bark of the tree and think about Smith's ability to blend into any circumstance. The sense of touch grounds me in the here and now.

"Olly olly oxen free," Smith says, rounding the tree.

Tossing my head back, I laugh. "That easy?" I ask. My smile fades when I see the intensity of his gaze. His body is lithe yet solid as he approaches.

With one hand on the tree, he shakes his head. "Quite the opposite, actually. Difficult. You're difficult," Smith growls. He rubs his fingers over his top lip.

I frown. "I resent that. Fully. I pride myself on being easy. Wait, that didn't come out right," I say, smirking.

Smith places both of his palms on the tree on either side of my head.

"I could be easy right now if you wanted, though," I coax.

He leans closer, his nose brushing the side of mine. His scent—the mouthwatering, fatally toxic scent of him —enters my body. I inhale deeply just as he blows out a breath.

"Difficult in that I don't think I can hold out another second," Smith says, his lips brushing mine on the last word. It would be the easiest thing in the world to lean up and press my lips against his. I want him to want me as badly as I want him. The feelings are so intense I have to close my eyes to block out one sense.

"Don't hold out," I whisper. "You can't hide forever." When I feel his hands on the sides of my face, I open my eyes. "Smith," I finish.

Instead of responding, he nods and rubs his thumb along my lower lip and ends by pulling it down to open my mouth.

I'm hyperaware of this moment. I know it's when everything changes. The setting sun plays peekaboo through the trees next to us, and the sounds of the children's shrill laughter lift on a slight breeze. Smith leans down and brushes his lips against mine back and forth. I taste his breath as mine mingles with his. My head, held still in his hands, is at his mercy. When I'm sure it's going to happen, I wrap my hands around his waist and pull my body against his. The muscles he's worked so hard to rehabilitate mold against me as if they were made to fit with mine.

"I'm going to kiss you," he says. And then he does. Before I can respond. Before I can scream at the top of my lungs, *Yes! Finally. Please. Kiss me and never stop,* our lips crash together in a hurried violence. It's a large amount of pent-up sexual frustration culminating in our mouths colliding—becoming one. After all of our interviews, my mind wandering to his perfect moving lips I could only dream about tasting, I finally get them. His tongue seeks mine out as his hands tilt my head to the side to ease us into a better angle.

I clutch the back of his shirt, tugging him into me until I think I may be hurting him. He releases my head and picks me up, turns so his back is against the tree, and continues his assault from here. My legs wrap around his waist, and in the midst of this frenzied lust filled with stolen breaths and shared emotions, his erection pressing against me, I decide that Smith Eppington is the only person I want to kiss for the rest of my life.

He's my morphine, the solitary reason my heart beats fast and slow in any single moment. I might as well be strung like a puppet and marched into an arena naked. This is how I feel when he asserts his control—his dominance—over me. There are so many things I want to tell him, but neither of us wants to be the first to break away from this moment of pure bliss. I've never been kissed like I'm oxygen, like I'm the reason one lives, kissed like I alone can keep a heart pumping. This is what I feel when Smith finally moves from my lips and trails his wet mouth down the side of my neck. Jutting my hips further, I seek out his hard bulge and wish we were naked. I wish we were back home in the one bed in our house.

I wish he were my first. I wish he were my last. I pray he will be the latter. He lets me slide down to my feet but keeps me against his body. Our kiss is broken, but emotions are running so high I can scarcely catch my breath. Gazing into his eyes, I find myself lost and found at the exact same time.

"And right before my eyes, one kiss tilted the earth," Smith says, flicking his gaze to different spots on my face, like he's cementing it to memory. "I don't know what it is," he says. His breathing is ragged as he drags a hand through his hair and promptly returns to touching me—light touches on my arm, my neck, the sides of my face, and ever so gently grazing his palms over my breasts on top of my dress.

"I know," I say. Licking my lips, I lock my arms

around his neck. "This is what it's like in romance novels." When it's real.

Smith smiles and shakes his head, still entranced with gazing at me piece by piece.

Because he can, he leans down and kisses me once more. And it's sweet this time—bittersweet. He doesn't, but I know how some romance novels end.

And it's not always with happily ever after.

CHAPTER FOURTEEN

Smith

IT DOESN'T FEEL like I thought it would. It feels better. Carina tastes like victory, solace, and truth. I can't stop staring at her, devouring every nuance of perfection. The high-pitched squeals of the children are drowned out by the sound of my heartbeat. They told me it stopped before I arrived at the hospital after my accident. Literally, I was dead—flatlined—sleeping with the angels. Scanning the planes of her face, rose-colored lips, and her soulful eyes, I realize why I came back. *Her.*

"A penny for your thoughts?" I ask, utterly lost in my own.

Tucking her hair behind her ears, she leans in to kiss me. "My thoughts are worth more than a penny," she replies, her wet mouth against mine. "But I'll tell you anyway." Carina pulls back but keeps her body entwined with mine. I'd take her right here and now if I weren't a stronger man. With one kiss, I'm convinced this woman is the reason I was born.

She strokes my lips with one finger. I feel that one small touch in every nerve ending in my body. "I'm thinking that you're an excellent kisser. You didn't forget how to do that." Her grin is intoxicating. I clench my teeth together to control the animal urges coiling every muscle in my body. If I had felt even an ounce of this with Megan, perhaps I would have tried harder for her and our dismantled relationship. As it stands, the emotions coursing through me are enough to bring a grown man to his knees—commit felonies.

I shake my head. "I've practiced this in my mind dozens of times," I explain. Thousands. She doesn't need to know that creepy statistic. It's the first time she's mentioned my amnesia outside of interview questions. Her mouth drops open, her white teeth peeking out, and I take advantage. I let my lips find hers and close my eyes with a relieved groan. "And not even in my well-practiced dreams did it feel this good. Tell me you feel this."

Holding her chin, I run my tongue along her bottom lip. Goose bumps rise on her skin.

"I feel it," she whispers. "The magnetic pull that surrounds us at any given moment didn't lie." She swallows loudly. "It's terrifying."

"What you mean to say is it's amazing. Maybe fantastic?" I ask.

"But still terrifying," she replies, smiling. Her eyes dance, and she bites her lip. "To have so much to lose. To have so much. I've never had that before. I thought I did, but you've made me realize I was sorely mistaken. Also..." Carina says, trailing off.

My breathing pace speeds up even further. "Also what?" I say. I lead her from our hidden spot behind the trees, but I never let my gaze flicker from her face. Megan was always easy to read, her emotions plainly on display. Carina, as a result of a hard life, hides much.

She keeps her hand in mine, and her large brown eyes tilt down a touch. "The also being what's it going to be like when we have sex?" A small grin pulls the corner of her mouth as she whispers the words.

"That's why you're terrified," I say. "Sex." When I say it out loud, I realize I'm the one who should be terrified of sex. Not because I'm concerned it won't be earthshaking, but because I've only been with one woman. Megan instructed me on how I used to perform, on what she liked. "I can assure you I have nothing that will terrify you." When she laughs, I wink.

"From what I've felt, it could be scary," Carina says, raising one brow. She tries and fails to hold a straight face. My dick responds to her sentiments immediately.

I clear my throat. "Don't tempt me. I'll take you upstairs to the bedroom I jacked off in at least a million times and scare the ever-loving shit out of you," I say. "I mean that in the most sexual way possible," I add on. Legitimately scaring her is a true fear of mine. "Then taking it slow will be out of the question and I'll be upset with my willpower."

She squeezes my arm. "Your willpower is stronger than it should be. I'm taking your clothes off as soon as we get home, Smith. Will you teach me about willpower then?"

A million scenarios of Carina naked come to mind. Her state of dress is unimportant. It's her eyes. The way her eyes scorch as she returns my gaze is the biggest turn-on. "Yeah. Yeah, I'll teach you all about willpower," I groan.

After she nods, a promising response, Carina's eyes land on the commotion in front of us. It forces a break in the tension boiling around our bodies. Never has a kiss ruined me in such a way. Even if I remembered my past, I'm confident that this is a fire that has never burned inside of me before.

Her voice draws me from my lust-hazed stupor. "I just wanted to drop by quickly and wish you a happy birthday," Megan says. She strokes my nephew Will's hair the way she always does when she sees him. He smiles up at her. The contents of my stomach turn to battery acid. Carina's grip tightens, and for that small gesture, I'm glad. I'm able to be the person who protects her always. Even in this uncomfortable moment, I will do my best. Next, Megan's eyes seek me out.

She won't be rude, I don't think. Megan approaches, her lithe gait swaying as she sizes us up—formulates the right thing to say. Now her phone call to my mother makes sense. "I wanted to bring Will a gift. That's all. I didn't know you'd be here, Smith. I'm sorry about that," Megan says. She stands closer than is comfortable, and I'm not sure why. "I was already on my way when I called your momma."

The tension in my arm eases a touch. "Megan. Good to see you again," Carina says.

"Loud, isn't it?" Megan asks, making small talk. Will's laughter rings out, followed by several more shrieks. "It looks like they're having a blast." Megan looks over her shoulder at the kids.

"They are," I reply. "We were just getting out of here."

Will runs up behind Megan and hugs her with one arm. "They were kissing by the tree, not hiding," Will says, a toothless grin wide on his face.

Megan's smile fades. "I see. Kissing behind trees was always Uncle Smith's thing."

Will wrinkles his nose and then he's gone, pounding away from us toward his friends.

Carina laughs uncomfortably while shifting her weight from one foot to the other. Megan folds her arms across her chest, eyes sad and angry. "Can I talk to you quickly, Smith?" Her gaze fixes on Carina. "Alone, if you don't mind?" she says to the scared woman clutching my arm. "It will just take a sec, darlin'."

"Of course. I'll go," Carina says. I don't let her pull

away. I use my hand to keep her entwined with me. "Smith, really. It's fine. I'll head inside to grab my purse." I understand avoiding conflict, but Carina's backbone bends at the subtlest hint of an argument. It's my job to make her feel secure in her place.

"No. You're exactly where you should be," I say, looking down at Carina.

She gives a small smile and bites her lower lip.

"You stay."

She nods. It's not an order. It's a strong request—me letting her know how secure she is in her place next to me.

Megan scowls. I aim a pointed look right back. "If you have something to say, you can say it in front of Carina." I take my free hand out of my pocket to send a wave in Fiona's direction. She's staring daggers at the three of us with bulged eyes and a mouth so wide it's catching flies. She waves back, folding her hand in half briefly, and retreats into the house.

Carina tightens her grip on my forearm. I don't have the heart to tell her she's hurting my scars. Megan sees, and she smiles like she's in on some inside joke. "I guess it's easier this way anyway. I wanted to see if you'd be against Carina and me getting together to talk. I wanted to get to know her better. Moose has so many wonderful things to say, and I think it's only fair if I get a small taste of what, or better yet, who is so utterly irresistible to the superhuman man who stole so many of my years," Megan drawls. Her blue eyes dart down to my forearm once again. "And maybe I can give her a few pointers on the care and keeping of Smith Eppington while I'm at it."

Ambivalence is key in moments such as this. I'm also not in practice. "Pointers in keeping me, huh?" I ask, smiling.

"That was rude, Smith," Carina whispers.

Megan clears her throat. "It's an expression. The lady is right. You mind your manners, sir," she says. "I mean no harm, Carina. I truly want to get to know you a little better. Call it curiosity. Nothing more and nothing less."

"That would be fine, I think," Carina says. Her voice is small, like that of a disobedient child. "If Smith is okay with it," she corrects.

I lean down and kiss the top of her head. Even the briefest moment spent that close to her has me inhaling the sweet scent of her shampoo. "You don't need my permission," I reply.

"Good. It's settled. Lunch and shopping next weekend? Fashion Valley?" Megan says.

Carina's vise grip finally relents. The assault is almost over. To be continued next weekend. "That sounds great. I look forward to it," Carina says.

The women exchange numbers while I watch, enrapt at this odd occurrence. I'm not sure if I can trust Megan, but I have to trust that Carina can hold her own. She mentioned talking to Megan on multiple occasions, so I know she'll be prepared. If there's one thing I know she's good at, it's spinning the conversation to make sure she's not the one divulging too much information.

Megan's voice breaks me from my worries. "You seem really happy. Really happy," Megan says. Her eyes tilt down in the corners, and her mouth turns down as she lets her eyes wander over my face, neck, and arms. "I'm glad," she finishes. She's not. My god, she's not glad. This is a show for Carina, and Megan knows I'm well aware of what she's doing.

Carina thanks her, but Megan only has eyes for me. I try to be tactful yet biting. "It's the happiest I've been in a long time," I say.

Megan swallows audibly and bids us a hasty farewell. She ruffles Will's hair one more time and heads back into the house. We don't go back inside until I see her car driving away.

"Try as I might, I can't blame her. If I were in her shoes, I'd be curious, too," Carina says. She twists her dress in her free hand. "I come in like a ninja and take what's always been hers." A sigh escapes her pretty mouth.

Turning to face her, I grab her wrist to halt the nervous twitch. A few years ago I wouldn't have noticed something this small and seemingly insignificant. I'm bothered terribly by the stupid gesture now. It's Carina's discomfort present with me. My stomach hurts. "You can blame her. When she broke up with me, she said she wanted a clean break. This isn't that. This is meddling with the one thing I care about. I won't lose you because of her, Carina. I can't." I lift my shoulders, then lower them again. Carina stops her hand and runs it through her pretty hair. "Also, it hurts my arms when you vise-grip me," I say.

Her mouth pops open, and she covers it with her delicate hand. "I'm so sorry. I should have known better. How will that affect you when you deploy and you're wearing mountains of heavy gear?"

I explain that all over pressure is different from tiny fingers digging into my skin pressure. I try to comfort her by telling her a joke because she feels bad, but I'm the one who ends up feeling uneasy at the prospect of leaving her. Soon. The time we have together is precious. The countdown is on.

Fiona is waiting for us when we make our way to the living room. "No one lost any teeth or hair," she says. "I tried telling Mom it was a bad idea to send her out there without warning, but she wanted to let the chips fall where they may."

I pull Carina into the seat next to me on the white,

linen sofa. "Were you taking bets?" I ask. "I'm joking." I turn to make sure Carina is aware. "She's been a part of the family for as long as I can remember. Which, uh, isn't much, kind of, but I understand. So does Carina. There's no bad blood between us."

"Just memories you don't remember," Fiona says.

I shrug. "Inconsequential at this point, don't you think?"

She shrugs back. Typical sister move. "I guess so. I'm sorry you had to endure that, for what it's worth, Carina," Fiona replies. "Once Megan has her mind made up, that's that."

Carina shrugs. "Can't say I blame her." With that, the conversation blessedly ends, and worry pangs my heart.

We talk for several more minutes when my parents join us. Mostly everyone ignores the Megan interruption in favor of my looming deployment and what exactly I'll be doing: which I can't say. Where I'll be: I'm not sure of an exact location yet. It has been changing daily. What I'll be doing: I make something up, because moms and sisters don't want the truth. They want a thinly veiled concept of safety and my comfort. I give them that. Everyone's concern is the attacks that have been increasing in frequency on American soil.

And with damn good reason.

CHAPTER FIFTEEN
Carina

WHEN THE MESS you get yourself into is no fault but your own, you can't complain about it. You roll with it with as much dignity and tact as you can. Growing up with my stepfather, I learned that lesson quickly. I made a mistake, I was punished for it. Now that I'm out of his rule and living my own life, the concept is still similar, albeit a little less painful. I fell for a taken man. The problem was he was only taken in a one-sided fashion. I can't stop putting myself in Megan's shoes. If I were the one to lose Smith, how awful the feeling must be. I shake the bad feelings away and try to concentrate.

My Bose headphones cancel out all noise. I don't have the music on, just complete silence. I'm at my small glass desk in my bedroom with the door closed. I'm pounding the keys, desperately trying to make headway on my manuscript.

As soon as we returned from his parents' house, Smith got a call and had to head in to work. He was not pleased. I've never heard him curse so much and so strongly as he did after he hung up the call. Part of me is happy to have a little space from him and what he makes me feel. Never in all of my years have I been so attracted to a person. His looks aside, the personality that shines through in every single moment of his life is enough to knock me flat on the floor, delirious with lust and...love.

Currently, I'm deleting more than I'm writing. It's a fight to get words on screen tonight—so distracted by his kiss and then by his ex. The thought gives me an idea. I pull up the chapter in which my characters have their first kiss, and I revise it. I close my eyes and remember his lips against mine. I write every detail, every feeling, every touch. Our first kiss becomes theirs, and even on paper the moment jumps off the pages as truth.

"This is how it needs to happen," I whisper to myself. Reading over the scene makes my heart pound. It's so real. I need an outside perspective to know if it's as strong as I feel it is. Dialing Jasmine is easy. She's speed dial number one on my cell phone. Like any best friend, she picks up right before it goes to voicemail in no-man's-land. No one listens to voicemails these days.

"I have to read you something, and I need an honest opinion," I say. I forgo a hello in favor of getting down to business.

I hear talking and laughing and then complete silence. "I'm ready," Jasmine says simply. There are no questions, no shit, because it's the weekend and I'm working. I remember she's out with our friends. An invitation I didn't accept because I thought Smith and I would be preoccupied with each other for at least twenty-four hours.

"I rewrote part of chapter ten," I say.

"The kiss," she replies automatically. Her agent hat has replaced her best friend cap.

I nod, glazing over the words in front of me with wide eyes. "Yes. I changed it...fixed it. I think. Here, listen," I order.

With a quick click I make my font larger and begin

reading. I made the scene resemble our first kiss so fully that I moved it outdoors by a tree and changed the dialogue to gel with the moment that is seared into my mind. Reading it back to Jasmine, I can look at it as a fly on the wall instead of breathing and loving in the moment, and it impacts me the same way: a sledge-hammer cracking my ribs apart. "A flower stands at its most beautiful just before it wilts away and dies. A black-and-white photo is timeless—it lingers in shoe boxes for generations. Words in black and white are eternal. This kiss, the one I feel in my soul, transcends any visual dimension the eye can see. It's more than forever," I read aloud the last part. My breathing is more jagged, and my throat is clogged. Tears sneak out of the corner of my eyes.

"Fuck, Carina," Jasmine says. Her voice is raspy with emotion. "That is beautiful. You've never written anything more...real. You know I'm going to ask, though."

"He kissed me, Jaz," I say, grabbing my throat with one hand. "And the world stopped cold. I fell so hard, and it only took seconds. It sounds real because it is real, and my life is strangely more appealing than fiction. How did this happen?" I'm doing this. It's down. My feelings and words are strewn about my laptop screen. My truths. Our secrets. There's no hiding them.

Jasmine swallows loudly. "This is unbelievable. If you can insert, no pun intended, more of your real life with Smith into this novel, the sky is the limit. I'm crying, and I don't cry, Carina. As far as first kisses go in books, you just devoured first through third place," she says. I can tell she's breathing heavily, just as affected by my words as I am. "Like maybe took over Jaime and Claire's spot, for Christ's sake."

I hit the save button and lay my forehead down on my desk. "This is what it feels like," I whisper.

"Yes. You lucky bitch. I can't even pretend to know what you feel, but your words? Those I can take and run with. Give it to us, honey. Give it all to us," Jasmine breathes. She laughs. "The first time you fuck him? Give me a few hours' heads-up. I want to grab a glass of wine and my vibe."

"You're atrocious. You think I'd give gory details about that?"

"Yes," she replies. "As your agent, I expect them actually."

I grunt. "I thought we'd be making details right now, but he's working tonight."

"Working?" Jasmine asks. "At night? Sounds suspicious."

I roll my eyes. "He's working. I'm worried, though. Did you see the news? The attack at the shopping mall in NorCal?" A conversation switch is mandatory now that we've delved into my sex life.

"Sick fuckers. Don't let fear run your life. Especially now that you have the hottest bodyguard on the planet."

"He deploys soon, remember? I'll be all by myself. Not that I'm worried about solitary confinement. Well, maybe a little bit." I don't even have to say his name.

"You haven't heard from him or seen him since the day you left. What makes you think anything will change?"

Leaning back in my chair, I tilt my chin up to stare at the ceiling. It's illuminated by the glow of my computer. "I have a feeling something bad will happen. I can't explain it."

Jasmine groans. "Then don't explain. Don't think about it. Just read me that scene again. I'm going to grab my glass of wine."

I laugh. "Shut up. I'll talk to you later. I'll send over the finished chapters in the morning."

"Good luck," Jasmine rasps.

"With what?" I ask.

"Smith. When he gets home from work." With a laugh, she says goodbye and ends the call.

Checking messages again without anything new, I toss my cell on the desk next to my notebook and headphones. I may need to move my desk into the empty bedroom. I've been working too late, and I think it's because my workstation is located a few feet from my bed.

I read my new words a few more times and stand from my chair to stretch my tired hands over my head. I throw on a nightshirt that hits high on my thigh, wash my face, and brush my teeth. All through the mundane tasks, I revel in the knowledge that I've written our first kiss. A kiss that will live forever in the pages of a book. It's freeing and terrifying at the same time. I've gotten used to my friends reading my work and assuming I write nonfiction. How will this be any different? Other than the fact that I'm dating the person who I'm writing about? Early on, Smith and I decided that he wouldn't read anything until I was finished—until it returned from the editor and the draft was final, final. He's got more willpower than me, that's for sure. If someone were writing a story about me, I'd have to know everything as it was written. Especially if it were sitting right under my nose. Smith doesn't even glance at my marker boards. He says his momma raised a gentleman.

Our wooden floors creak underneath my steps as I head for the kitchen. The old bungalow style of our house is brand-new to me. It's different than the house I grew up in and is much different than the house Roarke built for us. Surrounded by these walls gives me a new lease on life in more ways than the obvious. The water goes down easily as I stare out into the dark purple night, trying to quench a nagging thirst. A coyote calls out from the ravine several houses down, and lightning bugs dot across the window, flying so slow even I could catch them.

My eyes are heavy when I slide into bed and pull the cool sheet over my bare legs. I click on the small side lamp on the opposite end table so it's not dark when Smith comes home, and I close my eyes. My mind still whirs with the thrill of his lips against my own and the way he looked at me when he gently pulled away. Smith was starry-eyed. My stomach flips with excitement at the thought. Once his face enters my mind, I can't shake it. It's half tan and smooth and half red and scarred. Even his body is a representation of before and after. Pre-mortar and post-mortar. Or, in easier terms, Megan and Carina.

With no family of my own and the evil ghosts from my past plaguing me, this afternoon was a reminder of what will never truly be mine. Smith lost a lot, but he still has so much. My hope is that I can be a part of it for as long as he'll let me. I open my eyes once more, and the blue digital clock reads 12:07 a.m. I close my eyes for the final time, turn off my brain, and finally fall asleep.

First, sunlight peeking from the blinds wakes me. Next I'm acutely aware of the heavy arm slung across the middle of my body and his chest pressed against my back, creating a heat that warms me from the outside in. When I stir, Smith props himself up on his elbow and looks down at me. "What time did you get in last night?" I roll over to face him. The smile comes without my permission. Waking up to this sight makes me happier than anything in my past.

"This morning," he replies. "A few hours ago." A

quick glance at the clock tells me it's seven a.m. "I didn't want to wake you when I came in. You looked so peaceful in your drool-filled slumber." He smiles, and it melts my insides. I suck in a deep breath.

"I do not drool," I say, furrowing my brow. "I sleep like a Disney princess. Don't suggest anything to contradict that." I wipe at my bottom lip. It's currently dry. "You should go back to sleep, Smith. You can't possibly be ready to wake after only a few hours of sleep."

Shrugging, he pulls me into his warm, shirtless body and yanks the quilt back up to our necks, his hands now wandering over my body. "Sleep is the very last thing on my mind right now." His gaze burns into mine, and his hands find the hem of my nightshirt. His lips twitch. "You wear so little to bed. I can't help myself," he says. With a featherlight touch, his fingertips stroke the side of my thigh up to the string of my panties. He hooks a finger in and drags his finger underneath it, teasing himself. Teasing me, too. "It took all of my self-control to go to sleep with this much of your bare skin in touching proximity."

I blush. Big time. Everything below my waist cries out for attention in one wild rush of excitement. It's been too long. But it's more than that now because everything before this has been lukewarm. "What did you do at work last night?" I ask before all important thoughts flee my mind in favor of his touch—something that scrambles my brain cells. "Why did it take so long?"

His face changes. His hand stops on my hip bone and he grabs it, his fingers encompassing the whole side of my body. Breathing in and out makes his hand move with me. It's warm. It's demanding. "It's nothing for you to worry about," Smith replies.

I shake my head. "When people say stuff like that, typically there is almost always something to worry about, but you don't want to worry the person. Do you see how counterintuitive that is? Now I'm worried because you told me not to worry."

He sighs and then pulls the covers over his head and disappears under the blankets. In a fast maneuver that tickles and makes me pull away in mock protest, he makes his way between my legs. With the edge of the quilt in my hand, I lift it to see his smiling face between my knees. "You're trying to distract me," I say. Pressing my lips into a firm line, I try to hold a serious face. "Smith Eppington. You better tell me what I want to know."

Smith takes the sides of my panties and pulls them down and off my body with one fierce tug. It's playful, but so damn hot at the same time. Some noise exits my mouth, and it makes him smile, his good side wider than his bad. I shake my head. "Is it working?" he asks, then kisses the inside of my right thigh. "Are you distracted?" His warm breath on my skin clenches my core. He drags his lips up and down, inching his way higher.

I adjust my legs and try to calm my breaths. "I don't see how I can't be distracted with my underwear on the floor and your head between my legs. I don't forget," I say. Tapping the side of my head, I finish, "I'm like an elephant."

He licks the inside of my left thigh and runs his hands under my nightshirt, up and down the sides of my rib cage. I shiver. Tipping my head back, I close my eyes.

"An elephant isn't what I want to think about right now," Smith growls. "I'd ask you how you like this, but I honestly don't care. I'm starving for you. You're wet. I smell you." With his lips pressing against my skin and the disappearance of my panties, he's turned into a lust-crazed man. A man I've wanted to meet since I first laid eyes on him.

Taking the quilt, I throw it back so he's fully exposed and not lacking oxygen. "Don't think about an elephant. Think about me," I say, breathing in and out in a panic as I realize what's about to happen. His tongue traces lazy circles where my leg joins my body. "And whatever you do, do not stop doing that," I moan.

Smith finally moves his head where I want it. My own head, which feels like it weighs a thousand pounds, swims in sheer bliss. His mouth is warm, and his fingers stroke me deftly, slipping inside to rub just the right spot, the place most men don't even know exists. I moan out as the sensations—the connection—envelop every nerve ending. Smith is aggressive in his maneuvers, pushing my legs out to give himself better access, holding my hips down when I try to arch my back.

Knowing I won't be able to hold out much longer, I give in completely, as if I had a choice, and let myself grab his hair and ride the sensations. The noises coming out of Smith cause a riot of emotions. The dominant one being lust. There's no calmness or leisurely pleasuring happening. It's animalistic, a complete loss of control. I guide his head into me when I feel him slip another finger inside. He strokes a few more times, without halting his flicking tongue, and I lose it. The orgasm hits my body in waves, from my tingling thighs to the warm flush of pleasure cascading over every square inch of skin on my body. The waves go on and on, my muscles tense, and my eyes close tight.

When Smith is sure I'm finished, he rests his chin on my lower stomach but doesn't remove his massive hands from my thighs. The heat from his palms keeps me in a fog of bliss, unsure if more is coming. "And that is how it's done," I say, sighing. I haven't had an orgasm in months. I haven't had an orgasm that strong and body-consuming in my lifetime. He's smiling at me, his eyes lazily wandering over my face and exposed stomach. "I still can't catch my breath. No elephants in this room, huh?"

He kisses the flat plane of the skin stretched across my hip bones. "Who needs to breathe when you can have orgasms?" Smith smiles. It's predatory and full of promise. "Do you know how long I've dreamed of doing that? Of hearing your screams, seeing your face, knowing I'm responsible for making you feel good, tasting your sweet pussy?" He shakes his head and licks a trail from my stomach back down between my legs. He presses a soft kiss at my wet entrance. "Feeling you clench in release around my fingers while I envision it being my dick instead?"

I take a deep breath as my muscles contract from his mouth. "Probably as long as I've dreamed about reciprocating the favor?" I ask.

He stops kissing and fingering me. "You mean sucking me off?" Smith's gaze flicks up to meet mine, and I can tell it's painful for him to take his attention away from where he really wants it.

"Or a blow job. Your dick in my warm, wet mouth," I say. Tracing my lips with my thumb, I continue. "My lips wrapping around you as I lick and suck, taking you all the way back into my throat until you come." I smirk. My confidence is bolstered by the adrenaline and the pure power I feel being in his presence. He continues staring, a blank, unreadable expression playing across his features. "Unless you don't want that," I amend.

Smith doesn't take his eyes off my mouth as I speak. I'm unable to read his feelings on the subject and regret speaking in such a manner. He started the dirty talk, so I assumed it would be okay for me to reciprocate. "That's not your thing. It's okay. Sorry for mentioning it." I blush every shade of red, and I'm tan. I try to lean up, but he places a hand on my stomach to hold me in place.

"She's never done that," Smith says, voice so low I almost don't make out the words. "I've never had a blow job. Don't be sorry for mentioning it. I'm celebrating internally. I needed a moment to process what you said."

He's joking. He has to be. A full-grown man who looks like Smith gets blow jobs whenever he wants. He told me Megan was the only woman he's ever been with. I believed it, but I also assumed their sex life was top-notch. Look at her. Look at him. I never saw this coming. Not by a long shot. "Don't joke right now, Smith." My eyes are wide, confused.

"Say my name again," he growls.

I grin. "Smith."

Leaning up on his knees, he pulls down his black boxer briefs. His erection springs free, and I can't take my eyes off it. I haven't seen such anatomy in too long, and I've never seen Smith's. Envisioning it was my favorite game. Feeling it through his pants, pressing against my stomach when he hugged me, gave me a pretty good idea what he was packing, but it's nothing like seeing it in the flesh right now. It's long, a rigid nine or ten inches, with a girth much wider than I've ever encountered in my sheltered years. Nothing compared to Roarke. I have no comparison. It's beautiful.

When I finally pull my gaze up to his eyes, he bites his bottom lip. "One thing on my body didn't get fucked up," he says. "Still game to show me the ropes?" he asks. He lifts and lowers his thick, broad shoulders.

I sigh. The butterflies in my stomach threaten to rise into my throat. It's an odd sensation. A little bit of stage fright mixes with absolute passion. I've never been a fan of blow jobs, honestly. It was something I had to do because men like them, and it's how you return the favor. Right now my mouth is watering for Smith. I want to taste him. I want to own this first—something that no one else can say. "I don't think I've ever wanted anything more," I say, my gaze still taking in the lower half of his body. "Well," I stutter.

With his hands perched on his hips, he says, "Finish that thought, please."

His command draws my gaze up to meet his. Smith's warm voice is gritty with desire. It twists my insides into knots. "It wasn't really a thought," I reply. Taking his hand, I guide it back to my core. "It's more of a given. I want to have sex with you."

Smith sucks in a breath, bites his lower lip, and closes his eyes. His eyebrows knit together. He's holding himself back. It's a look I'm not familiar with. In my previous relationship, holding back wasn't ever on the agenda. Roarke took from me exactly what he wanted regardless of how I felt.

"We aren't in the living room right now, so it's obviously not on the agenda," I say. I scoot forward to give him better access and tentatively reach for his hard-on. I watch as he swallows hard and then raises his other hand to my face, and I lean into it.

"All this time, I've gotten to know everything about you on the inside. The outside was a tightly held treasure of a mystery. The promise of the eighth wonder of the world. I've wanted to touch you like this for a long time," Smith growls. My eyes flutter closed for a brief moment as his fingers play me like his favorite instrument. "It's not a disappointment. In case you're curious. Every curve," Smith whispers, dragging the hand from my cheek down my neck and trailing over the swell of my breast. "Every beauty mark." The tip of his finger grazes the spot right next to my belly button. "Every single line, dip, and hair on your entire body." He leans in and kisses me. A breath-stealing kiss. A life-altering kiss. Into my ear, he says, "Is my favorite memory."

"No more memories. Just now. Okay?" I say against his lips. "Our future," I promise.

He agrees with a megawatt smile and just the right words again. My heart flutters like the wings of a bird. This takes courage—a facet of my personality that's buried deeply inside somewhere that hasn't been accessed for years. Since I was a little girl and hugging my knees and praying for a miracle. My miracle happened. Just later than expected.

"Well, this one last thing can go into memory. If you think it worthy enough," I reply.

Smith smirks as I lean over and push his boxer briefs further down his sculpted thighs. I take him into my mouth and relish in the hiss of air that leaves his mouth when I slide him in deeply. He swears. Every curse word in the book. Words I've never heard before pass his lips. For a man who has never received oral sex, he finds his role quickly. One hand is wrapped around my hair and the other is pushing the back of my neck in the fast rhythm that I quickly realize he enjoys most.

My hand is tired, and my jaw feels like it may never shut again, but the pressure is on to give him the best first of his life. It's all I can give him at the moment, and it feels glorious. Smith tells me a few times to slow down because he wants to last a while longer, wants to feel my wet mouth around him longer. I know it won't take much longer when the grip on my hair tightens. I keep my hand pumping and take him to the back of my throat. He comes in several hot, long bursts down my throat. On the last jerk, he falls back into the kneeling position.

I keep my mouth latched around him until I'm sure he's finished and swallow the remnants. His grip loosens on my hair and neck. Taking a deep breath, I sit up again into the kneeling position. "Finish your thoughts, please," I say, taking his words.

"Best orgasm of my life. You swallowed it," he says, eyes wide.

I smile. "What did you think I would do with it?"

"Spit it all over my body and break out into a thankless argument about how female ejaculation isn't real," he replies.

Smith and I break out into laughter at the same time. He pins me on the bed. His weight is welcome and warm. The urge to have him deep inside me surfaces, and I wonder if he knows how deliriously happy he makes me.

I cover my mouth with one hand to stifle the laughter. Grabbing my wrist, he pulls my hand down. "Never cover that blessed device. Do you understand me?"

I giggle and shrug. His beautiful eyes crinkle in the corners as he smiles down at me. "I understand," I say, feigning obedience.

His mouth turns down as his smile disappears. "I'm sorry for being rough with your head. Surprisingly, I had little control of that in the heat of the moment."

His concern gives me pause. "Don't apologize. I know you would never hurt me purposefully. You would never hurt me in any way." How I hope this is true. How I hope he is my forever. He runs his fingers through my hair gently. "Would you?"

I know him well enough to know he will read between the lines like a pro. His eyes glaze over. He kisses my forehead and then the tip of my nose. I close my eyes when he kisses my eyelids.

When I open them to find his true emotions playing

across his face, for the very first time, I know my hopes will become a reality. "I love you, Carina. I love you forever."

And nothing can steal them away.

Nothing.

CHAPTER SIXTEEN
Smith

IT DOESN'T HAPPEN VERY OFTEN, but when it does, it's a big deal. Rain in Southern California. It comes down all day long, and it's a harsh, unrelenting flood because the streets and landscapes aren't made for weather as such. When it stops and the sun shines down like a soldier staking his claim, it's a sight to behold. You've missed it, and you're more than glad the warm beams are beating down on your skin. It's a feeling like nothing else. That's the only comparison that comes close to describing what it's like to be with Carina intimately. To hold her body next to mine. To touch the skin that's usually covered by her clothing. To see the parts only a lover is privy to.

She's the fucking sun. The rain, too. I can't control myself around her. Carina has triggers after suffering abusive relationship after relationship. Yelling is one. Sex after an argument is another. Apparently, she closes herself off. Nothing sexual in the shower because it's a small space, and she's claustrophobic, and thank God hair pulling is not on her list.

After the blow job, which will go down in history as the best in the world, she left for a meeting with Jasmine to talk about work. I met Moose at our work gym, and now we're at the outdoor shooting range, practicing. It's high-tech and tracks everything: precision, speed, and distance. These skills will prove to be of the utmost importance soon.

A sense of clarity washes over me as my body goes into autopilot. The world melts away for an hour as I pull the trigger, aim, and repeat. I feel so much when I'm around Carina, it's almost a relief to think about nothing except the task at hand. When Moose finishes, we head back to the high bay to hang out. He grabs a drink from the bar and hands me one.

"I made it light. It is a workday," Moose says. Smiling, he pats me on the shoulder before he takes a seat on the leather sofa opposite me. "What's on your mind?" He looks at me over the rim of his glass.

I shrug. "Nothing and everything," I admit. "I've never been happier, but it's the beginning. The tenuous part of any relationship, and we're about to ship out." My palms, the same ones that scored almost a perfect score at the range, begin to sweat.

Moose shakes his head. "There are no promises on that front. You heard the brief," he says.

Swallowing down the liquid fire, I relish the burn every step of the way down. I'm nervous. The state of affairs that our world is in is too big for a quick fix. "Regardless, we don't have enough time to cement the relationship before I leave."

"You haven't had sex yet," Moose says. His eyebrows rise in surprise. "Not that I want you to talk about it because you know details aren't my thing, but you're living with her. How is that possible?"

I drain the rest of my drink and slink back into the cool, brown leather. We nod as a few guys pass through, gear bags slung over their shoulders. "I've been gone." I sigh. "And I wanted to take things slow because this is different. I know her. I know her so well. And I don't want to scare her off or fuck things up before they have a chance to get off the ground." I can't make eye contact. Not when talking about something this personal. It's about Carina, not Megan. It's awkward, and he's my best friend.

Moose huffs out a breath and runs both hands through his longish hair like a shaggy dog. "God, I hate to say this, but are you sure? There's still time, man. If you haven't taken it to that level, there's still time to go back to her." Megan. Like I assumed.

I nip his train of thought in the bud. "I'm in love with Carina. I love her. I want to be with her forever. We've done everything but, Moose. My allegiance will always be with her," I say, using my hands as I speak. Moose understands words like love and allegiance. "Megan made her choice, and I've made mine. Carina is meeting her for lunch tomorrow. It's working out. I've never been more sure about anything in my life, bro." I think about how she makes me feel—how important she is to my mental and physical health. "I'd give up my career if I thought the relationship was in jeopardy. Bow out. Get an office job and a closet full of suits if that's what made her happy."

It's a strange, foreign thought. It's true, though. My happiness is her happiness. Never in my wildest dreams or nightmares would I conjure up leaving the Teams. It's my identity. Finally...finally, my true identity has been exposed.

Moose is staring at me, eyes wide and mouth ajar. "Now you're talking like a crazy asshole and *I am* going to butt in with my opinion and tell you that you need to get laid as soon as humanly possible." He claps both hands down on his sizable hamstrings. "You're changing, man. I can't say I like it, either."

"Or actualizing who I really am," I return. Taking the glass out of his hand, I return the two to the sink by the bar and wash them out without looking. I'm lost in thought, translation, and in truth.

He stands, shaking his head with a stymied look on his face. He puts his hands on his hips as he surveys me. "Back to what I said before. Fuck this bullshit out of your system. We have a job to do, and you need to realize what's important. We need you. Look around, Smith. The world is going to shit. If there's any time we need some of that superhero shit you spout, it's now. Don't have a mid-midlife crisis, please. You are a fucking SEAL. The best one I've ever known. You owe it to yourself. You owe it to Henry." Once spoken, Henry's name and a million memories troll through my mind.

"I'm working on remedying the issue today, actually. If you ever let me leave," I reply, ignoring the emotions that threaten my good mood. "No mid-midlife crisis. Okay?"

Hesitantly, Moose nods.

We talk for a few more minutes about work stuff and head to our lockers to pack a few more gear bags. He thinks I'm crazy. That I'm not thinking with the right head. I tell him I know what's important, and for once, since my accident, I know exactly who I am.

It brings him up short. He passes me several zip ties. When I take them, he says, "I hope you know what you're doing, man."

So do I.

It took a lot of convincing to get her to visit. My own internal struggle was pretty rough, too. It could change her mood and turn her off so completely that we may never have sex. I need to have sex with her, and a lot of it. It's important to be here, though. To both of us.

Carina's hand shakes as we turn the corner onto a dead-end street lined with trees and shady sidewalks. She stares out of the passenger window in a trance.

"It's right there. On the right. The white one," Carina whispers.

It's a plain, nondescript house. The grass is longer than the neighbors', and the shutters look like they could use a coat of fresh paint. If I didn't have firsthand knowledge of the atrocities that occurred here, I would think it a fine middle-class home in a nice neighborhood. Carina is shockingly silent when I pull into the driveway.

"It's been so long. It doesn't look the way I remember it," she says. One hand on the door handle, she pauses, looks over at me, and blinks once slowly. A tear trickles down her face. "I need to close this chapter once and for all. Thank you for understanding."

Scooting over, I drape my arm around her shoulders. "Hey, I wanted to come here with you. You're brave, Carina. It shows your strength," I say.

Turning her head to the side, she seeks out my lips. I kiss her because it's the least I can do. I kiss her because I can taste the salt from her tears, and I kiss her because I love her, and you embrace the good and the bad.

This structure standing tall in front of us is her bad. All of it. It's what set the course for her life and the string of abusive relationships. You see, it wasn't just Roarke. First, it was Jake, a boy in high school who thought it was fun to fight and fuck, and then it was Eddie, who liked drugs and alcohol. By the time Roarke came along, he appeared as Prince fucking Charming. Sure, he was nice when he wasn't drinking, and for all outward intents and purposes, he was the perfect fiancé, but beneath the surface, he was the worst of all of Carina's past relationships. He was responsible for verbal abuse so strong that his words set fire to the core of her personality. A beating was something she was familiar with—could withstand within reason. His words, that fucker's words, tore her to shreds. Her confidence slowly returning, I see what she used to be—what he stole—and it's infuriating.

Carina exits the car slowly, her gaze turned to the front door and her hands fisting the sides of her skirt. It has bold colors weaved into the pattern, and she told me it's her favorite because it has flounce. Bunching in her hands, it looks like an overused dishrag. She removes the key from the lockbox, inserts it into the bolt lock, jiggles the handle a few times, and pushes the heavy door open. It creaks. Her heels echo as she takes the first step inside. I give her space. I let her walk in without disturbing her thoughts.

"I need to sell it. Before it rots from the inside out," she says. Carina doesn't turn around. Instead, she heads to the kitchen, her head held high.

I follow her in, closing the door behind us. It smells musty and unused. Not that it bothers me. The places I've slept and lived in overseas are more disturbing than an empty house in America will ever be. I once slept on sand, without a pillow, for two weeks straight. I used leaves to wipe my ass and ate meals out of pouches for more days than I can count.

Sighing out a deep breath, I take in my surroundings. "I don't know. I bet if you had someone come in more frequently, you could sit on it for as long as you wanted." Anything to stave off her having to deal with more hassle and pain. "I can handle the sale if you want."

She turns around, both hands on the kitchen counter

behind her. "You don't have to do that. I can handle this, Smith. You don't have to worry about me, okay?" Walking toward her, I realize she's right. There are no tears or any sign of an internal struggle. "I mean it," Carina says. "Having you has changed everything for me."

I shake my head and take her face in my hands. Her skin feels like velvet against the palm of my hand. "I can't fix you, Care. I can't. I'm flattered you think I can, but I know for a fact that only you can fix you." I sound like I'm quoting the text written by my own psychologist.

She leans up and kisses me and wraps her hands around my neck. "Maybe I fixed me. Because of you," she says.

My heart pounds against my chest, and Moose's words come to mind. *What is important?*

I take another small step to press her back into the counter. Mounting her in this kitchen won't solve anything. "I want you. You're so important to me," I growl, taking her bottom lip in between my teeth. "Just you."

I can taste her lip gloss and smell her skin—that scent that no one else has. It's like makeup and her natural scent combined into one intoxicating flavor made just for me. I inhale greedily as she tilts her head and leans into the kiss. "I've always wanted to do this," she says on a breath. "Erase the memories that inhabit this place."

It takes a great deal of willpower, but I push away from the kiss, keeping her in my arms. "That's what this is then?" I ask.

She lets me keep her at a distance and then leads me out of the back sliding glass door into the yard. "No. It's not, but if I can kill two birds with one stone, I can't see how that's a problem. You're a practical man. What do you think?"

After she asks the question, the shed in the far corner comes into view.

Bile rises up my stomach, and my feet are leaden as she guides me to it. There's no pause as she walks, but I do feel her tighten her grip on my arm as we near it. The padlock dangles to the side, unfastened. "I think that this is a horrible idea," I say, honestly. I feel my pulse in my neck as the stories she told me about what took place in this shed surface. What must she feel like in this moment? "I'm here for you. I'm here," I say. Support. That's what she needs. Not my opinion on the matter.

Carina lets go of me to toss off the lock and throw the door open. A shiver, completely visible, rolls up her entire body. She throws a hand over her mouth, the first sign of distress she's shown since we arrived. "My god," she says.

Dust wafts as the empty shed sees light for the first time in who knows how long. It smells like old, mildewed wood and the earthy scent of dirt. Somewhere behind us a bird chirps out a melodic song, and a car horn honks. I hold her upright. Even if she doesn't want my support, I need to give it.

"It's so much smaller than I remember it," Carina whispers, leaning her head back into my chest. "It doesn't smell the same either, but it kind of does."

I nod, knowing she can feel my response. My arms drop by my sides as she takes a step toward the small, painted-over window and stoops down to jiggle one of the floorboards. Carina is actively crying now, and it takes all my power not to pull her out of this shack and torch the motherfucker to the ground. Hell, maybe I'll set the whole house ablaze while I'm at it. I know what she's looking for, so when she stands with an almost black children's book clutched to her chest, it takes a second for me to catch my breath.

"Got what you came for then?" I ask. My tone is low and gruff. It's angry. I exit because I can't take one more second of the putrid air. The air that stole her oxygen. The air that stole her life. The air she breathed for days on end when Greg was abusing her in every single way. Somehow it feels like breathing this air makes me closer to him. Closer to the devil incarnate. Farther away from Carina. I don't like it.

She nods, walks backward, and jumps when her shoes hit the step outside of the door. I steady her with one hand and close the creaky door with the other. "Let's get the hell out of here. Or did you want to see my childhood room?" she asks. Her face is tear-streaked, but there is a sense of relief washing over her features. "I did it."

"You did," I reply. "I wanted to see it, Carina. I did. But now that I know, now that it's real, I'm not sure I'll ever be able to get over this. I'm so sorry. I'm so sorry." There's nothing else to say to her. She looks like a ten-year-old girl clutching her favorite book, broken. Her skirt floats in the slight breeze as we make our way across the lawn, back into the house, and to my truck.

Once we're seated, she tells me another story. A happy one about her grandma visiting and teaching her how to crochet. I tell her I want her to crochet me something. She laughs, a painful sound through her sobs, but I see her face contemplating the request. Finally, she agrees and leans her head onto my shoulder as I make our way back home. "Thank you for showing me," I say. "I feel selfish now."

"No. No. I needed that, Smith. It's different now with you. You didn't change me, but I think you've fixed me. The awful memories are still there, lurking in every corner, but loving you and having you with me dulled the pain," she says.

I turn quickly to look her in the eyes. I force my lips into a smile.

"Sometimes, regardless of what you think, knowing someone gives a new clarity—a true sense of what matters."

"And what matters?" I ask. Gripping the steering wheel, my heart lodges in my throat.

"Letting go of the past completely and admitting that I'm worthy of a future. Our future. I'm worthy of you and your love. Despite what I've been through, I know I can be good for you. What matters is that I can trust myself and my love for you. I love you." I can't take my gaze from the road, but from my peripheral, I see her clutching that weather-torn copy of the book she loves and hates in equal measure.

I resolve to trust my gut. Carina is what's most important to me. "I love you, Care," I say, squeezing her leg. "You're all that matters to me."

She sniffles. "Doesn't seem very honorable and moral to say that," she says. Her tone is light and joking.

But her words hit me directly in the chest.

CHAPTER SEVENTEEN
Carina

THE PIT in my stomach melted away the second we pulled into our quaint little driveway and entered *our* home. "I'm going to take a shower. Wash my face," I say, waving the book in the air like an explanation.

Smith smiles. It's almost the smile from a man who feels sympathy, but it's not. He teeters on that line very gracefully. I give him mad credit for that. I don't want anyone's sympathy. Especially from the man I love. With a nod, Smith says he's going to his room to return a few phone calls and asks that I come get him as soon as I'm finished.

Nerves hit me in spades. I shower slowly and shave every square inch of my body. I wash my hair twice and let my face mask soak in longer than I usually do. It's not because I'm nervous, it's because I'm trying to forget what this afternoon made me feel. I don't want to confuse emotions. I want to compartmentalize my time spent in the house of horrors. The shed. The pit in my stomach rears as do images of Greg on top of me grunting, his alcohol-laced breath wafting in my face as he drilled me into the wooden floor, his eyes screwed shut and his shirt rubbing against my cheek. He never took his shirt off. Not even once.

I lean over and vomit into the drain. My stomach is empty, so it's just bile and bad memories. I wash my face one more time and exit the warm shower. There are two sinks, so I make my way to mine and take my time brushing my teeth and blow-drying my hair while I go through Smith's products. He keeps them in his Dopp kit on the counter because he's always leaving. I smell his cologne and open the top of his shaving cream and smell that, too. It makes my mouth water. Yes. Smith. That's what I need to focus on now. The rest of today is gone... buried with Greg.

"Pull your shit together," I say. Smith makes me feel good about myself. He makes me strive to leave the weak, hurt girl in the past. It's not one particular thing he does, it's merely what happens when he's himself. I know what's going to happen when I leave this room and find him. I want it to happen. I need to be in the right frame of mind. I want this to be something to be remembered. Something more fantastic than fiction. It can be that just by the fact that it's us. Smith and Carina. A fact that is frightening as much as it is amazing.

Dabbing my finger on my lips, I gloss on some clear balm. I hear the low, manly timbre of Smith's voice, so I know he's still on a phone call.

Hanging up my towel behind the door, I cross the hallway naked into my room. "Time to get dressed," I whisper. My closet is a rainbow explosion of colors. Most of the time I wear black, but recently I've been taken with brighter, more daring colors. Folded in the back on a shelf, I find what I've been saving for just the right time. "This is it, guys," I say to the lace bra and panty set. I purchased it at the high-end boutique one day while

Jasmine was next door at the market. It's teal and more risqué than anything I've ever worn.

A man like Smith is accustomed to sexy pieces like this, I'm sure. Blue is his favorite color, and I know he likes lingerie. He didn't come out and say those exact words, but through a story in the beginning of the interview process, he mentioned it. It had to do with a video chat session and his ex-fiancée while he was deployed.

Delaying our intimacy has been a challenge, and since we moved in together, it's always at the forefront of my mind. At first, I thought something was wrong with me. What type of man delays sexual gratification? From a woman practically throwing herself at him? The answer was a resounding *no man I've had previous experience with.* And that's a good thing.

I slip the delicate lace into place, put on my silk robe, and then sneak past the office door and into the living room. I have several candles hidden in drawers and cabinets I've been planning to light when the moment was right. If this isn't the moment, then I'm not sure about anything else. Our time together is dwindling. He's leaving. Also, I can't face Megan tomorrow being the woman Smith refuses to have sex with. I'm standing my ground. This is happening. We live together.

We're in crazy love.

I'm lighting the last small candle and sliding it into place on the ledge in front of the bay window when Smith finds me. "You were supposed to come and get me," he says. I watch his neck work to swallow as his eyes take in my appearance.

I smile. "I was busy. I wasn't ready to come and get you," I say.

Smith leans against the open doorframe, crossing one bare foot over the other. "Well, I wanted to be the one to introduce the romance. I'm a little offended you didn't let me help." He bites his bottom lip in a smile. Butterflies invade my insides. It's the opposite reaction of what happened in the shower. It heals the raw, jagged place where I keep bad memories.

"Perhaps you can introduce something else?" I edge.

He taps his chin. "Would it be a true introduction if you've already met him?" he says.

His joke makes me smile. Pressing my lips into a firm line, I send my gaze to the side wall for a couple seconds. When I look back at him, I nod. Smith laughs, the low tone more erotic than any other laugh I've ever heard in my life.

The coffee table is in the center of the room. I bend my leg and push it backward and out of our way. It makes a scratching noise as it goes.

"Are you sure you're okay?" he asks, standing straight. Through the dim glow of the candlelight, I see the contrast of every rippling muscle on his stomach. Absent-mindedly I lick my lips. "After today," he continues when I don't speak. My eyes find his face, and his amused smile morphs into concern. "It has to be perfect." He crosses to me in a few large strides.

Taking my face in his hands, he says, "It's the first time. More importantly, I want it to be my last first. Our last first."

Smith is so close I can taste his breaths and smell his skin. "I'm okay," I reassure him. Placing a kiss on his chest, right over his heart, I tilt my head up to look at his face. "I want this. You mean everything to me. I'm okay when you're with me." With his soulful eyes wandering over every inch of my face, I gather what confidence I need and drop the silk robe. The light fabric flutters to the ground around my feet. "Do you like?" I ask, backing away slowly so his view is unobstructed. His chest rises and falls at a more hurried pace, and he doesn't have to answer me.

With one hand bent behind his head, he reaches down to unbutton and unzip his jeans. "I want you badly," he says. "You look amazing. Beautiful."

"Right here?" I ask. Turning in a slow circle so he can appreciate the shards of lace from every angle, I move my feet slowly and let my body sway seductively. "This is where you want me first, right?"

While my back was turned, Smith stealthily closed the space between us. My back against his front, he leans down, moves my hair out of the way, and kisses my neck. "You have no idea what this means to me," he whispers in my ear.

"Show me," I reply. Pressing my bottom back and against him, I feel his erection. "Show me now because this means everything to me, and I want it so badly I'm not sure I can take another second of not having it." I spin to face him and let my hands find the waistband of his jeans and boxer briefs. In a quick movement, I pull them and follow them down to the floor until I'm kneeling in front of him.

Peeking up, I see his look of awe and utter lust as I take him into my mouth slowly. I let my tongue wind around the tip briefly before I slide him into my mouth as far as my gag reflex will allow. Smith moans, but he doesn't take his eyes off me. I stroke his thick shaft and lick his balls until I find just the right tempo. His legs are shaking, and wetness floods my core in response.

"That feels too good, Care. Enough. Enough," Smith says, trying to still my head with his hands. "Slow," he chides, stepping out of his tangled pants.

"I'm too worked up to slow down now," I pant. Standing, I wrap my hands around his waist as he pushes me back to the center of the room. He kisses my cheek, my forehead, and then my lips. The wet sounds of our mouths and our breaths are the only sounds to be heard. Smith slips his pointer fingers under my bra straps by my collarbone and eases them down until my breasts spring free.

He licks his lips. "We shouldn't slow down then," he says. "You're so fucking beautiful." Taking one breast into his mouth, he pauses before going to the other. "So goddamn beautiful. I can't help myself, Care. I want to devour you. Keep you here forever." I stroke his hair and close my eyes, oblivious to anything except what's right here and now.

My mind clears completely for all that isn't Smith Eppington. His muscles are coiled and hard, and his eyes are truly only for me. First, he tosses down a faux fur throw blanket from the sofa, and then, bending over, he easily takes my body weight in his arms and lowers us onto the floor. He never stops kissing me. It's the delirious feeling of floating and falling and consuming him right back. He breaks away briefly and remarks how my panties are his favorite color as he slides them down my legs. I don't tell him that's why I chose them. I smile and tell him something more true. "I love you. You know that, right?"

I'm completely naked, and my words give him pause. The soft glow of the candles and the moonlight infiltrating our safe place transform this moment into something magical. "I think I do know that," Smith replies. "I've never heard words that made me happier. Or frankly, more turned-on." His cock pulses up in protest. "You have no idea how you affect me. How you've always affected me."

Smith doesn't give me a chance to respond. He bends his head down and kisses me between my legs with his tongue. He licks me deep and slides a finger in at the same time. He's just as turned on by it as I am. His breaths come fast, and my own hands become frantic. Pulling him closer, writhing under the strong weight of his hands pressing me down. Breaths turn into panting and then into moans. He's a quick study—knows exactly what gets me off. Tonight I want something more than his magical tongue and fingers.

"I want you inside me, Smith," I beg. With the sides of his face in my hands, he raises his gaze to look at me. "Inside me."

"That's an order I can't ignore," Smith says, sitting up. He scoots over to sit on the blanket and takes me with him. I walk on my knees to straddle his legs and lean forward to kiss his lips—taste my wetness. "How's that taste?" he asks.

"Like I'm ready," I reply. I kiss him again and glide my lips down the side of his neck—the bad side—and trail soft kisses across his wide shoulder and back again. His dick is beneath me, warm and hard as steel, flexing and throbbing. "Are you ready?"

He doesn't reply with words. Smith reaches between our bodies to position himself, and with his free hand, pushes my ass down. I cry out. It's pleasure. It's pain. It's unlike anything else in this world. A small groan escapes his lips and into my mouth. "Did I hurt you?" he whispers.

I lean back to look at him and slide up a touch. "You could never hurt me," I reply. Then I lower myself back down onto his slick cock. It fills me so fully that I don't want for anything else in this moment. I ride him several more times, connected, melting into blissful oblivion while watching the forever memory dance in his hooded eyes. He works my clit with his thumb, a gentle assault compared to the girth of his member splitting me in two.

I throw my head back and relish all of my senses. The

sweet smell of the floral candles burns through the air, as do the crickets chirping outside the window, Smith's lips dragging down my throat as he makes the sweetest of love to me. His body is hard, but his heart is so soft—so ready to love freely without reserve.

"I'm going to come. Where?" he grinds out in between clenched teeth. "Where?" he asks again.

We spoke about the fact that I'm on birth control already. "Inside me. I'm coming. Inside me," I say. It's jumbled because my thighs are tingling and my whole body is about to fire into the atmosphere, but I'm sure he's understood. With both hands on my ass, he brings me up and down at the speed that he desires. It's punishing and erotic. I slump over his shoulder and hug him around his neck as I come around him. It's fast and slow at the same time. The waves of pleasure are so severe that I see stars, my whole body overwhelmed with the satisfaction of release.

Smith brushes several strands of hair away from my face as I continue to slide up and down on top of him. "I need to see your face," he says, holding my cheek lightly.

"I'm here," I say.

He licks his lips a moment before his mouth crashes into mine. He kisses me with his eyes open for a second or two, and then, with his gaze locked with mine and his hands still on my face, he comes. His eyes flutter closed briefly as he unloads several hot bursts deep inside me. I wrap my legs around his waist and clutch him as tightly and as closely as I can.

I think from this position we can't be closer. Him inside me, his heart beating against my chest, his chin folded over my shoulder. His breaths falling down my back. It's all so personal, so vehemently different from what I'm used to. Regardless if this was the right choice —he and I—I now realize this was my only choice.

"Is it wrong that I already want a second time? And a third after that?" Smith asks. I feel the rumble of his spoken words in his chest as he speaks them.

I press a kiss to his shoulder. "You're still inside me. I don't think we can count this one over yet," I reply.

He lets his palm graze down the center of my back until he finds my ass. Then, he lifts me up. Almost to the point where his cock leaves my body, but not quite. When I don't think I can take another second, he lets me fall back down, taking him all the way in, filling me completely.

I moan, the noise echoing loudly in the room. He hisses out a long breath. "You're still hard," I rasp. I run my teeth down the edge of his ear and let my tongue glide along the rim.

"Care, I'm going to be hard anytime you're in the same room as me for the rest of our lives." He groans when I suck his earlobe and assault him with a slow ride. "I'm ruined now. In the best fucking possible way."

I circle my hips in a small circle, forcing a new sensation. "This was beyond all expectations and dreams. Ah, yes. Keep doing that. Fuck," Smith growls.

"This feels so good. Your cock is so big and thick. It rubs me the right way. I want to come again, filled with you," I reply. The motion of circling and grinding is the perfect angle for my clit, and I feel the sensations of orgasm building again.

He takes my face in his hands. This time he tilts my face to the ceiling and licks a trail from the hollow of my neck up to the bottom of my chin. "Do that. Around my dick."

I push myself down a little further. And in a quick move, with one arm around my back, he leans me down so I'm resting on the floor. Smith rubs my clit while he thrusts inside me, rubbing my G-spot with the head of his erection. I close my eyes with the uncontrollable bliss of this position. I tell him I'm going to come, and he leans forward so he can kiss my lips while I explode, my core clenching as much as it can around his girth.

I pant several long, drawn-out breaths, my chest heaving with exertion and pleasure. "I can't even breathe, that was so good," I whisper. The scent of sex and the candles warps my reality. It's like coming to Jesus. Being rescued. Something burned into the core of my being.

"Please breathe. I wasn't trying to kill you. I promise," Smith says. "I wanted to make you feel good."

Feel good. He wanted to make me feel good. Does he have any idea how trivial that sounds coming off the lips of a person who has saved my life? "Smith," I chide, rubbing the good side of his face. "We knew the sex was going to be like this. This breathing entity of its own. We were made for each other." His half grin fades as he realizes the magnitude of what we're feeling together. "Now it will be a chore to keep us off each other because we've opened Pandora's sex box."

His eyes crinkle in the corners with that comment.

"I'm just glad it meant as much to you as it did to me. It's why I wanted to wait. To make sure this was it," he says. Smith winces as he draws himself out of my body. "That was the most pain I've ever been in," he proclaims, grimacing as he wraps a hand around his slick cock.

I smirk. "Your invitation is open. Anytime."

He kisses me on the nose and pulls me up to a seated position.

"The fur blanket is going to be sullied in mere seconds." I raise one brow when I feel his come leak from me, warm and wet. "I never understood that in movies and books. Why do people have sex on fur? It can't be cleaned easily, and it's possibly the most impractical fabric to use." I sigh and shift positions to try to dodge the inevitable. Smith pulls me into him, kissing me breathless.

"Maybe they want to mimic a There's *Something About Mary* hairstyle, though? Except on fake animal fur."

"That's just weird," I say, my lips brushing his. With his arms wrapped around me right now, I feel something I've never felt. "You make me feel so safe. Like no matter what happens, I'll always be okay because you'll protect me. It's so cliché." But also so true.

"Always," Smith says, his face buried in my hair. "I'll always protect you from everything. On my honor."

You know how when you're a little girl playing dolls, Ken walks Barbie down the aisle when they get married? It's mostly because you don't know any different, but also because he's the only man doll. Even when I grew up, I liked that idea more than a father figure doing the walking. It's Ken who is changing your life. It's Ken who will drive the convertible back to the pink mansion. It's Ken who is rescuing. It's Ken who is protecting.

Now that's cliché.

And it's also the one truth I'm now positive of because Smith Eppington is my Ken. And I want to marry him and keep him forever.

CHAPTER EIGHTEEN

Smith

I LEFT Carina sleeping in our bed. The windows were wide open, and the fresh air was cool and smelled like morning. Her naked body was half concealed by white sheets, and parts and pieces of her skin played peekaboo. Long brown hair fanned across her pillow and mine. Her eyelids fluttered as a signal of deep sleep. As I stood there debating on whether I wanted to wake her up to kiss her goodbye, I took stock of everything I love. Every breath passing through her plump pink lips. All of her: every last fragment. The weak ones, the strong ones, the ones that can't be defined.

I left her sleeping. I didn't wake her. I didn't kiss her for fear of waking her and disturbing the perfect moment. *I didn't say goodbye.*

"Epp. Epp," someone calls.

I turn toward the voice, dragging myself from my daydream. I raise my brows and nod in my chief's direction. "What's up?" I ask.

"You need to go sit in on the brief. Now," he says. Everyone is on high alert. The offices are bustling with people who aren't usually here. Phones are ringing off the hook, and smiles and jokes are replaced by serious expressions and goddamn briefs. I always do as I'm told.

"Yes, sir," I reply with a quick head tilt. I set off for the conference room and walk in to a bunch of men in uniform talking loudly.

There are always reports of horrendous attacks that may happen. Few actually come to fruition, but today, we're dealing with intel of something larger. Something much, much larger. Moose slides me a tablet when I take a seat next to him. Zane, a SEAL seated on my other side, rambles curse words under his breath at record speed.

"It's happening," I say, as much as I ask. I've been preoccupied, my mind revisiting making love to Carina on replay. We had sex in three rooms of our house last night. I took her in every position imaginable. I came more than twice in one night, and I'm still hard just thinking about it. So while this horrible news isn't unexpected, it's surprising.

I click on one link. And then another. Sweat beads on my forehead even though this is the conference room where the AC is broken, and it runs constantly. Maybe it's purposeful. I'm not sure of anything right now. I can't be.

Zane murmurs back in my direction, "It's happening."

I click another link. There are photos attached here. My mind goes black. When I'm inside the situations, it's different. I'm in control. There are several plans in case one goes bad. What I'm looking at now is something I can't control. Something I can't fix. Not in the present, anyway. It does, in fact, remind me why I became a Navy SEAL to begin with.

I was a precocious little boy with wide eyes and a penchant for getting into mischief. Not real trouble, though. The kind of trouble you get into because you're always trying to figure something out. Always asking questions. Always trying to fix things. Even if they aren't broken. It reminds me I'm due for the yearly apology to my mother for blowing up our washing machine when I was thirteen. The whir the noisy machine emitted was normal, but I tried to fix it anyway. I don't think she'll ever forgive me for that.

I grew up in an upper-middle-class neighborhood where a lot of us planned on going into the military after high school graduation. Living in SoCal, the allure of the Navy was close geographically and emotionally. After 9/11 happened, it strengthened my resolve to serve even more. I watched those towers crumble to the ground in a pile of smoke while sitting in my high school English class.

We weren't sure right away what it meant or why it happened, but it didn't take long for the pieces to fall into place. No one wants to believe a tragedy so great can occur. Especially on American soil. The news portrays these types of disasters, but typically they're always in another country. Might as well be another planet for all that it directly concerns us. September 11 showed America that it can happen here, and it can happen easily. My soul was forged in fire and dipped in iron when our president confirmed they were attacks of terror.

I would become the terror and reflect it back onto anyone who threatens our way of life. Anyone who doesn't fight fair. Anyone who is owed deadly retribution. Hell Week was hard, but I knew what I would face after it would be more difficult than anything a screaming BUD/S instructor could deal out.

There was an even divide with my peers. September 11 either sent them far away to college to study for a degree that would keep them away from the trenches, and then there were the men like me, who wanted nothing more than to dig the trenches, shoulder to shoulder, to help defeat the traitorous monster regardless of the cost.

"The televisions. Turn on the news," Moose says, next to me. I'm gripping the side of the tablet harder than I should, and the case makes a straining sound.

People are going in and out, and all of the phones in the room are in use. Someone is teleconferenced in and is on the screen on the wall—face blank and words monotone. I can't hear above all the chaos, and I stand from my chair.

"It's real time. We're getting the intel only minutes before it happens," Zane says. He glances from his tablet to the television. "It's unreal," he finishes, eyes wide.

I bend over the screen in front of me and click another link. Another terror attack. And another. The news broadcaster on the television announces the one I read a few minutes ago. Another link pops up in our system. "Another one," I whisper.

Moose is sitting down next to me, scribbling a list as he goes. "Chicago, Tulsa, Austin, San Francisco, Miami, Vegas, Biloxi, Detroit, Phoenix, Virginia Beach," I say, reading over his shoulder. "There's no pattern," I mutter.

Next he starts another list with the international terror attacks happening right now. He can't write as quickly as they're happening. No one can. Hundreds, then thousands of huge attacks in minutes. It's like a spiderweb encompassing the entire planet. My breath is stolen. My whole body feels weak. The images are coming faster than I can process.

"They're sporadic in location but planned in action. This was planned. It was planned. How did we not see this coming?" We did. My god, we did. We had so much warning, but how could this possibly be stopped? Our enemy has no rules of war. They don't fight fair. They're organized, and yet they aren't.

The tragedy in this room is deafening.

Guns. Suicide bombers. IEDs. Bombs in suitcases. Cars turned into bombs. Every imaginable and unimaginable way to create mass death is reflected on every surface in the room. Airports, sports venues, parking garages, the Statue of Liberty, the Eiffel Tower, Times Square, Plaza Mayor, trains, Tower Bridge, subways, the Chunnel, grocery stores, hospitals, Musée D'Orsay, cruise ships, theme parks—nothing, nowhere is unscathed. The terrorists have stolen freedom and lives in every corner of our world.

The attacks are happening quicker and more frequently than anyone knows. The ones we aren't hearing about are probably the worst. No survivors to report anything.

I hear someone throwing up in the corner. Others have tossed their tablets aside in favor of calling their loved ones. I can't stop watching the tablet, the live video feeds of terror happening and destroying. How many lives are gone right now? Morbid curiosity rears its ugly head. How long was this planned? Not long. To have such a stronghold and so much power to be capable of this is terrifying.

"San Diego," someone shouts. "San Diego has four right now." That draws my gaze away from death. That makes my heart kick into a gear I didn't know existed. It steals my breath.

"Where?" I ask.

"World War III, men. This is it. Grab your ready bags. We are shipping out. Orders are in directly from the president," the officer says. He's a tall guy with always perfectly manicured hair. He's stoic and no-nonsense. I trust him. "Our priority will be the home front. We will go to the major cities and locate leaders, financiers, anyone who is remotely connected will hear from us." A couple of excited shouts echo. "This will be different from anything we've ever dealt with. Be ready to improvise."

I hear orders, and I understand them, but I can't go there yet. "Where in San Diego?" I ask louder. Someone must know. We are *in* San Diego.

Zane clears his throat. "Balboa Park. The museums, Gaslamp, and a mall." This is where my world comes apart at the seams.

"Which mall?" I fall back into my chair, the weight of today adding a hundred pounds. How was everything fine ten minutes ago? I drove to work. The air was nice. The traffic wasn't bad. Life was beautiful. This can't be reality. It can't. I'm trained in death and destruction, and I can't grasp this. "Which fucking mall?"

I put my head into my hands to cover my face. I already know what he's going to say. This is how it ends. It's how it has to end. Carina is at the mall with Megan. Today was their meeting. It's impossible to push everything else aside to think about my own interests completely. "This can't be fucking happening." It's an odd combination of terrified honor. The large picture and what this truly means for the world takes a back seat to the fear I feel for Carina.

"Everything tech is pushing through is shaky cell phone video feed and Twitter updates," Zane says, lowering his voice. Men funnel out of the door quickly. Others linger on phone calls. Some, like me, are glued to the spot. "But it's Fashion Valley, the food court at the very least. Possibly another IED in the west parking garage."

With wide, terrified eyes, I turn to Moose. He's already busy trying to get an outside line out, a strained look on his face.

I glance at my watch. She's there. They're there. The tables in this brief room are structured in a big square wrapping around the room. I hop into the middle pocket to reach the closest free phone and dial. The infrastructure outside of the base has to be in complete disarray. Cell towers will be down and flooded with unanswered calls. Cable and electric companies inundated, if they even have the capacity to be inundated, that is. Several attacks were on or around power plants.

Memorizing phone numbers isn't something I've ever done, but I know hers. I call her even though I know I won't get a response. I dial her to comfort myself—calling my girlfriend is a normal, everyday thing to do. Calling Carina means she has to be okay—her cell phone ringing in her oversized bag right next to her notebook full of words. I get her voicemail. "It's Carina. I can't reach my phone. You know what to do after the beep!"

She can't reach her phone. The harmless phrase makes my head swim. I lean over the desk, placing my palms flat against the cool metal. Taking deep breaths, I hang my head. I catch sight of my trembling hands. They remind me of what can be lost.

"I couldn't reach Megan," Moose says.

I see his boots between my legs, standing behind me.

I can't respond. I close my eyes as the shakes that were contained in my hands stretch up my arms and into my shoulders. I grab a forgotten tablet in front of me and find the San Diego info. I scroll through panicked social media messages and find the clearest video. Screams of terror ring out as the black smoke skews the camera's view. In between wisps of smoke, you can clearly see it is indeed the food court at the Fashion Valley Mall. I need to see it for myself. I watch it again and again, trying to discern the screams of death and terror. Is it Carina's cry? I've never heard her voice in that particular pitch. It angers me I can't decipher it. I can't confirm. Or deny.

"Goddammit, Carina. Be okay," I whisper. A funny

thing happens while I'm worrying about Carina and the state of her being. I contemplate life without her, and the sick feeling in my stomach wreaks havoc on the rest of my body. I let her die in my mind and taste that pain, let it leak out of every single pore on my body. It's unbearable. Then *it* happens. The cruelness of my own reality overrides everything else.

I remember.

I remember Megan.

I remember everything.

CHAPTER NINETEEN
Carina

I CAN'T OPEN my eyes, but I hear voices. More importantly, above the buzz and chaos, I hear *his* voice. "She'll be okay then?" he asks. In response, I hear mumbling from someone whom I assume is the person he's talking to. High-pitched beeping embeds itself into my mind every several seconds. It's an awful reminder that I'm not completely aware or in control of my own body.

"Take this and assure me she will be okay here and will continue to have a bed," Smith snarls. What does that mean? "My number. Call me daily. Do you understand?" There is a tension in his tone I can't comprehend. Mostly because I can't see the face that goes along with it.

"There's no need for this. Yes, sir. Of course, sir," the other man replies. They speak in hushed whispers a while longer, unintelligible words my foggy mind can't comprehend. I don't even know what happened or where I am. I feel his warm lips against my forehead. They linger longer than I think they should for a harmless kiss. I smell him. It's different. It's him, but it's also smoke, sweat, and an indescribable scent I'm not familiar with. I want to reach for him and pull him to me. I need him to tell me what's going on and why I sense such unease. Also why I feel so much pain deep within my bones.

Somehow I know I won't get that chance. "I love you, Care. Forever." His presence disappears from my weak awareness. Even unable to open my eyes, I know for a fact he's gone. My voice doesn't work. I can't call out for him to tell him I love him too. There's nothing now.

The beeping continues, now at a more hurried pace. It's incessant and skull piercing. It seems to grow louder and louder, echoing in the empty places Smith created when he left. "There, there," a male voice soothes in my ear. It's the wrong voice. My arms are leaden now that I feel them and try to use them. "Calm down." I must be tied down.

A fire starts in the crook of my arm and spreads. The panic I felt seconds ago vanishes, and I gladly accept the black cloud that spreads over me like a warm blanket. I don't have to think, or try to think, now. I just have to sleep.

There were signs—foreboding symptoms of a world infiltrated by evil. Mostly they went ignored as isolated threats and sporadic, spur-of-the-moment decisions made by unpredictable enemies. They were unsuspecting war declarations. That's usually the way until something so damning and heinous happens you can't ignore it. Our generation's Pearl Harbor massacred hundreds of thousands. It's the beginning of World War III.

Martial law is a bitch. Curfew is a bitch. Guards that patrol the streets are a bitch. Well, they're around to make sure we're safe, but they're still a bitch. They represent what's been taken. Not just from me, but from everyone.

The terror attacks on the 9/11 anniversary were so widespread that almost every person on the planet was affected in some way or another. Everyone knows someone who died, was injured, or was friends with someone who knew of someone who is now gone. Weeks have passed, and it still feels like it happened yesterday.

The television in my living room is on nonstop. In this state of emergency, the news plays twenty-four hours a day. The worn-out news anchors feed us information directly from the president. He himself will give news conferences from the Oval Office once a week. I think it's supposed to boost morale or to let us know he's working on the problem. How are we ever supposed to feel safe again? That's what I want to ask him. That's the issue I want to address. I've never had safety until very recently. It was snatched away, in all forms, in mere seconds.

When I finally got out of the hospital, the city was in complete melee. I was battered and bruised, but I would heal. The world? It will never be the same. I shuttered myself in my perfect little house after a terrifying ride home from the hospital. Jasmine stayed a few days, but eventually she returned to her house. Cell phones work sporadically. I blame the fact I haven't heard from Smith on that.

And the fact that he's off saving the world. The note stuck to the fridge with a cat magnet said, "Chicago. Then NYC. Call when I can. I love you. Be safe." The yellow sticky note is now taped to my laptop—the only reminder I have of our relationship that is tangible at this point. It seems like a whirlwind. A dream. Something that happened to someone else. Something that ended so brutally and quickly that I'm unsure how to feel.

So I don't feel. Anything.

We're supposed to carry on our everyday life like nothing happened. That's what they keep telling us, their voices monotone and robotic. Like it's even possible to consider that for even a second. My heart pounds out of my chest anytime I open the front door.

The sun still has a murky haze in front of it. If I were a more religious person, I would think this is the rapture. The apocalypse. The end of times. Earth going to hell in a handbasket, wrapped neatly for the devil himself. The image reflected on the TV presently is that of our planet from space. Earth is crying in the form of thick, black smoke.

It makes my stomach pang with unease. Turning up the volume, I retreat to the bedroom to work. Smith's novel is finished. I haven't given it a title, and I'm not sure about the ending I've written. But given the circumstances and the fact that I'm not sure where we stand in our relationship, it's poignant at the very least. Jaz will hate it. Even though she's asked to read it a dozen times, I've told her it's not ready. I've edited it more times than I care to admit, and I can't put my finger on what needs to happen for me to call it *done*.

Reading it is the only thing that takes my mind off reality. I lose myself in a love story so swift and so simple that it blocks everything else out entirely. Because if I remember Megan the way I portray her in my story, I can forget how the blast that gave me a scar on my right ankle disfigured most of her face and half of her body.

Tears come, and the well of guilt that resides in my chest forces labored breaths. I picture her with her long, silken, blond hair and her pageant-ready features. Her petite, toned body and her flawless skin. Her smile. Her laugh. Her perfection. The vomit rises when her new reality, her new, destroyed body and face, comes to mind.

"I never thought I'd say this, but I'm happy for Smith. And you. After talking to you this morning and hanging with you one on one, I can call Smith and Megan done," Megan said.

"*He was mine for so long I forgot what life was like without him. But when I stopped to think about it, after he healed from his accident, he wasn't my Smith. I've been living without him for a while now, Carina. That man is so obviously yours it's embarrassing.*" She smiled at me and took my hand in hers. She swallowed, and it looked like it was difficult. She had to work hard to get those words out. The emotion reflecting in her eyes was almost too much to bear, so I looked down at our joined hands.

Her long fingers folded around mine, and her nails were so perfect, so goddamn perfect, that I couldn't look away. The French manicure. The perfectly filed natural nails. The moisturized skin. I was thinking, *My god. What if he remembers this beautiful, kind woman?* when the bomb went off. I didn't know it was a bomb at the time because I was knocked unconscious right away. I think it was the blowback that took me out. Megan, seated mere feet from me, got the bad end of the stick.

After I finish today's crying jag, the sun is setting. US residents aren't permitted to be outside after dark. A facet of Martial law I find odd because terrorists don't require dark. They relish in the light—in taking it—in snuffing it out completely.

I get out of bed when I hear a knock at the door. Sean, Jaz's brother, is bringing me groceries. I don't bother putting pants on underneath Smith's oversized T-shirt. It hits right above my knee anyway. I shrug and open the door a crack to peer outside.

"No," I say.

Roarke shuffles from one foot to the other. It's a nervous gesture I've seen him do in meetings. "I want to talk. Please, Carina. I promise not to come near you. I just want five minutes of your time."

"How did you find me?" I ask. I know damn well with today's technology you can never disappear completely. He's known where I've been since I left him. I want to watch him squirm for an answer and to see if he'll admit to violating the restraining order.

He swallows, looks behind him at the setting sun, and blows out a breath. "I don't have time for that. The sun will set in twenty minutes. Five. Please, babe."

I open the door and fold my arms across my chest. Roarke isn't the most evil villain in my world anymore. How sick and twisted is that realization? "Talk," I command. "And never call me that again."

He blinks several times quickly, right in a row. Another nervous twitch. I've never seen these habits directed at me. I've never made him nervous, I suppose. He hasn't met the new Carina. "I wanted to ask how you were doing. When it happened, I was so worried for you. You have to know I still think about you every day. I still love you. That didn't go away. I've had all this time to think about what a horrible person I was. What I did to you," he says, his voice breaking on the last syllable.

I can't even look at him without feeling ill, so I look away. Maybe it's because I'm tired, or because I miss Smith, or perhaps it's because I'm reflecting my anger and guilt on him, but I don't want to sugarcoat anything anymore.

"There was a time when you were the worst thing in my world. I worried about leaving the house because of you. Because of what you might do to me if I ran into you. I don't miss you, Roarke. I definitely don't still love you. It didn't even go away," I say. Looking at him seems important right now. I finish, "Because I never loved you in the first place. Not even one bit. You are a bad person. You aren't reformed, Roarke. A bad thing happened in our world. A nasty, bad thing that makes men like you look like saints, but I'll never forget what you did to me. The things you said when you weren't even trying to be mean and vicious." The lump in my throat appears, and it angers me. I want to tell him everything I should have said all those years ago. The first time he said something mean or condescending before he started beating me for invalid reasons.

I take a second to breathe. "Apologize if that's what you came here for. Your mom will be happy if you get that out," I say.

He hangs his head. "I'm sorry, Carina. I'm so sorry. I hope one day you'll forgive me. I can't ask you to forget the things I did to you. I never would. I am a bad person, you're right. I've been talking to a therapist." *Because it's court-ordered*, I think. "And she says that I projected a lot of my insecurities and problems onto you. I took it out on you. Because I loved you and trusted you."

I roll my eyes. "Now is the part where you tell me you've found a new outlet for your negative energy and will never do what you did to me to another woman again. Am I getting warmer? Boxing? Running?"

He blows out a breath through his mouth. "You're so different now." He ignores my question because I'm right. A twinkle in his eye suggests I'm irritating him. I'm not afraid of it, though.

"How am I different? Now that I'm with someone who respects me? Wouldn't dream of hurting me? Or am I different because I'm not a person who will take your bullshit anymore?"

"I guess," Roarke says, shaking his head.

I start closing the door. "Sean will be here with my groceries any moment. I'm pretty sure the cops have better things to do than enforcing a restraining order."

"You look good," he says. "You don't feel the same way, and I understand why, but it was good to see you. I'm glad you're doing well." Such menial talk from a man who has the ability to break bones with his words.

"Tell your mom not to call," I reply. Shutting the door, I lock it. When I hear his vehicle start, I slide down my front door to sit.

Mentally, I pat myself on the back. Then seconds later I curse myself for all the things I should have said. It makes me so angry. My doorbell breaks me from the audible tirade I'm having with my foyer.

"Oh, good," I say when I open the door to Sean. "My groceries."

He has four large, reusable sacks full. Walking into my kitchen, he sets them on the counter and turns to face me. I lost power for several days after the attacks, and I've slowly but surely built back up my freezer stash by way of Sean's trips.

"How was the store?" I ask. "Is it still terrible out there?"

"You're going to have to go out eventually, Carina."

I start unpacking bags. "Don't you start, too. I hear it all day on the news. I should go shopping like a million people didn't die in horrific fashion, mind you, mere weeks ago. Don't you tell me to return to normal life when I have to keep a pile of cash stuffed under my mattress."

My writing is the only normal I've established.

"I started your car again," he says, voice monotone.

"Thank you, Sean. I'm sorry. I'm in a mood right now." *Because of Roarke*, I want to scream. How dare that rat bastard try to take anything else from me? Another breath would be asking too much. I'm so mad I'm practically seething.

He clears his throat. "Perhaps if you changed out of your pajamas, you'd feel better?"

My cloud of anger abates a touch.

"Hey!" I shout. "This is a dress. It's as long as a dress, anyway." I smile from ear to ear. "I was thinking of visiting Megan. Jasmine said she's been transferred to a wing of the hospital that can have visitors now," I explain.

Looking down at my bag of canned vegetables and fruits, I get even angrier. Fresh produce is a thing of the past. The TV tells me it won't be long before the farmers are up and on the roads again transporting their goods to stores, but it feels like it's been forever. These are the new First World problems.

"Is that a good idea? Why don't you start with the grocery store? The hospital is still pretty awful. The structure was dismantled fully. You remember how many beds they had in a room when you were there. It's just as bad as when you left." No corner of the world was left unscathed, copiously so.

I open up the bag of bread and shove a slice into my mouth. It's white bread, so it sticks to the roof of my mouth. "I don't know why I was lucky. Why her and not me?" My words are jumbled because of the food.

"God wanted you to OD on carbs. And luck has nothing to do with it," Sean says. "Have you heard from Smith?" An unwelcome change of subject. Awesome.

I shake my head. "Nope. Still nothing. And I think that's why I'm going crazy."

Cracking open a bottle of water, I drink half and set the bottle on the counter next to the other twenty or so empty bottles. No recycling trucks are running. Garbage pickup resumed shortly after the attacks in an effort to keep society clean. The reminder of yet another way my life has been upheaved pisses me off. I knock the bottles over like damn bowling pins.

"You'd feel better if you left the house. It's scary, but at least it's real. Sitting here and pretending isn't doing yourself any favors."

"It's how I'm coping. Not even a single email telling

me he's alive. Not a text message. Nothing. Is this real?" I ask, waving my arm out to the side. Our cozy house, our life so briefly lived. "Because it feels like a fucking joke. A cruel fucking joke!"

Sean hangs his head. "I'll see you in a couple days. Call. Email the work address if my cell doesn't work, or tell Jaz what you need, okay?"

I feel like a jerk. "I'm sorry, Sean. I'm spun up today." I make a move to approach him.

Sean throws both hands out, palms facing me, and I halt in my tracks. "I get it. It's fine. Everyone is on edge. It's understandable. Just remember who's here for you," Sean says, walking away from me. His hand on the doorknob, he turns his head to the side. "I'll be here for you as long as you want me to." He opens the door, shuts it, and then uses his key to lock up behind himself.

I think this is when I realize everyone else knows something I don't. Smith and I are over, and I'm the last person to figure it out.

CHAPTER TWENTY
Carina

ANOTHER THREE WEEKS PASS, and I haven't heard from him. The infrastructure of America is making progress in small increments—a slow, moving process, or so we're being brainwashed to believe. I've visited the grocery store and the salon. My friend, who is a hairdresser, opened her salon for a half day once a week to ease back into life. I figured it was as good a time as any to dip my baby toe back into the new real world. Today I'm headed to the hospital to see Megan.

I've put the errand off for so long that now it's awkward. Then, by calling it awkward, I've also labeled myself important. It's a serious case of self-contrived bullshit. I dwelled on the decision for so long that it came back full circle, and here I am heading in the hospital's direction, my hands on the steering wheel at ten and two.

Driving is scary. There are roadblocks and guard checks every few miles along the freeways. It makes traffic almost unbearable. The radio has the same feed as the televisions, and it barks out orders about curfew and the importance of adhering to our new, normal rules. I turn it off as I enter the crowded parking lot. Cars are parked everywhere in a haphazard nightmare. There weren't enough spaces, so visitors park wherever they find an empty spot. The curbs and sidewalks are lined with cars, and the grassy area in between lots is slammed full. There is no way I'm going into the parking garage. Not today, and maybe not ever again.

The empty space I find is at least a mile away from the hospital. Sweaty and out of breath, I show my driver's license, walk through a metal detector, sign in at a security checkpoint, and then sign in at the hospital's front desk to obtain my visitor's pass. A gruff nurse with a wart on her chin directs me to the area where Megan is. I focus on my breathing as I ride the humid elevator up to the fourth floor and turn down a barely lit hallway. The faint scent of antiseptic and blood clings to the air, tainting my oxygen and reminding me why I'm here. She's inside the last room on the right. There are more beds shoved inside the space than there should be, but it's still easy to spot Megan right away.

A large, hunched male figure is slumped over, resting on the side of the bed by her thighs. My heart catches in my throat, and the scent of rubber gloves and betrayal mixes with the former smells, and I throw a hand over my mouth. My stomach flips.

"Carina," Megan says.

I gag. It is perfect timing, really. Her face has healed by leaps and bounds since I last saw her. The blond, silken perfection that she calls hair is patchy but returning to its former luster. I plaster a weak smile on my face and walk toward them.

He lifts his head. "What are you doing here?" he asks, lifting one brow, his face washed out with confusion and accusations.

I sigh. "Moose." I let my shoulders slump in relief. Not that I have any right to be relieved, but it gives me some piece of hope. Hope of what, I'm still not sure. "I wanted to see how you were doing," I direct at Megan.

She smiles, and the warmness draws me nearer, like a moth to a flame.

"I didn't know I had to go through you to see her," I say, flicking my gaze to Moose. Huge arms on the bed and his looming size force the image of a watchdog to mind. Moose loves Megan. It's so clear to see. Does she love him? Or is it blatantly ignored in favor of a past nothing can compare with?

He leans back in his metal chair and folds his arms behind his head. "You don't need my permission. I figured you'd want to see Smith. That's all."

The room spins. His words seem a different language for a beat or two. "What do you mean, see Smith? I haven't even heard from him." Saying his name out loud brings a whole new set of emotions. I can practically feel him here with me.

Megan coughs, then grabs her side as she winces, her pretty nose scrunched up just so. Moose lays a hand on her arm in what I think is a comforting gesture. "He left here just before you walked in. He's headed to your house," Megan says.

"Oh my gosh," I whisper, slumping down into an empty chair on the other side of her bed. "Why didn't he call me? I didn't know. How could I possibly know?" A tear sneaks out. "How long are you guys back for?" I ask. Dread turns to panic when I gauge Moose's appearance for the first time. He's tired—dark circles look drawn underneath his drooping eyes. His T-shirt is stretched out, and his jeans look five days worn. I close my eyes.

"We leave again soon. In hours, not days," Moose says.

I won't make it back in time. There's no way. The traffic. The security checkpoints. It's futile.

"For how long?" My voice cracks. "How long will you be gone this time?" I forget to breathe, so I place a hand on my stomach and force my exhale to move it in toward my body.

Megan takes my hand. "Thank you for coming. I understand if you want to leave, Carina." Her nails are absent of polish, and the red scars are almost completely healed. They remind me of Smith's scars. Smith. My heart cracks into two.

"Why did he come here first?" I ask. Either Megan's or Moose's reply will satisfy me. They don't reply, but they do share a look that scalds me to the core.

"It's not my place to say," Moose responds. I think it's mostly so Megan doesn't have to, and he's all about sparing her any grief or pain. I hear the patient in the bed next to Megan laugh, and it makes me enraged.

With a small squeeze she says, "This is part of it. You're not familiar with the deployments and his absence, but it's part of loving him. You have to trust that everything will be the same when he comes back. If you don't, then you're wasting your time." She swallows, and I can tell it is painful. "Even if you know nothing will ever be the same, you have to allow yourself to believe it will."

How morbid. How unromantic. This isn't anything like how I pictured our relationship. Or lack thereof.

I close my eyes once again. To think about Smith and to block out her pain. "He hasn't called me once. He hasn't emailed me once. I didn't know if he was dead or alive. He came here before he came home. What am I supposed to make of that?" Now I'm angry. "How can everything eventually be the same when a person is gone? No communication?"

"It's like riding a horse," Megan says, nodding her head. She's trying to comfort me, and something about it irks me. "He comes back, and everything falls back into place until the next deployment comes around."

I should want her advice. She has firsthand knowledge I don't, but I can't get the image of Smith here, visiting her, out of my mind. I thank her for her advice and wish her well. I tell her I'm sorry and I'll never forgive myself for choosing the left side of the table. She tells me not to worry over it another second, because that's just how she is.

"I should go. Where are you flying out of? Any chance I can catch him there?" I ask, turning for the door.

Moose shakes his head and explains they're flying out of the airport on base. No one is allowed except those authorized, and with the heightened security, there is no way they would make an exception.

I rush out of the door and hold my breath all the way to the elevator.

"Wait up, Carina," Moose says, coming up behind me. "I want to talk to you."

"We just talked," I reply.

He sighs and leans both palms against the wall next to the elevator. "It's better if you miss him right now. He's not himself," he says, chancing a glance in my direction.

That makes me want to see him even more. "What's wrong with him?"

"You know he's the most loyal and honest person I've ever met. That's no secret. It's deeper than what it seems on the surface. After Henry died, he promised to live a life in his honor, to warrant barely escaping a fate he thought he deserved. I guess, right now you could say he's in the largest moral dilemma of his life," Moose rasps. Taking a deep breath, I wait for him to finish. "He's wrapped himself in work so completely that it's no surprise you haven't heard from him. He loves you,

Carina. Remember that, okay? He's not even calling his parents."

"That's supposed to make me feel better?" The elevator pings open, and I step in quickly. What would I say to Smith if I could talk to him face-to-face? Would I fall into his arms and forgive him because of all he's dealt with? I'd like to hope I wouldn't. I've grown stronger than that. "Do you know how my mind has played tricks on me all this time? I doubted he even existed. Sometimes I even wondered if claiming me was a fun game. Make Carina fall in love with me, have sex with her...finally, and then pop, smoke," I say, stabbing a finger in the air. It's not Moose's fault, but seeing him is as close to seeing Smith as I'll probably get until God knows when.

He shakes his head. Standing in front of me in the elevator, the doors close behind us. "It's not like that at all. Trust me. He'd be devastated if he heard you talking like this."

"Him? Devastated? He came here to visit her before seeing me," I say. Traitorous tears flood my vision. "I saw you hunched over her bed when I walked in, and I thought it was him. I thought it was Smith. And that would make perfect sense. Then you looked up, and I was relieved. Maybe for one more minute I could pretend he truly is still mine." Sniffling, I wipe my nose with the back of my hand in the most ungraceful way possible. "He's not mine, though, is he?" I turn my head to meet his eyes.

Moose winces, looks away, and then down at the floor. Shaking his head, he says, "He was never yours to take, unfortunately."

An arrow shot directly into my heart would hurt less. "I have to go. Thanks for the talk." He follows me out of the hospital and into the parking lot. I sense him close behind. "And for what it's worth, I think you should tell

Megan how you feel. She deserves more than an honor relationship."

He stays silent, but still follows me all this distance out to my car. To make sure I get there safely, I assume. It irritates me, and at this point I'd do anything to hurt him the way he's hurt me. Even if it's truly Smith who has hurt me. The hot sun beats down as I stew with the words on the tip of my tongue and my heart hardening by the second. "I've got it from here," I whisper, grabbing the door handle of my car to unlock it.

Moose clears his throat. "I respect Smith too much to ever pursue her in that way. I can be her friend. I can try to fit in the spaces that he's left, but he's all over her body. He owns every inch of her skin, her soul, her heart. Forever."

An angry sob rises in my throat. "Never forever!" I yell, remembering the words Smith whispered before he left me alone in that hospital. "Forever doesn't exist. Only dimensions of time that can be calculated by happiness or sadness. Sadness? That lasts forever. Happiness is never forever, Moose. It's not. Don't fool yourself into thinking any different. I got a few months of it, and I'll take it for what it's worth and move on. She won't love him forever. Not after what he's done. Reach out and take what you want. Not because I think it would make my life easier, but because who the hell knows how much longer we have on this planet?" I sob again and start my car with the door open. I point to the hazy, smoke-covered sun. It still doesn't look the way it did before.

Moose is leaning over, one hand on my side panel and one wrapped around the side of his head, soaking in my words of wisdom. Maybe someone will have a better day than I am. "I have to go. If there's any chance of catching him, I'll never forgive myself if I don't try." I close my door and roll my window down.

He's still silent and stoic.

"Tell Megan I'm sorry and she's beautiful, okay? This wasn't how I envisioned this visit going."

He nods. "Thanks, Carina."

A dimpled smile is the last thing I see before I pull away and head toward the freeway. I use my Bluetooth to call home and alternate with Smith's cell phone dozens of times. The lines are down right now. It's useless. With each security check, I become more and more impatient. The officer that's checking my trunk and back seat at the entrance to my neighborhood is friendly enough, but I might as well be spitting nails instead of pleasantries. It took two hours to cover several miles to get home.

Smith's truck isn't in the driveway when I pull in. I cry some more and beat on my horn like a maniac. The radio blares some news about an impostor attack at the White House. The perpetrator didn't get close, of course, but it's still a suicide vest with intent to kill. I cry some more for the state of affairs that ripped my life apart. Pretending isn't an option anymore. I exit my car with a face full of wet mascara and my oversized bag full of mace and empty notebooks.

The second I push open the door, I smell him. Smith was here, and the tragedy of that forces a pit in my stomach that powers me to a toilet to be sick. The house is warmer somehow. Complete. And he's already gone. I can't ask him anything. Or talk to him about how he's doing. I can't tell him about Roarke or Sean or show him my new hair color. Truthfully, it's as if a stranger passed through my home while I was out.

I open the door to the room where he keeps his gear. A few large Tupperware boxes have been shifted. I close the door quickly and head straight for my marker board to write down the title of the book. I know without a doubt what suits it best. With shaky hands and a red Expo Marker, I tell the world, and myself, too, what this story will be. After I write it down on the board, I sit down to open my laptop to email it to Jasmine. It's ready. I'm ready for her to see my scars. I'm ready for her to sell them to the highest bidder.

That's when I see the letter. It's one page, written in Smith's neat scrawl on a piece of computer paper. It's not folded. It's sitting on my keyboard, sandwiched by the screen and the keyboard. "What have you done?" I ask him, as I glance over his words.

My beautiful, sweet, kind Care,

I missed you. I walked into an empty house that felt like you. Missing you has been painful, but feeling you and smelling you and not seeing you is heartbreaking. I don't have a lot of time as I'm headed out again, but I need to tell you a few things.

I haven't contacted you because I needed space. You consumed me so wholly that I wasn't sure who I was anymore. It sounds like a pretext, but given my circumstance, it bears more weight than the average man giving that excuse. Don't get me wrong, I love you so fully that I can't imagine the world without you in it, but I feel I may have taken advantage of our friendship by pursuing more.

I'm not calling you weak, or saying I have some superhero powers of persuasion, because I know that what you felt for me is real.

Our love is real.

Something changed when the new 9/11 happened, while I was wondering if you were alive, dead, or otherwise harmed. I stopped breathing. I made deals with God. Nothing in this world made sense if you weren't going to be by my side. It's so selfish. It's wrong. All my life my goal was to be a SEAL. Loving you detracted from that goal, I've realized. Loving you changed me completely. Loving you is painful. It's truth. It's lies. It's the past. It's my future. Loving you is always.

Loving you is immoral, Carina. Because long before I loved you, I promised my love to someone else. It wasn't coerced. I gave it freely and of pure heart, entirely. Megan needs me now more than ever. If I've learned anything about the fickle, trivial things of life, it's that you need to honor your commitments. What else can you do? How else is a man formed except by his word?

When I proposed to Megan, I got down on one knee and asked her to marry me. I told her I would be there for her until the last sunset and the moon refused to rise. I told her I would be her rock in any storm of life—her protector, her guardian, her provider. Most men say these things during their wedding vows. I promised them when I proposed.

Do you know how horrible it makes me feel?

Because of how it must make you feel? You're not second best. You're not runner-up. You're the love of my life.

None of that matters. Sometimes men must sacrifice for the greater good. Sometimes men must sacrifice for honor. I must sacrifice because I can't in good conscience love you so fiercely and turn a blind eye to my past promises. It would make what we had less. And it's not less. Quite the contrary. Care, you are everything.

From this moment forth, you'll be that gentle sunlight that wakes me on a weekend morning. That first scent of fall when the air begins to cool. The smile on my face when I see a couple lounging in the park. You'll be the wind in my hair when I jump out of an airplane. The stars in the sky as I fall asleep at night. You'll be that soft second beat of my heart every other moment. The fog during a morning run. Your name will be the first thing I think when I wake up and the very last thing I mouth before I fall asleep.

Please know that nothing could change this, and it really has nothing to do with you. This was the decision I was always destined to make when the time arose. Some may say it's not fair to Megan to give her the pieces you didn't claim in her absence, but I know you'll understand I have to try. I have to make it right in her eyes.

I have to honor my word. I have to work to convince her of these things.

I know you'll be more than okay because of how amazing you are. The things you've overcome don't define you, they add to your charm—your backbone. I hope one day I can look at you and not feel everything. I hope one day I can think of your face without wanting to curl into myself and die of longing. Mostly I hope you can move on with your life without a backward glance in my direction. If you love me, you will. As soon as you can. It's my plea. My dying wish.

I'll long for you always. I'll love you even though I shouldn't.

I remembered. And it changed everything and nothing at the same time.

Yours always,
S

CHAPTER TWENTY-ONE
Carina

IT SEEMED SO convoluted and complicated at first glance. Given our difficult histories, it was hard to come to terms with how it truly boiled down to something so simplistic—honor. Smith's honor. I wouldn't love him as fiercely if he didn't have it. I think it's the single most appealing quality in a man because so few actually have it. It's poetic because that's what stole him away from me. I'm trying to move on as Smith asked, but it's been slow going for various reasons.

Sean kisses like a wet dog after a swim in a pool. I broke things off with him before they evolved into anything more than friends who kiss. He was upset, and in turn it made Jasmine upset. She forgave me when I wrote her a detailed scene of me kissing her brother. I think the words she used were "utterly disgusting." It's not easy going into the dating world knowing no one will ever stack up to *him*. Not ever. Not even close.

I haven't heard from anyone in Smith's life since the letter either. I can't bring myself to contact Moose or Megan. The jagged wound he left in my heart is still raw and bleeding. I'm still trying to figure out how you can love a person too much, because that's what his words boiled down to.

It's been several weeks since I read the letter that changed everything. "Come here, Poppet," I say, then click my tongue. The solid white juvenile kitten jumps into my lap. Moments after I finished reading Smith's words, I heard a tiny meow from the hallway. Smith broke my heart and left the white kitten to mend it. I hated Poppet and loved her in equal measure for a long time. My overall desire for this cat won out in the end, and now she is basically the most important thing in my life. She has a red-and-white striped collar that reminds me of a peppermint stick. She licks my face and pounces on my feet anytime they're under a blanket.

"I'm three months away from becoming Bridget Jones, Teala," I say into the receiver of my phone. "Can I come over tonight?" I ask.

"Are you bringing Poppet again? Last time she chewed the handle of my Louis Vuitton, and who knows when I can get it fixed." The mail is still incredibly slow. Mailing the handbag in for repair isn't an option. I checked into it after my sweet girl teethed on my friend's bag. "Macs is here right now. Give me an hour or two." She giggles. I close my eyes at the sound of her happiness. Macs is a SEAL Moose introduced her to when their date didn't go as planned.

I clear my throat.

"I'm sorry, Carina. I shouldn't have told you that."

"Ugh. Stop it. I'm not some wilted flower. A love-scorned woman without any prospects," I reply. "A woman who has multiple book and movie offers about the above-mentioned scorn. A woman who has a life." I lighten my tone and laugh as she groans with each of my points. My work will tie me to Smith for the rest of my life. It's worth reconsidering, and I have several times.

"And a woman with a bitch cat," Teala jokes.

Smiling, I scoff. "Take it back now, or I'll poison your chai." Coffee shops are coming back into business after the attacks, but the one by my house is still closed. I've taught myself how to make a mean chai tea latte. I bring them for my friends when we get together. "Jasmine will be over before me, I think. I have a quick errand to run first."

"Finally entering the world. I like the new Carina." She wouldn't say that if she knew where I was headed. "Don't make it so sweet this time. I haven't been to boot camp lately, in case you weren't aware." We're finally at the point where a joke about the sad state of affairs in our world is acceptable.

"Your ass is too big to fit through the door even if it was open for business," I say. "We can try that workout video tonight if you want?"

"Nah. Less sugar. That will take care of the problem," she responds.

I smile and agree to make hers with less sugar.

"Oh, and for your information, I entered the world a long time ago. If you came up for air out of your sex cloud, you might notice it." Macs is with a troop of SEALs that are stationed here in San Diego. Oftentimes I wonder if I would even know if Smith was back here. I'm sure he would try to be, to be closer to Megan. "Will he be here long?" I ask, fishing.

She giggles again. "He's here long," she says. I hear a satisfied male grumble in the background.

"Oh, ew, Teala. Get out of here with that."

She sighs. "Smith is still gone, Care. That's what you're asking, right? I don't know why you just don't talk to Moose. You said he's called you a few times. I'm sure he has all the information."

I shake my head. "I have to go. Remember I'll be a little later. Go…have fun," I say.

"Drive safe," she says. "Quit. Stop it." I roll my eyes at my friend's obvious daytime romp. I bet she's naked right now. Lucky bitch. "Remember to just breathe and turn off the radio. It distracts you. Nothing will happen that you can't find out about when you get here, okay? Pack Poppet some fucking toys, please."

I laugh. Because I can't help but smile when I think about my cat, and hastily agree. With a quick goodbye, I hang up the phone. "Sleepover tonight, Poppet! Let's pack!"

I send a quick text to my errand. *I'll be there in an hour. You'll be home?*

His reply is immediate. *Waiting 4 u.*

I get ready quickly and have everything packed and in my car in no time. I head in a direction I don't typically drive. The security checkpoints are run differently than the ones I'm used to, and it makes me nervous. I put Poppet in her carrying case, and she hates it. The officer asks me to unzip the flap. I raise a brow but oblige his request.

"Curfew is soon, ma'am. Get to where you're going," he says, satisfied that my precious cargo isn't something more sinister. Teala would disagree and show you the handle of her expensive handbag.

"Of course. I'm almost there," I say, motioning to the road in front of me that he's blocking. A car honks behind me and beside me. It's annoying and it makes me nervous.

He waves me through, and I turn into the gated community while I talk to my cat about how the politics of the world are a clusterfuck of epic proportions. She listens and doesn't judge. She even meows back in irritated intervals. I can tell her anything. Talking to my cat distracts me from the stupid thing I'm about to do. Jasmine would kill me if she knew, but I'm determined.

Pulling into the driveway sends shivers down my spine, but it's not enough to stop me. I have everything to prove. The car stays running because I won't be long. I unzip Poppet's bag to give her freedom to roam while I run this quick errand. I kiss her on her white fuzzy head and leave a smear of dark pink lipstick.

The sight makes me smile. As much as I hate to admit it, Poppet is the best gift I've ever received. She represents something so dark and painful. If I can love her, maybe one day I'll be able to love the wounds that accompany her existence.

"I'll be right back," I whisper. Then I walk up the driveway and ring the ornate doorbell.

The same doorbell I chose a few years ago.

Roarke answers the door. It takes him a long time. He's finely dressed and presentable, but a bad feeling lodges in my throat. A hint of distrust creeps in and my fight-or-flight kicks into gear. *The car is running,* I remind myself.

"Carina. Come in. Please," he says. His voice is clear, in control. Not like the last time I saw him.

I hold my shoulders up straighter in an effort to portray confidence. "Poppet is in the car. I have to be quick," I explain, hiking my thumb over my shoulder.

"Finally got a dirty rat of a pet, did you?" Roarke asks. I slide by him. He stands too close, so my shoulder rubs against his chest as I pass into the foyer. The scent hits me at the same time a wave of bad memories does. This place. This horrible, horrible place where an emotional prison sentence was served.

"Stop it," I say. You don't call my cat a rat. "Is my legal file where it used to be?" There's paperwork I need that was long forgotten when Jasmine and I moved out of here in a frenzied rush. Roarke eagerly agreed to let me pick it up when I texted him last week. That's when I was trying things with Sean and I figured he'd come with me to keep things on the up and up. After proclaiming him fish lips, I couldn't very well ask him to escort me here.

"Join me for a drink," Roarke replies.

"Are you drinking?" I ask. My heart pounds out a warning against my chest. This, this is the moment I should turn around and get into my car to leave, but that odd tether that always appears when he asserts control shows itself.

He cocks his head to the side as he eyes me up and down. "I've had a few." I shake my head and head for my old office. It's redecorated, and my filing cabinet is nowhere to be seen. Roarke stands behind me. Too close for comfort. "Come here, Carina. I've missed you."

"Fuck you, Roarke. Where is my file?" Spinning on my toe, I face him. He glowers down at me. The scent of expensive bourbon lingers in the air surrounding his body. "Do you even have it?"

He laughs—a caustic, evil sound. "I burned it. But it was the perfect excuse to get you right where I want you, wasn't it? And he's not even here to save you this time," Roarke says, accentuating each word in a drunken slur.

I take a step back. There's a lamp on the table next to his mahogany desk. It's stainless and solid. Another step back. He follows, leaning over me, trying to scare me. It works because it's always worked.

"This is how it's going to work. You're going to fuck me. The way you used to. Like you love me. Maybe I won't beat the shit out of you after. I haven't decided yet. You ruined my life, you know? I can't forgive that easily. Now, I'm going to make you a drink. Your favorite, and then I'll show you how my girlfriend redecorated the master suite." I taste the bile. It mixes with hot anger as I watch his back disappear from the room.

Scurrying like a frightened mouse, I head for the lamp and unplug it. I test the weight in my hand. On second thought, I grab my cell phone and send a text in the group message with Jasmine and Sean from back when they were doing all my errands. I type, *Help. At Roarke's. Sorry.* I picture Jasmine's face as she reads my message. Horror. Anger. This was backup. I'm going to take care of myself this time.

I walk out to the wraparound porch out back. The cement is this beautiful lavender color. When he selected the color, I thought it was odd, but it's stunning with the décor, and I do miss this room a little. The mace is in the pocket of my sweater, and the lamp is in my hand when Roarke walks in with two martini glasses. The cops are too busy to deal with trivial things like domestic disputes.

"Don't be rude. I made you a drink," he says. "I like your choice of room. Drop your weapon. I told you I wouldn't hurt you. It's me, babe. I took care of you all those years. Remember?"

I want to beat him to a pulp. I want to cry, but the feeling that overrides them all is that of love. I do want to go to his embrace. It's fucked up, and I know it. He set this trap specifically for me.

"You said you wouldn't hurt me if I fucked you. That's not happening, buddy. Not by a long shot. So either you let me go right now, or I'll use the weapon," I explain. "I can't believe I trusted that you've changed. Do you beat her too?" How does he do it? Keep women under his control. There's nothing special about him.

I need to buy time and make him think I'm not actually scheming. I'm going to kill him. It's the only way out of this for good. Deep down I think I knew this would happen when I agreed to come over here tonight. That's why I slipped the mace into my pocket.

My phone buzzes in my pocket. That draws his eyes from my face. It's a phone call, not a text.

"Did you call someone?" he asks. His face transforms into something resembling a monster. A dangerous one. He drops both glasses, and they shatter on the beautiful cement. A million pieces of glass dancing across the floor where horrible memories call home.

He springs, and I swing the lamp like a baseball bat. The phone continues to buzz against my leg. It keeps me grounded in this moment—it focuses me on what I need this outcome to be. I hit the side of his arm as he blocks me. Stumbling, I catch myself on the back of a chaise lounge. Swinging once more, I miss.

Roarke is strong. Much stronger than I will ever be. This is a fact I shouldn't know firsthand. I have to use my wits to beat him.

I take a step back as he strikes out, a clenched fist aimed directly at my face. I cry out, a loud, ungodly noise of fury, as I swing the base of the lamp at his head. It connects this time because my war cry distracted him. He wasn't ready for a determined Carina. He wasn't ready for my bloodlust. The crack is satisfying, and he goes down hard. Blood trickles from a deep gouge by his eye as he brings himself up to his elbows. I'm breathing heavily, adrenaline pumping through my body when he gets to his feet. I'm frozen to the spot as I watch the dark red liquid pour down his face. It doesn't look like I dreamed it would. My phone vibrates again. He's incapacitated, so I take it out and look at it. The text from Jasmine says she's here.

He sucker punches me, and I hear the whiz of his knuckles the second before they crunch into my cheek. I've taken worse from him, but I lose my grip on the lamp and it falls down by my feet. I cry out. Jasmine is going to get hurt. Why did I text her? Through the stars and dizzy sensations, I yell for her to stay away, to let me solve my own problems. Roarke kicks me in the ribs like I'm some animal, something not worthy of standing upright. The mace in my pocket is within reaching distance. It's my only chance to right the mistake I made.

The words of rage passing his lips are incoherent at this point. He won't stop until I'm not breathing. And neither will I. There's a lull in his abuse, so I'm able to get the small bottle palmed in my hand. I scream out and through searing pain I make a lunge toward him, grabbing his pants with my free hand to help myself up. He can't shake me off.

As I'm spraying the repellant in the general direction of his face, Smith is breaking down the screen door on the side of the porch with Jasmine and Sean close behind. He makes light work of the titanium masterpiece Roarke had specially made for this room. I cough on the fumes of the potent spray.

"Get the fuck away from her," Smith roars, charging toward us like a battering ram. I think it's the blood leaving my body, but time starts slowing down—the moment crystallizes in a dreamy sort of way.

I can compare it to how I feel when I'm writing a scene. I'm there, and yet I'm not. I have control, but no true power.

Smith's beautiful, tired eyes turn to me on my knees, and the grimace on his face shifts to that of fury— untamed, unmatched, tangible in quality. I could reach out and touch it, taste it, hide from it. Roarke goes down in one solid blow from Smith. I don't know what he looked like moments before it happened. I wish I could have seen his face as he watched Smith rush him, knowing what terror truly looks like. But Smith is here.

He's real, and he's alive, and there's no way I can turn away from the sight of him.

Jasmine has me wrapped in her arms in the next second. While her gesture is tender, her words are sharp and cruel. "I deserve this. It was a stupid decision to come here," I reply, nodding my head into her chest.

After confirming Smith doesn't need help, Sean stoops down next to us. "I would have come with you. That was the plan. First and foremost, I'm your friend. How could you do this? Come here?"

I shrug. Blood trickles down my face and falls onto the shoulder of my blouse. "I needed the legal file. He came over a few weeks ago to apologize. He seemed different. As dimwitted as it sounds, I thought he would give me the file and I'd be on my way," I explain. "What's he doing here?" I whisper, nodding toward the living, breathing caricature of anger and jagged, life-altering beauty. He's restraining Roarke with plastic zip ties even though he's knocked out and looks to me like he'll stay that way for quite some time.

Jasmine closes her eyes and takes in a deep, long breath. "I've been in contact with him. Just quick calls so he can check in on you. He happened to be over at my house when you texted. It must be fucking fate, Carina, because you'd be dead if he wasn't." This wasn't part of the plan. He wanted me to move on so he could be with Megan without guilt. I was a piece of his past he was moving on from, not checking in on.

Fate is a bitter, lying bitch. I shake my head. Not only am I in physical pain, but my best friend went behind my back. It stings.

"You act like I wouldn't have stopped it," Sean says, pride wounded.

Jasmine sighs. "They took away your guns, remember? There's no way you could have gotten in here as quickly as Smith did."

Sean sits back. "Whatever, Jaz. Fuck you," he snarls. "I'll be in the car. You need anything, Bulldozer?" he tosses Smith's way.

"I need to talk to Carina. Alone."

I take my sweater off to press it to the cut on my cheek and hobble to my feet. Not taking my eyes off his, I walk past him, over the bloody glass, and into the house. He's following me, his gaze boring a hole in the back of my head. I feel hot and cold at the same time. The blood is rushing to my head and not to my heart. It's the oddest of sensations. This hasn't been my house in a long, long time, and I feel at home as I open the freezer and grab a bag of peas to press against the side of my head.

When I turn around, I find Smith inches from me, seething mad, his teeth clenched together and his arms coiled. "How could you be so stupid? How could you do this?" he asks. Smith is controlling his breaths, and I realize I've never seen him angry. Not like this. Not like Roarke.

I swallow down the sweet emotions I feel at seeing him and focus on hurt. "Seems to me you gave up the right to worry about my actions and my stupidity. I don't understand why you're even here."

He shakes his head and takes another step toward me, his presence more sinister than ever before. "I don't understand how you could be so fucking stupid!"

I take in a sharp breath. "What? Are you going to bounce me off the walls? I'm out of practice. Just so you know." The metallic taste of blood makes my stomach heave, and the headache I knew was coming arrives. Closing my eyes for a moment, I try to make sense of all of this.

He backs away immediately. "How dare you say that?

How fucking dare you, Care! I'm angry, yes. I'm so angry that I can't see anything but red, but you came here knowing what he's capable of. If you recall, the only thing I'm bouncing is your fiancé's head off the fucking ground. Don't you ever insinuate I would harm you again. That's not fair. Why did you come here?" His tone takes on a desperate plea. "Look what he did to your face. This wasn't how it was supposed to be."

I lick a drop of blood off my lip and smile. "Tell me how it was supposed to be then? This is always how it's been for me, Smith. Tell me! You enacted this master plan without consulting me. How is that fair? You go behind my back to talk to my best friend. You crush my heart by way of a written letter. You don't call me. Or text me. Or email me. You proclaim to love me so much that you have to honor your word to Megan. Tell me, Smith. How was it supposed to be?"

He leans back on the island behind him, his muscles causing his dirty shirt to pull across his wide chest. This side of him, this avenging angel dipped in dirty charcoal, is breathtaking.

With his face aimed at the floor he says, "You were supposed to find a nice guy, fall in love, and stay the fuck away from your past. The past being me, but mostly that asshole outside. Nothing was worth coming here for. You know that. I know that."

"If I want to play Russian roulette with my life, it's mine to gamble. Pardon me if I can't find my Prince Charming and settle down with my two point five kids after having everything I thought I knew about love turned on its head." I cough and then wince at the pounding heartbeat in my head. "And I write romance, so that's saying something. There aren't nice guys anymore, Smith. There are men like Roarke and men like you—the type that pretend to be nice—but then use superhero, fake rules to crush anything good in their lives. At least Roarke knows who he is and what he wants."

Narrowing his eyes, he shakes his head. "You're cruel." Biting his bottom lip, he looks at me from under his lashes. "I'm sorry if you think I didn't handle the breakup properly."

I hold up one finger. "Correction. It was a letter, not a break-=up. I thought it would take more than a piece of paper to tear us apart." I was so, so wrong.

He throws his arms wide out to his sides. "This is war, Carina. You can't even imagine the things I've seen happening on American soil, how much blood is on my hands. It's a different kind of combat without rules or plans. It's enough to mess with anyone's head. It's not fair," he says. The urge to ask him to elaborate rises, but I squash it quickly. My heart is about to leap out of my chest.

"Nothing is fair in love and war," I reply. A profound sadness washes over me as I realize the truth in my own words. "Whoever said the opposite was acutely wrong. I think we can both agree."

Smith inhales deeply and closes his eyes. "Seeing you. Merely seeing you standing here makes me whole. I'm so angry I could spit nails, and that anger is directed at you, and still, I want nothing more than to hold you, to touch the skin on your face with my palm." He reaches out his hand, then fists it back to his side as if he's lost control of his own reactions. "To touch all of you."

His expression is earnest, and my heart is thudding in agreement. I shake my head and remember his letter of words. I studied them for hours and days trying to decipher a hidden message. "The worst strain of heartbreak is when both parties are unwilling participants, when life forces your hand," I say. My voice catches. "War forced your hand, and I went along with it because you didn't give me a choice. I was the one left behind without a choice." The days of black, dark depression gut me. The memory leaves me feeling weary and unprepared for the conversation.

Carefully, I peel the bag of peas off my face. Smith winces when he sees the cut.

"I have to know something," he says, approaching me slowly. He closes the space between us in seconds. Just when I think he's going to take me into his arms, when he's close enough to kiss me, he stops.

"We've gone from verbally abusing one another to this in no time at all, so by all means, ask away," I say, studying his beautiful features up close. It takes me back to a happier time. I'm transported to Balboa Park. My head nestled on his shoulder, the red-and-black blanket spread beneath us. I'm gazing off at the trees swaying in the breeze, and Smith is telling me a story about his friend Henry. I play with his blue T-shirt and tap my fingers on his chest to the rhythm of his pulse. The war never happened, and his memories and promises to Megan stay buried. Like broken glass in a landfill no one ever sees again.

A sob escapes as my vision turns to dust and cracks into a million pieces on the floor next to the olive laced vodka. "What, Smith?"

"I need to know the honest-to-God truth. Had tonight gone differently, had Roarke really shown you a changed version of himself, would I have walked in on a different scene? Would you, I mean, could you, really have taken him back?" Pain resonates in his tone, and a grimace transforms his face as he envisions a totally different scenario.

I could lie. That's always easiest when given a question of this magnitude, but I want to give him an answer he can believe. I turn around, grab a glass from the cabinet above the sink, and fill it with water. I drink a full cup and set it down next to the sink. With my back turned to him, I find it easier to coerce my thoughts. Seeing him makes everything foggy. I want him so badly. More than anything else. I spin on my toe to face him. "There's one man I want, and I can't have him. That's the truth, Smith."

He sighs a long, drawn-out noise. "She may be the gun aimed at my chest, but you're the only one who can pull the trigger," Smith replies, his eyes tilting down in the corner. His proximity is too near, and I'm not sure how much longer I can avoid touching him. The last time he was this close, I wasn't able to see him or understand what happened. "I want you," he says, swallowing so hard his neck works.

When he lays his hand on the side of my face, I sigh. He clears his throat. "I don't feel anything," he whispers. He drags a thumb down the rest of my bottom lip. I watch in awe as he looks at me, truly taking in my every detail. "That's what remembering got me. I'm devoid of everything." I have to close my eyes. His pain is so blatant and strong it's taking us both down. He continues, "I found myself and lost everything. Loving you made me myself. Without you I'm this," Smith growls, palming his chest with his free hand. "Empty and alone. How easy it would be to pretend I still had amnesia. A joy—it would be freedom. Blissful ignorance. I'd have you. I wouldn't have to look at you and feel this pain deep in my gut." One solid tear runs down his face. "A longing so profound I know I'll never escape it. It's unbearable."

I sob, and it hurts my chest when I try to control it.

"That's why I spoke with Jasmine. Knowing the tiniest things about you and your life ease my pain and heartbreak. Going cold turkey wasn't an option. I'll never stop caring about you."

I fall back against Roarke's counter because I can't hold myself up any longer. Dizziness hits me in a wave, and stars cloud my vision. "Why fight this, then? Why escape it? Why not embrace it? The honorable thing to do is to honor your heart, Smith." Henry would respect a decision made out of love. I don't dare bring his name into this already emotion-fueled conversation.

I wipe a tear from my cheek, and the stinging burn of my own salty tears reminds me of the deep gash. Smith lets his hand fall from my face and steps away from me. His chest moves deeply, up and down. It takes more effort than I realize for him to distance himself.

He shakes his head. "You don't understand. My feelings mean nothing in this equation."

His decision is solid. I'd bet a wedding date is set. I sniffle. "You should have let natural selection play out tonight. The reason for your pain and angst would be gone. You can't love me for the rest of your life, Smith. How honorable is it to marry Megan and have feelings for me?"

He turns to the side. It's the profile of the uninjured side of his face. From this angle I can imagine what he looked like before. What he looked like as Megan's Smith. "Natural selection, my ass. You made a bad decision. I will never let anything bad happen to you!"

"People like me always make bad decisions. You won't be able to stop me from living life and making decisions. This is it. Right here and right now. It may be the poorest decision I've ever made, but you need to stop this. You can't profess this tragic love for me and be with her. I love you. I'll always love you and want you. But I won't be the other woman. Megan deserves more from you. And me." More guilt rises to the surface.

"Go to her. The memory of me will fade away until I'm merely a black-and-white snapshot in your new memory. Or kiss me. Embrace your feelings. Don't stalk me or talk to my friends to keep tabs on me. A clean break or a sharp love. Your choice." They're strong words, but I feel anything but. My voice is hoarse, and my face is throbbing. My stomach is coiled with anxiety, and my ribs sear with a sharp pain anytime I sob.

"One last kiss, then," Smith says. He's asking permission.

I nod, the finality of our situation hitting me hard.

Smith closes the distance between our bodies, and when I think he's going to take me completely—mouth, heart, and soul—he leans his head to the side and kisses my cheek, right next to my wound. His hot breath sends shockwaves to my core, and I hear him moan as he breathes me in. His warm hands run down my arms as he separates from me. On a second thought, he kisses me on the other cheek, down by my jaw.

"It will never be enough," I say, tilting my head to the side to give him better access.

"It has to be," he replies. His lips press in a firm line. He shakes his head and runs both of his hands through his hair in frustration, looking at the ceiling for some divine intervention telling him to make the other decision, I'm sure. "It has to be the right choice, or nothing in this fucking world makes sense."

I could convince him otherwise, but this isn't my decision to make. I just have to live with it. "You should check on him," I whisper.

He nods, looking around the kitchen—any place except at me. He walks out of the room with more confidence than he should have at this moment.

I slide down to sit on the floor. Leaning over, I open the freezer and grab another bag of frozen vegetables and hold it against my face. I let a few tears fall, but I ration them. I know tonight the flood will break. I'll be alone with the new, horrible words he's given me.

"Poppet," I exclaim. When I throw the front door open, I see Jasmine inside the cab of my car with the white cat on her lap. She rolls the window down and asks how my conversation went. I shrug and grimace when the tears begin. I hold my hands out and she puts the cat into my arms. Jaz talks to me for a few more moments, tells me to call her when I can, and she leaves with Sean. Smith's truck is parked next to mine. After a longing glance and a tearful thank you to my friends, I return to the house of horrors.

The kitchen is silent when I breeze in, so I make my way into the back porch. With one hand on his head, Smith squats next to Roarke, two fingers pressed against his neck. Cocking his head to the side when he hears me, he raises his brows. "One less person I have to worry about," he says. Standing, he looks at me cautiously, pausing to give me room to take in his words.

My eyes widen as I realize what he's insinuating. He nods several times as I try to catch my breath, clutching my scared cat to my chest. Smith's gaze darts down to the cat, and I catch a hint of a smile on his full lips. It seems twisted as hell, but also sweet.

"Go in the house. I'll take care of this." He slides a cell phone out of his pocket and dials quickly. I look down at Roarke. It's the most helpless I've ever seen him. I wish I could take a photo. I'd develop it in black and white. "It was in self-defense. No one is going to doubt that when they see your face or when you tell the story." It was a single punch that did him in. It's been that simple all along.

Sean returns with a few of his coworkers. They all look tired, and they aren't wearing their police uniforms.

They're here to help off duty. Next, several large, hulking men enter the house. I stay glued to the white sofa in the living room. The men have names that match their muscles and sheer size. Smith peeks in every so often and assures me that everything will be okay, that neither of us did anything wrong. Sean is here on the side of the law, and the SEALs on the government side. Under Martial law, the government side runs everything anyway.

Roarke's mother. His family. I think of all of the personal attachments of a person who is gone. That's what I mourn in this moment. I don't mourn him. How could I possibly?

"We're almost finished. You didn't do anything wrong," Smith reiterates, his head behind me over my shoulder. Lost in thought, I didn't hear him approach. The men have been cleaning up and taking care of whatever loose ends need to be tied up legally, and I assume removal of the body.

I don't say it, but I think it. *We did everything wrong.* We fell in love when we had no right, and the resulting chain of reactions led to this moment. The goddamn love didn't do anything for either of us except cause pain.

For the first time I'm completely free, but my deepest desire has been taken away. Loneliness smells like flowers—gardenias. Now devastation has a scent. I inhale deeply and let it tear the rest of my heart to shreds.

CHAPTER TWENTY-TWO

Smith

THE SUN IS SETTING. We're out past curfew, and even though Sean and his officers assured us we'd be fine driving to Carina's house in separate vehicles, I want her to ride in mine. The appropriate badges and paperwork will be with me in my truck. Seeing my unease, Sean offers to drive Carina's car home so he can make sure she gets home without hassle. I'm mollified when she accepts and even more sick when she hugs him, the white cat meowing between their bodies.

"I want to check one thing before we leave," Carina tells Sean.

He nods and says he'll wait for her in the car.

Swallowing down stabbing jealousy, I follow her down a hallway. The dim light from the wall sconces projects creepy shadows on the opposite side of the hallway. This house is large. It gives me chills because I know what these walls have seen. They'll see nothing more. Not where Carina is concerned. I'll always protect her. Silently, from a distance—or even close if the need arises. She turns into a room, and I follow her in, closing the door behind us. The glow from a bedside lamp shines against her back when she turns to face me. Her features are masked by shadow.

"I need to talk to you. Not here, though. I need to tell you something."

"You've said all you can possibly say," Carina whispers, shaking her head. She puts Poppet down on the bed and strokes her fur when the cat sits down. The love she has for the cat is visceral. It encapsulates her pain. Does it erase it, I wonder? She stoops down and fishes for something under the bed. "It's hard to see you, Smith. I wish you'd go." Her words slice me to the bone. Carina slides a long, skinny safe out from under the bed, and it comes away in her hands with a click.

"Stupid bastard never erased my fingerprint from the system," she says, opening the heavy metal box with ease. "And he didn't burn my files either." She scoffs as she pulls out a few manila file folders and tucks them under her arm. She's so calm in this situation. Any other woman would break down—be hysterical. She's matter-of-fact, taking the documents she came for and securing the safe back into its place. The practicality is what confuses me.

"I really am sorry, Care." I clear my throat, hoping to garner a look from her. That sorry is supposed to encompass many things.

She picks up the docile cat and leaves the room. Over her shoulder she says, "I'm going home now. I need to get ice on my face so I don't look like Quasimodo in the morning. You should go to Megan."

I should. But I don't want to. "I need to explain something to you now that I'm not fuming mad."

"And murderous?"

Oh, Carina. If she only knew my body count for the month. "Please?"

She merely nods and then leaves the house. I follow

behind her all the way back, the odd sensation of driving at night forcing me to realize how fucked up everything has become in such a short time. The radio, which is devoid of music for the most part, is talking about how airports will be up and running next week. I tell the radio and the empty cab of my truck it's a bad idea.

Sean's friend picks him up once we've arrived safely in the driveway, and Carina leaves the front door open after she's entered. Her scent clings to the air, and like Pavlov's dogs, my mouth waters. I close and lock the door behind me. My cell chimes in my pocket, and I know who it's going to be before I check it. Megan. Asking when I'll be home. I don't respond. It feels like cheating. Right now *I am home*. The cat winds around my legs.

"I'll be out in a second. I need to change and call Teala. There's some coffee in the pot if you want to warm yourself a cup."

Sitting on the couch, I stare down at the spot in the center of the living room. I catch sight of movement, and my gaze tracks to the end of the hallway where Carina is pulling down a T-shirt over her head. I see the perky swell of the bottom of her breasts and her toned stomach. I avert my gaze back to the coffee table and pray to God I can keep my shit together. It's harder than I thought it would be. The last time I was in this house, she wasn't home.

"You didn't have to pay the rent, you know. I would have told you that and thanked you, had you, I don't know…called me over the past months?"

I wanted to take care of her.

"Financially I'm doing well, Smith."

I took care of her rent for the next two years upfront.

I shake my head and swallow. "It's the least I can do."

She sighs and nods, like perhaps she does think I owe her something. I've hurt her.

"What did you want to talk to me about? It's been a long night. I'm probably going to try to go to sleep early. The nightmares will try to keep me from that, though." She laughs.

"Why are you laughing?" I ask.

She disappears into the kitchen and appears with a cup of coffee and an ice pack on her face.

She offers a sideways grin. "Because a dead man isn't the worst thing I've seen. It should be. A normal person would be affected by it, but I'm so messed up that all I felt tonight was relief and a bit of sympathy for his family. You can tell me how messed up it is."

"You just described the last few months of my life. How is that for messed up?" I reply. I smile back at her and lean back, away from her and her intoxicating scent and wet, pink lips. She sips her coffee as Poppet jumps up and into her lap. "Are you okay? Your face?"

She strokes the cat on the head, and it immediately purrs. "I think I'll become a cat lady. Maybe I'll collect white cats." She laughs, but her smile falls away quickly. "I'm fine. Say what you need to say, Smith. This is hard."

Making small talk isn't the only thing that's hard. My dick didn't get the memo about Carina taking a seat on the bench.

"How's the book?" I ask.

She raises her eyebrows in surprise. "Finished. It's being edited."

I can't remove my gaze from her hand as she sets her coffee down. Everything about her turns me on. Even minuscule gestures no one else would ever notice. She folds them in her lap.

"Of course, when it's finished, you will have to okay it." Her lap distracts me even more than her hands do.

"I need to tell you a story. You might want to grab a pen," I respond. At this, her face brightens. This is neutral territory—a place we've perfected coexisting inside of.

She excuses herself and comes back with the tape recorder.

"Only because you know I can't help myself," she explains, shaking it side to side.

"Maybe that's why I offered it in this way," I say.

She smiles, and it's genuine. Nothing else touches it— not the fight with Roarke or the fact that I abandoned her for months. It's just Carina and Smith. Her questions and my answers. Falling and catching. Loving and leaving.

She hits the record button, and the tiny machine whirs to life. A nod in my direction lets me know she's ready. "Tell me then," Carina prods. I take several deep breaths and prepare to tell the story I haven't told anyone. Not even Moose. He got the CliffsNotes version.

"We'd been planning a mission for days. Not just eight-hour workdays, but twenty-hour days for almost a week. The target was clear, and we were going to head out the next day and begin the mission that night. Henry and I were in our room, a fact we were upset about at first, because who the hell wants to share a room with another dude for six whole months?" I smile to myself when I think about Henry and his jokes. He always had a way of making me smile while also getting anything he wanted. I can't look at Carina for fear of losing track. "We were so tired, but he wanted to video chat with his wife and baby one more time before bed. The time difference is always significant, so it's always a crapshoot when you make calls back home. He got ahold of his wife on the first try. I put on my noise-canceling headphones, like I always do. Out of respect and because it's an unspoken rule when you have to share a room."

Carina leans over and touches my hand. At the sight

of her fingers on top of my own, I close my eyes. "I read a magazine for a few minutes until he tried to get my attention. Henry wanted me to tell her the story about one of the guys and his hair obsession." I shrug. "Henry always thought I was funnier, so he liked when I told stories, but he was more thorough. I'd pick thorough over funny."

Carina smiles weakly. "You are funny, though," she says. "She liked the story you told?"

I nodded. "She did. I saw their little newborn boy sleeping in her arms. The laptop was always a little pixelated because the Wi-Fi is awful at camp, but that night it was so clear, Carina. You could see every hair on that baby's head. Henry wouldn't stop talking about how clear Marie looked, how beautiful she was, how her smile was brighter than the sun." Emotion clogs my throat. and I have to stop talking for a moment. I take Carina's mug of coffee off the table and take a sip, mindful to place my lips directly where hers were.

"I'd say you don't have to finish, but I'm honestly not sure when I'll see you again. If you want me to incorporate this into the novel, you'll have to go on."

One more sip of lukewarm coffee slides down my throat. "Ruthless tonight, aren't you?"

Pressing her lips to one side, she sighs deeply. "I'm not sure what to call it. Numb. I guess I'm sort of numb. I know where this is going, so it's probably a good thing I've lost all sense of feeling." She's numb because of me, and I'm numb because I can't have her.

Ultimately, Carina is right. "I want you to know," I reply. I pass her back her mug. She places her lips where mine just were. She looks at my eyes over the rim of the cup, knowing, taunting.

"Right before they said good night and hung up the call, his wife remembered to thank him for the flowers he sent her the day before. She was upset she didn't mention it earlier in their conversation," I say, recalling this memory that's been buried for so long. "At that point I thought about putting my headphones back on, but call it curiosity, I listened instead. She gushed about how beautiful they were and how special they made her feel. Henry was excited that she loved them. He told her he would be home before the roses died."

I shake my head, and Carina looks out of the large, dark window. I have to finish.

"He promised her that they were the last flowers he'd have to send. The next gift she'd get to unwrap was him. Marie laughed. A true belly laugh so joyous I couldn't even make fun of Henry for the lame joke." I smile when I remember how happy it made him to hear her laugh. Carina wipes a tear from underneath the eye that isn't wounded.

"Marie laughed so loudly she woke their baby. Henry cooed and told him how much he loved him, promised he would see him soon and rock him to sleep and tell him cool stories about how awesome his daddy was. Marie told him how much she loved him and then spoke a little more loudly to wish me a good night."

"No," Carina whispers.

I ignore her. "I told her goodbye, and he hung up the call."

"Then the mortar hit?" she asks, eyes wide with horrified curiosity.

"No," I say, giving her word back to her.

"He asked me about Megan. I told him she didn't like flowers much because they died so quickly. Flowers were best suited growing in the ground. That's what she always told me. He asked if I was happy. I said I was. He told me the key to happiness was always being completely honest—that's what makes a relationship work. It made a lot of sense. Henry always made a lot of sense. A young Buddha," I say. My chest tightens. "He sent Marie flowers because he promised to always remind her how much she meant to him. True to his word. Always."

Carina is crying, wiping her eyes with the hem of her shirt. It does nothing for my willpower. Her taut stomach is visible.

Sucking in a breath, I close my eyes and focus on Henry's words. It feels like an oxymoron to be here right now telling his story and the reasons for my actions. "He loved Megan, thought we were perfect together. He made me promise to make her happy, Carina. Because our careers would fade away and the only thing left will be the person sitting beside us. Wouldn't we want to treat the one constant in our world with the utmost care and love? Wouldn't you honor your words given to the person who will stick by you through thick and thin? You take the moral high road, always. In my career path, many men don't take anything close to the high road with regard to their relationships. They cheat and take what they want. Henry never did that to Marie. He made me promise to never do that to Megan."

"Oh my god. Just stop, Smith. Stop. Please," Carina whispers. Her sobs are so loud they're moving her chest up and down. "I can't take this."

"You need to know why I made the decision I did."

"I don't. Not at this cost. This depressing, life-altering cost. It's unbearable to know this. Okay, go be with her. You don't owe me anything. I get it. I understand now. There was never any other woman for you. It will always be Megan. Even if it's not. You made a promise to your best friend. You honor your word to a fault. To a deficit even."

"Carina," I say. She shakes her head. "I never expected to fall in love with you."

She stands from the sofa in a brisk movement and paces to the window, her back to me. "Henry told you that before he knew your circumstances," Carina whispers. "You honestly think if he were here right now he'd tell you the same thing?"

"I sat back in my bed, the top bunk, and closed my eyes. I'd loved Megan for so long that I wasn't sure what it meant to do anything except that. I would never cheat on her. I thought I was already on the moral high road with my engagement to my high school sweetheart. Watching him with Marie made me question things. To the point where my promises to Henry made me feel like an impostor in my own skin."

Carina turns from the window but stays silent, her eyes rimmed with red and the hem of her shirt soaked with tears. I go on. "It was because we had the big mission the next day. I'm sure of it now. He had no idea what was going to happen in mere seconds. He was putting his ducks in a row just in case. Henry asked me to always be an honorable man regardless of circumstance. He used those words, Carina. I never thought much of it because I remembered him saying that after my accident, but it was before I remembered Megan."

Carina wilts. She sits on the floor, on her knees. She can't bear my words any more than they sear me leaving my mouth. "He doesn't even know me," Carina whispers.

"He doesn't," I say, holding my hands out to the side and then clasping them over my knees. A clock ticks somewhere in the background, and Poppet approaches Carina on the floor, nudging her head into her hand. "And it's criminal he doesn't."

"I love you so much," she says. "I always will."

"I agreed and told him to mind his own business. I was joking, of course, and then the mortar careened into the housing trailer," I say. I lay my head down on my knees. "It was the last thing he said to me. He was my best friend." Cruel reality seeps in and makes everything inside my body ache. It's wave after wave of grief and regret. "I promised him."

"You should go," Carina says. I hear her quiet footsteps as she crosses to me. I hear her stop the tape recorder. She places a hand on my shoulder. "Promise me something," she says. This gets my attention. I chance a look up to find her pain-seared face grimacing.

"Anything," I reply.

She sniffles. She closes her eyes as tears fall gratuitously down her face. "Be happy with her. Truly happy. That's what he wanted. It wasn't about honor or morals, Smith. It was about your happiness. Her happiness. I don't even know him, but I could gather that much from your story. Promise me you'll be happy with her."

I want to tell her that I could never be as happy with Megan as I could with her, but I don't. It seems a moot point in this time and place. It wasn't a favorite promise, it was about honoring my first promise. My engagement to the woman who first stole my heart. Not the one who holds it now and probably will for the rest of time. "I promise," I lie.

"As the author of the book about your life, thank you for that. As your former girlfriend, I can't look at your face anymore. We'll be in touch." She walks to the door and opens it as wide as it will go. Carina still has an ice pack in her hand, and she presses it to the side of her face.

I leave without another word, my hollow promise lingering in the air like a rotting body.

CHAPTER TWENTY-THREE

Carina

SHE CALLED ME. I didn't answer, so Megan left a voicemail.

The boot camp class was practically empty today, and it's a good thing. I was angry. Angry that when I finally tried to move on and had gone a few minutes without thinking of Smith, her call reminded me of everything I try to forget. I'm fooling myself to think anything will take his memory away. The voicemail she left was vague, only that it was important that we meet up to talk. I text her that she can meet me at a café in Gaslamp in ten. There's no way she'll meet me on such short notice. It's my hope anyway.

The drive to the coffee shop I've been writing in is a short distance from the gym and from my house. It just opened back up a couple weeks ago, and it's always quiet. Most people still stay home as much as possible. Those with full-time jobs have returned to them, and sometimes I forget 9/11 happened. It's only a brief memory lapse, though. So much has changed.

The way society functions is warped completely, and not for the better. There are metal detectors everywhere, and there are still checkpoints along freeways and state borders. Airlines are so strict that it's almost quicker to drive wherever you need to travel. Civilian militias have formed in backwoods communities and even in some large cities.

Our borders have been closed since the attack, and families have been separated all this time. The news still plays constantly, but now stories of Americans trapped in other countries trickle into the mainstream. It's sad, but it's reality. The television in the café is playing such a story right now. My phone buzzes when I take a seat by the window. It's a guy I've been seeing, confirming our plans for tonight. It's the fourth date and he's expecting to get laid.

My friends approve of him, but it's not quite right. Nothing will ever be just so, though. Smith ruined that. Our relationship clogs everything.

Taking a sip of my iced black coffee, I open my laptop and start writing an outline for the next chapter I'm working on. It's a thriller, something completely different. I almost didn't even want to give my heroine a love interest, but Jaz threatened my life, and when it's all said and done, she knows what's going to sell.

A blonde approaches in my peripheral vision, and I know who it is before I glance out the window. She still has the it factor. The thing that draws attention from men and women alike. Men want to love her, and women want to be her.

She sees me and waves. It's a small gesture that doesn't line up with the scowl on her face. She bypasses the counter and heads straight for my table. "If I thought you would actually show up, I would have changed," I say, wrinkling my nose. "I came from the gym," I explain.

Her hair is glossy and has grown back in. Makeup

can't hide her scars or the rough, red, uneven skin, but it's easy to not notice it. "It's important."

I eye her bare ring finger.

"Obviously," I reply, closing my laptop and folding my arms on top of it. "No coffee. This must be really bad."

"An attorney called the house attempting to schedule a meeting with Smith about your book," Megan explains.

I feel her staring at my face as she speaks. I keep my gaze focused out of the window.

"He mentioned that you wouldn't be at the meeting."

I nod. "It's for the best if I'm not there. I'm confused. Why are you upset? We live in the same city, and I'm doing everything I can to avoid Smith...and you." I contemplated moving away, setting up shop in some Pacific Northwestern town. Somewhere I could wear rain boots every day of the year and drink chai tea and do yoga and sleep outside if I felt like it. A place I could start over away from everything in my past. "I'm not ready to move yet. I will, I think. Eventually." That way Smith won't haunt every corner and every single favorite place in this city. Living in the house is bad enough, but I haven't been able to return to Balboa Park either.

Megan untucks her hair from behind her ear so it hides the side of her face. I have to look away. "He says I'm supposed to plan the wedding, Carina. He reassures me a million times a day that he's excited and can't wait to get married to me. Every single night he stares at the ceiling, oblivious of everything and anyone around him. It's not bad memories either. It's you. You live in my house. You live inside him. It doesn't matter if I marry him. He's owned by you."

My breath hitches. This is unexpected. Smith didn't count on Megan rebelling away from his master moral plan. "Does he know you're here?"

"Of course not. Do you know how jealous he'd be if he did know?" She scoffs. It's a high-pitched noise made out of annoyance. Rubbing her hands together, she says, "I can just see his face when I tell him where I've been. He'll pretend to be mad, but then he'll ask me questions. Not because he's curious, but because he's addicted to you, and like a junkie, he wants any piece of you he can get. I'm not an idiot."

"Why do you stay? If you know...then why?" My mouth is dry. "You're not an idiot, Megan."

She motions to her face and body. "Look at me. Even if I didn't look like a burn victim poster child, my heart has always belonged to him. When he came to me and told me he remembered, I thought it would go back to the way it was before. You have to understand because you know him—I had to give it another chance. He's been my love for my whole life. That's not something you let go of easily. You fight for the important things in life. Giving him another chance was my weak attempt at fighting for us. I didn't anticipate one thing."

"What?"

"That what he feels for you doesn't even touch what he felt for me at the height of our love." Her eyes turn down in the corner, and she covers her mouth to hide a sob. "Competing is exhausting. We have years of memories, and your months with him are enough to take me out completely. He lies to protect my feelings. He doesn't think I know. I'm not sure how he can be so oblivious. He's pining. He's broken."

I brush away a tear with my pointer finger. The news in the background barks out a warning about the militia staging a protest in DC. They have guns and signs. I take in a breath. I can't focus. "What do you want me to do? I've moved on. I'm done. He made his choice."

232

"You don't love him?" she asks. "Tell him then. In person. That you don't love him."

I close my eyes to try to block out the background noise. I can't understand what she wants, and the things she's saying are confusing me beyond belief. Megan presses her lips together in a firm line. It reminds me of Smith. The way one half of his face is perfect and the other half is marred by scars. Megan's face looks different than his, but it has the same feeling. Beautiful destruction.

"The meeting. You want me to go," I say. This has to be why she began the conversation with it. When she sniffles and then nods, I go on. "He won't believe me."

"Because you do love him."

It's my turn. "It doesn't go away. I will tell him I don't love him. That he needs to move on with his life, but you need to plan for this to go badly. The last time I saw him…" I explain, trailing off. I didn't mean to go this far, but now that I'm here, I might as well be honest. "He said a lot of things."

"Oh, god. I knew it. How am I supposed to get over him again?"

When I do, I'll let you know, I think.

"Don't. Live with it. I'm done. I'll contact my attorney and let him know I'll be there. It's to sign the final paperwork for the book and movie options and his percentage shares. If he approaches me, I'll tell him anything you want me to."

"Thank you," she whispers. "It won't be enough. That's my fear." She is so self-conscious it's hard to be around her. The way she fidgets and looks down. It reminds me of the woman I used to be. That's the real reason I want to get out of here as quickly as possible. That, and this new information about how sad Smith is. I think deep down every woman wants to know her ex is miserable after a breakup. They say nice things such as wishes for their happiness, but it's a surface truth. Because if their ex is happy, then something must be fundamentally wrong with them and how they conduct their relationships. Humans are selfish to the core.

"This is hard. It's hard for everyone involved, but you have options. You're beautiful despite what you see in the mirror. You are the same person. You have so much going for you that any man would be lucky to have you. Smith has to see that."

She shakes her head. "I have to go. I'm glad to see you doing so well," she says.

I look down at my sweat-soaked workout gear and smirk at her, raising one brow. "Thanks, I think. Sometimes you have to ask questions. Even hard ones," I explain. "It goes along with the communication clause, you know?"

I hope she knows what I mean. If things are as bad as she says they are, nothing is saving their relationship. After she leaves, I call my attorney and schedule the meeting for the soonest available. The thought of seeing Smith sends butterflies to my stomach, and my core clenches. I wonder how long he'll have this hold on me.

"Forever," I whisper.

Opening my laptop, I write a scene between my characters. They fight and yell, and then they make love. For a moment, I feel better.

I'm shaking. The office is cold and smells like fresh donuts. My attorney, the fat bald guy who Jaz uses to vet all my contracts, is sitting at the head of the table, prattling on about how awesome it is that we had so many high-priced offers for the novel. I'm also shaking because Jasmine mailed Smith a copy of the book last week. He's read it.

He's read my words. My scary, heartrending words. His stories, but my words swirled with fiction in a love story so tragic and beautiful that Hollywood has never seen the likes of. Obviously, hence the reason we're here to begin with.

Jasmine presses her hand in mine. "You look beautiful, Care," she says, her lips whispering close to my ear. The blinds are open, letting in enough sunlight to brighten the room. With a shaky hand, I sip my coffee. "No more coffee or you're going to buzz right out of here," Jasmine chides.

I slide the cup away from me.

"You're right," I reply, checking my watch. "He should be here any moment. Do you think he's going to be mad?" I look at my friend, eyes wide and terror transforming my whole demeanor.

She shakes her head. "He was always going to read it. He had to. Remember in the beginning when you started this whole crazy project? You wanted to help people. You wanted to write a story that would mean something to someone. He's that someone you have the most chance of impacting. The whole world is going to read this story, and you need to get used to that fact. Smith is just one of the firsts."

My heart pounds, and the palms of my hands sweat with unease and uncertainty. Moose walks in with the same terrified look on his face. "Thank God! Finally! I thought you weren't going to show," I say. Standing, I leap into his arms to hug him. "They'll be here any minute. Are you ready for this?"

"Hi to you too, Carina. You're insane if you think this is a good idea. I almost didn't come in. I circled the parking lot fifteen times while saying aloud every reason this was going to end badly." Today he has more to lose than I do.

I swallow hard. "This is the last chance, Moose. And no one will think it's odd you're here. Your character is a huge part in the story, remember? Isn't part of your job description to go with the flow? Form a plan while a horrendous situation is unfolding?"

A sidelong smirk appears. I knew I should play on his strengths. Moose likes his ego stroked.

"They're controlled messes, though. Usually ones we create ourselves," he replies.

"But I did create this mess. I'm enacting you as the king's hand. Clean thy mess and confess thy sins," I say, joking. His blue eyes twinkle with mirth. When his dimples show, I know I have him. "You have to be at least a little bit excited?"

"More like ready for the biggest letdown of my life, but hey, in the spirit of your book, one in which you spill so many details and tenuous secrets about my best friend and his bedroom habits, I'm willing to play ball."

It never occurred to me Smith would have spoken to Moose about the book. "Oh, god. What did he say?" I blink a few times very slowly. I'm pretty sure it's a defense mechanism because all of a sudden I feel faint, my vision morphing into a tunnel.

The door creaks open to my back, and the time is finally here. Moose flashes me a grin and turns a megawatt, exuberant smile at the door. Megan. "I'm sure he'll tell you himself," he says, through clenched teeth.

He puts his hand on my shoulder as I spin. Jasmine joins us to my left. All air leaves the room when I see him. I can't put up a wall or even false pretenses around this man. Smith forces a smile when he sees Moose, but I watch the confusion and hesitance arrive in the same breath. Smith avoids looking at me, which makes it even more awkward because it's so obvious he's trying not to look at me. With one arm he's holding Megan around her waist, like he alone is keeping her standing, but in the other he's holding my book. The spine bent as if it's been through the dryer seventeen times in one week. My heart jolts, and I feel I may be sick right here on the carpet in front of everyone. One glance at Megan's face and I know she's read it. What type of horrendous torture must that have been for her? I can't even imagine the pain it caused. The anger. The absolute terror of realizing how in love someone else is with her fiancé.

"What are you doing here?" Smith asks Moose. He's so stunning, standing tall and proud with the air of confidence only worn by those who claim it truthfully. It makes me weak. The last thing I need right now is any form of weakness.

Jasmine squeezes my hand. "I asked him to be here. He plays a large part in Greenleigh's novel, and in turn the character will play a large part in any future movie role. Our attorneys have cut him into the deal as well."

Moose squeezes my shoulder. I hadn't told him that yet. It's a thank you for being here today. The least I can do with my pain money I don't need. That's what I refer to it as now. Looking at the cover alone makes me squeamish.

"What she said," Moose replies.

Smith doesn't buy it. Not even for a second.

Megan watches me so intently that I feel like an actress putting on a show. Do I look pretty enough? Am I missing a line?

"Please sit down. Let's get the process going," the attorney says.

Smith and Megan sit across the table from Moose, Jasmine, and me. Smith's attorney meanders in and makes his way to a seat near Megan and opens his files. When we're all seated, Smith drops the book in the middle of the long conference table. The loud thud makes everyone jump.

I swallow, close my eyes, and take a few beats to clear my head. He's so angry I can feel his tremors from across the room.

"*Never Forever*," Smith says, quoting the title.

I open my eyes, but he's pointing a glare at Jasmine. It's meant for me, but he won't risk that move. He doesn't intend to make this any harder on himself.

"A Navy SEAL's tale of loss, love, and honor." He reads the tagline through gritted teeth.

"It was beautiful," Megan says, already tearful.

Great. This is how it's going to go. I turn to my attorney and give him a nod. *Make this fast.*

He starts in on his speech about the contracts and percentages and all of the other boring math things that go over my head but are too important to ignore. No one else is listening. They're too busy tasting the air so thick you can cut through it with a knife. The tension is so visceral that no one is unaffected.

Megan speaks over the bald man. "I said it was beautiful."

So, it begins.

Jasmine sighs. "It's incredibly beautiful. They're already billing it as this generation's Romeo and Juliet," she replies to Megan. "Carina wouldn't budge on the title. I think it suits it fine enough. It's simple so people will remember it, yet it still remains integral to the story."

Smith's hand shakes as he reaches out for the worn-out proof copy of the book but ultimately merely lays a hand on top of it. Like a Bible. "This wasn't what I expected," he says. "It's...it's...too much."

"Too much what?" I ask, willing him to turn his gaze my way.

He doesn't, though. He slides it back in front of his chest. His resolve is faltering. I see the cracks in his front. He knows how much this will cost. The price has never been higher. Still, he doesn't realize Megan already knows. It's why she's crying, a mess of tears and insolence as she stares at our story, now a tangible item lying in front of her.

"I don't want any money from this. I know my name won't be associated with it, but that's the only thing I care about. I want to leave today being reassured that this will never come back to me. No matter how big this thing blows up, I don't want to be this person." He speaks to me while looking at Jasmine, at the same time pointing to the cover of the book.

"You are that person. You can't pretend you're not. The rest of the world will never know, Smith. But you will. And that's the only thing that matters," I say.

He stares to the right, his jaw working back and forth.

Megan looks at me, her makeup-stained face a wash of confusion. "What do you mean?" she asks.

"Why are you so upset with your portrayal, Smith? Look at me," I command. When he doesn't budge I yell, "Look at me! You owe me that much!"

Finally he turns, and I see the wetness in his eyes—the burning rage. "Because it's not fiction," he says. "Because you told the truth." His words are laced with pain, and everyone in the room silences. In this moment it feels as if the air we're all breathing is too loud.

I nod. "That's right. I did. It's our story, and you chose the ending. Megan," I say, bouncing my gaze back to her. "Moose has something he wants to tell you."

Smith slits his eyes as he glares at his friend.

Moose opens his folded hands and then clasps them again. "Everyone loves a good underdog story, right?"

"I'm confused," Megan replies. "Don't you have something to say, Carina?"

"I'm not telling any lies today, or ever again. I'm sorry. This right here is the table of truth. Let Moose finish."

Jasmine grabs my leg under the table. We're both a ball of nerves. If I were a smarter person who had a knack for planning I would have had security here with big, metal sticks. Megan looks at Moose, wipes a few tears from beneath her eyes, and flashes him a small smile.

It gives him the confidence he needs. "I've been in love with you for longer than I care to admit," Moose starts. He looks at his friend across the table.

Smith stands, turns around, and stares out of the window, both hands perched on his hips. Megan stays glued to her seat, her wide, beautiful eyes enraptured.

I puff out a breath between clpsed lips.

Moose stands. "I loved you when he loved you. Before the accident. I know it was wrong, and I never would have admitted these feelings to you under any other circumstance, but I want you, Megan."

"You've got to be kidding me," Smith mutters loud enough for the whole room to hear. He doesn't turn around, though—his back broad and his stance wide.

"Oh my god," my attorney says.

I shut him up with a glare, and he takes a seat, eyes flicking back and forth between Smith and Moose. Jasmine giggles. It's unfolding exactly how I knew it would.

"I wanted you when you were standing next to him at BUD/S graduation and when you stood by him through every deployment. The envy I felt at watching you love him is something I'm not proud of."

Megan stands and rounds the table slowly.

He goes on.

I smile.

Smith remains unmoving.

"When I saw his feelings change, I thought yours might too. It was a shot in the dark because how do you penetrate a heart that's belonged to only one person? Maybe I didn't have to. Maybe your heart would recognize I've been there all along."

Jasmine leans over. "Soap opera bullshit at its finest," she snarks, and I shush her.

Finally, Smith turns around, just in time to see Megan stop in front of Moose. I can't read his expression, but if I had to guess, it was indifference and relief, also just as I predicted.

"Why didn't you say something sooner? You were there for me all that time and I always thought it was because Smith asked you to." Why would a man in love ask his best friend to be there for his woman? Megan is beyond blinded at this point. It's sad.

Moose shakes his head. "I wanted to be there for you, and I prayed Smith wouldn't catch on."

"Enough," Smith says, cutting an arm through the air. "I've assumed this for a long time." He crosses his arms and, if possible, stands taller. "Why not come to me first? Why not tell me first? Your best friend." He enunciates the words "best friend" harshly.

"What type of best friend would I be if I admitted feelings for your fiancée? I've lived with this for so long it's become second nature. Telling you was something I never planned on doing. Seeing her happy was the only thing that mattered."

Megan's face right now as she gazes at Moose is that of the sun saying hello to the moon for the first time. Relieved. She's tired. He's her sanctuary.

Moose turns back to face Megan. "And you aren't happy right now. You haven't been truly happy since Smith's accident. Admit it. I know I make you happy. You laugh and smile when we hang out. I can make you happy. Please let me make you happy."

Megan sobs and covers her face with both hands. When she's had a moment, she looks at Smith. Smith looks at the floor. "He's right. It's true. I love him. He does make me happy." There it is. The simple words I hoped for, but never in a million years envisioned her saying out loud in a room full of people. I thought this conversation would play out in private. "I don't know how this happened," she says.

Moose goes to wipe away a tear from her face but thinks better of it and fists his palm by his side.

I stand, tears running down my own face. Jasmine follows quickly, her hand still entwined with mine. "Finally. Finally someone gets a happily ever after inside this nightmare," I say, closing my eyes and letting a sad smile creep onto my face. "I've signed all the paperwork. Smith, if you could do the same, this will be finished."

"Why did you do this, Carina?" he snarls.

It's my turn to turn my back, and I clear my throat. Jasmine walks to hug Megan and it's to give me some semblance of peace with my thoughts. You never say the right thing when you need to. It's the curse of a writer.

"I didn't do anything. Your absence did this. You have no one to blame but yourself. Sometimes life throws curveballs, and you adjust. I think that hanging onto the past is a good thing until it turns into a detriment in your real life and your future. That's what happened to me. I became the things that happened to me in my youth." A tear falls from my chin and lands on the flowered blouse. "The evil translated into personality flaws. Your promises transformed into failed attempts at honor."

I laugh once. A painful cackle. "And I'm not my past anymore." Shaking my head, I stand straighter. "Good or bad, the past doesn't control me." I turn to Moose. He's watching me carefully. Like I'm a loaded gun about to fire. "You both deserve each other. Be happy," I say.

"You only have one life," I whisper. Mostly for my benefit, but I know Smith heard too. It's ironic, because he's had two.

CHAPTER TWENTY-FOUR

Smith

I'VE FUCKED UP EVERYTHING.

In a world where general safety isn't promised and evil villains are your next-door neighbors, that's a mighty feat to admit. It's hard to focus on work when my personal life is in such upheaval. It's hard to focus on work when part of the reason my life is in such upheaval is sitting next to me talking to my ex-fiancée on the phone. The high bay at work in San Diego is full of SEALs. We've been here all day, attending meeting after meeting.

Macs, the dude with perfect hair and a penchant for Armani T-shirts, saunters in through a side door. "We need the prettiest motherfuckers over here on this side of the room," he barks. "I'll need five. Maybe six if we have that many decent-looking men. It's for Hero Hair," he explains, smiling. It's the mission name, and I immediately know why we need to send good-looking guys.

Laughter breaks out, booming around the room. "Who is deciding who's the prettiest?" someone yells out.

It's a welcome change of subject.

Moose's voice and his words still carry. Megan moved in with him almost immediately after the book meeting.

I'm stuck at a house full of shit I don't want, lonely beyond belief. It's ironic now that I'm stationed in San Diego, there's no reason for me to be.

Zane stands. "I volunteer as tribute," he shouts, raising one arm in the air, three fingers pointed skyward.

"Sit down, dude," someone says. The tactics we have to employ are different than they are in usual war. It's a guessing game, but one that we're picking up on quickly. The head figures use financiers to back their initiatives. The financiers typically live an upper-class lifestyle. We've discovered it means lonely, drunk wives with loose lips. Zane argues his finer attributes but in the end gets shut down by Macs.

While the guys squabble about who has more symmetrical features and better abs, I think about how badly I fucked up with Carina. I don't have a dog in this fight. My looks are long gone. They send me when they want to scare people with sheer muscle mass and jagged scars—similar to the bad guy in superhero films. I feel like the bad guy.

It's hard to say who is at fault. Some would argue I am for trying to escape my feelings and for leading Megan on for so long. Others would say it was Carina for meddling in fate. I can't be mad at her for speaking the truth. I can be irritated she won't return my calls or emails. Her attorney returned one of my emails because she'd forwarded it to him. I'd asked a simple question about the book, but it was mostly begging for her to meet with me.

Never Forever is slated for a summer release, and with the current state of affairs, reading is the number one pastime in every age group. Given the subject matter, it's also highly anticipated. The military and all the facets of SEALs are a mystery. People know the basics, but chances are they don't know a real SEAL. That's different from actors portraying them in movies. It's real. It's life outside of combat. It's me. Advertisements are everywhere. Every single one reminding me of the only true love I'll ever experience. One that I was lucky to have while it lasted because it changed me—it saved me.

She's so damn beautiful. Her headshot side by side with the cover. She's smirking—her full, glossy lips tilted to one side. It's not the shy smile of a girl I met on the floor of a theater. It's the confident, knowing smile of a woman who has risen to such great heights that nothing in the world can touch her. Her brown hair is waving well past her shoulders, and her almond eyes are taunting me, reminding me what I'll never have again. At the rate I'm going, I don't know if I'll ever see those eyes again in person.

My stomach coils with anger. In a situation I can't control, my mind dives to dark places. It transports me back to a hospital bed when I was unable to move or talk or do anything for myself. Those were my darkest days, and this feeling right now is comparable to that.

"Moose. It's you. Get up here, you beautiful bastard," Macs commands.

Moose stands, laughs, and makes his way to the pretty group. Guys slap his back as he saunters to the other side of the room like he's won an award. I'm relieved. It means his conversation is finished and I don't have to hear the warble of her voice on the other end of his phone. Do I feel guilty? Yes. She made sure I wouldn't for long, though. She dove headfirst in with my best friend. It wouldn't surprise me in the least if they took our wedding date and made it their own. I wouldn't care.

Moose throws his arms in the air when he reaches his mark. "Thank you. Thank you. I'd like to thank the academy and my mother. Because without her genes, I'd look like a wolverine mated with a grizzly. Sorry, Dad. I love you," Moose says, throwing one arm out to take an awkward bow. "Most beautiful," he shouts in an accented tone.

Macs groans. "Okay, okay. Go to the meeting room and make sure your ready bags are packed."

Everyone sighs. We're tired. Several troops are overseas, but most of the SEALs are spread across the US. We've infiltrated big cities and small cities, going wherever there's a lead. We have to take big and small tips in the same manner because no one knows what something small may snowball into. "The rest of you, train."

I pull my cell out and check my messages. Nothing. "You should call her from the office line. She won't have that number blocked," Moose says over my shoulder.

"She has my number blocked?" I ask.

He shrugs. "I spoke with her the other day, and she's traveling this week. Manhattan, I think? Maybe LA.? PR is gearing up for the release." When he reads my face, he adds, "She called me, bro."

"I swear to God I will fucking kill you, Moose. End you—if you screw up this part of my life. Do you have feelings for Carina too? Do you want to adhere to polygamy just so you can fuck every woman I've ever been inside of?" It's harsh, and I know for a fact I've pissed him off. A few guys overhear and sidle in closer in case a punch is thrown. Fuck, I should throw a punch.

"Fuck you, Smith."

I push his chest, and he stumbles backward but rights himself quickly. "I've stayed quiet for too long. You don't get to ruin everything and talk to her too."

He holds his palms out in front of his body. "I don't want to fight you. I didn't ruin anything that wasn't already ruined. She's not yours anymore, either. Like I said, *she called me*."

Rage boils, and I think I will hit him—clock this

asshole in the face so many times that his face will never be considered pretty. "Why did she call you?"

He clears his throat. "Let's get out of here. The gym, yeah? We can talk somewhere else," he says, subtly glancing around us to force me to notice our audience. Everyone knows our business anyway, but he's right. I don't want to be the unstable bastard of the bunch. There's always one.

Brushing his shoulder on my way by, I storm out of the room and head for my locker. Someone catcalls, and another person growls. Goddamn animals.

Moose follows me. I hear his boots heavy on the cement floor.

"You're supposed to be my best friend," I say.

"I am your fucking best friend. I should have knocked you the fuck out in there, Smith. You're raving mad."

I turn. "I've lost everything. Everything."

He shakes his head. We're alone in the hallway leading to our cages. "You have your life. Or have you already forgotten how lucky you are to have that? I surely didn't forget. You haven't lost everything. She calls me to ask about you," he whispers. His gaze turns serious.

"Isn't that fucking bullshit? She forbids me from talking to her friends, and yet she's allowed to do whatever the hell she wants? She breaks up my engagement. Well, you both did that, and Carina gets to come out on the other side as the good guy." I'm vibrating with anger. I'm going to hit something, and I don't want it to be Moose. The wall is closest, and I punch it swiftly once. The crunch echoes, and blood sprays everywhere, splattering against the white stucco.

"Jesus Christ. I won't tell her that," he says, shaking his head. "The fact she cares enough to call me is a good sign. Go over there. I have to get to the meeting room. We're taking off tonight. Are you going to be okay?"

"I'll be fine," I growl. Grabbing my wounded fist, I pull it against my chest. "I'm going to call her from the office phone."

"That's a fabulous idea," Moose says, using a tone you'd use with a child. "Smith. I'm sorry. As fucked up as it sounds, I kind of did you a favor. Until you realize that, know I'm sorry. Okay?" He hasn't said that to my face yet. Part of me doesn't want to hear it, because it validates the fact that he disrespected our friendship. I meet his gaze only briefly. It's enough to tell exactly what he's apologizing for. Everything. "I'll see you soon." He clears his throat, unsure if I'm going to respond.

I nod. "Don't mention it. Kick ass," I reply.

He turns and leaves with a nod and smile. I've forgiven him, and I'm not sure I had anything to forgive. He's the better choice for Megan.

I try to put my fists through solid walls because of Carina. It was never fair to hold on to Megan. I was selfish in my pursuit to honor Henry's memory. I'm not ready to admit it, but Moose did do me a favor.

If I can't be true to Henry with my final promise, it makes me feel like he didn't exist at all. As more and more time passes, I can't recall certain things about him and our friendship. His memory is fading from existence in the opposite way of his death. His death and life were swift. I'm grasping at straws of his being. Of his memory. To keep him alive, I need to find my happiness. The way I see it, there's only one way to obtain that.

The office door is unlocked, and I head for the closest phone. I move a bag of almonds out of my way and dial to get an outside line. Like Moose said, Carina answers on the first ring.

"Hello?"

The number that pops up on her screen will seem odd: maybe only a few digits instead of a whole phone number. Horns blare in the background, and there's the static of people talking.

"Care," I reply, breathing out deeply. I clear my throat.

"Ben, is that you?"

My heart drops.

"Where are you calling me from?"

"Who the fuck is Ben?" I ask.

She waits a beat of two, then says, "Smith. Where are you?"

"Answer my question first."

"My boyfriend. What's up? Did my attorney not give you what you needed? I told him to answer any questions you have."

A female voice calls out for her. It must be Jasmine.

"You have to be joking," I reply. The hand holding the receiver shakes. I look down at the blood on my hand to watch it roll off and onto the desk. He'll forgive me. Whoever owns this desk has to forgive me. "To answer your question, I'm at work. I called you from here because you don't answer my calls or texts coming from my cell phone."

"I've been busy," she says. Like that's why she hasn't answered. "Listen, I'm in Gaslamp right now. I'm about to go into a meet and greet at the bookstore. Was there something you needed?" Her play at nonchalance is too good. It's ripping my heart out and slamming it back, like a rubber band vibrating. She's not in NYC or LA. She's here. Close.

I clear my throat. "I need to see you."

She remains silent for a while. I count my breaths. Nine. It takes her nine breaths to make a decision. "I'm not sure it's a good idea." She's moved away to somewhere quieter. The background noise has vanished.

"Why? Your boyfriend won't like it?" I'm so surprised about this turn of events I can't get angry about it. Yet.

"Because I'm finally doing well. I'm afraid if I see you I won't be able to control myself. I need to keep myself, Smith. I don't think you realize what it's taken to get over this. Whatever this was…with you. You have some idea because of *Never Forever*," she explains.

"Don't mention that, please." That fucking book tore my heart out of my chest while making me long for her so badly that I couldn't breathe. I read it three times in one week to see if it affected me differently when I wasn't surprised by what happened next. It did. Because it was honest. That's what makes it so good. The truth. That's also what makes it so painful.

"Still upset about your character?" she asks, eager to change the subject.

"What you don't realize is that this has been just as hard for me. Harder even. Forgetting you is impossible. And I'm not using some random girl to erase you. I need to see you, Carina. I'm glad you're doing well, but I'm not. I need you."

"It's taken me a long time to come to this conclusion and to have the courage to say this, but I'm not a second-place woman. I'm not the woman you get to run back to because Megan left you for Moose. I want to be someone's first choice—their only choice. Ben is my boyfriend, yes, but he doesn't erase you. You're still inside my soul like you'll remain for the rest of time, but to Ben I'm number one. There's not anyone else vying for his love. It's not complicated. He has helped me get over you in some ways. Your hold was so strong that I couldn't function in life. I've closed our chapter. Literally."

I run my bloody hand through my hair as panic sets in. "Don't say that. Never say that!" I yell. "You were never second place. I tried to do the right thing, and I fucked up. You said you understood that. You were always first. Always. Never, not for a second since the day I met you was there any doubt that you were the one for me. I fucked up. I'm sorry. I'm sorry. You have to give me another chance. Think about us together. You won't have that with anyone else." It's a bold statement, but one I think I can truthfully admit. She said so in the book.

"I gave you another chance, and you still chose differently. I won't even say you chose Megan because I don't think it was her you were choosing. It could have been any person, really. You chose your promise to a dead man over your love for me. It's not fair to put me in this twisted game. I've gotta go, okay?"

"Don't hang up on me. I need you." I feel out of control. Wild, even. I'm fearful of what I'll say and do next. I need to get out of here before I self-destruct.

"Smith, people are lined up to meet Greenleigh right now. It's the pre-release meet and greet. I have to go. As much as Jasmine helps me, I don't think she can pass for me when there's a poster of my face behind the table. I have a date tonight with Ben, but maybe we can get together another time?" Another time is as good as a nail in the proverbial coffin.

"Sure," I reply, voice monotone. "Goodbye, Greenleigh."

I hang up the phone softly, then taking it in both hands, I throw the fucker against the wall so hard it shatters into a million pieces. The door cracks when I slam it on my way out. I run out of the building so fast that people give me odd stares. I pay them no attention, and I don't respond when my brothers ask what's up. They can't help me right now.

When I pass a car in the parking lot, I catch sight of my reflection in the side window. Blood runs down my face from my knuckles. I'd forgotten. I take off my uniform jacket and wrap it around my hand in a makeshift bandage.

I'm supposed to be training right now, but there's only one thing on my mind. One task I need to complete. I look like an insane psycho, but maybe it will add to the desperation of my plea.

There are so many people here. It makes me uneasy. I'm in work mode and personal mode at the same time and that's a dangerous place to be. In uniform, I'm able to carry my weapon without issue, but my bloody appearance attracts a lot of attention. There are both men and women flooding the street outside of the bookstore. Parking was so crowded that I ended up in a lot several blocks away. It gave me a chance to scope out the situation from every angle. Two hundred people? Maybe even more? Some have copies of her book in their hands. Others clutch handbags.

Handbags are dangerous. I don't remember hearing about any events this large in San Diego since 9/11. There is security here, but not enough. Uneasiness washes over me in spades. My anger transforms into fear for her safety. Fuck. I swallow down the terror and function in stealth mode. I'd give anything to have on civvies right now. I slip my bloody jacket back on, remove my name tag and trident for anonymity, and run my hands over my face and hair to try to smear away the dried blood. I'm out of regulation, but it's a chance I'm going to take.

I enter the back of the crowd and try to keep a scowl off my face as I assess threats. These people look harmless, but harmless is the new norm. I've hunted harmless for months now. It sends a shiver down my spine. I should call for backup, but I'm leading with my heart right now. I nod at a security guard, who narrows his eyes in my direction. When I'm close enough to the window, I chance a glance away from the crowd and see Carina sitting down at a small table in the center of the store. She looks like a sitting duck. A beautiful, stunning author who wrote a novel about a SEAL: a target. The prettiest target there ever was.

She fixes her hair, pulling it over one shoulder as Jasmine sits next to her and brushes an eyelash from the top of Carina's cheek. She smiles, but I see a sadness in the pull of her mouth. From talking to me. I did that. It makes me happy and fucking miserable at the same exact time. I'm caught up in thoughts when the doors open. It's like cattle pouring into a barnyard. Carina's eyes widen as she sees the flood of people, and she smiles a false grin.

I watch her. Caught up in this moment viewing a woman I don't know. The author. The person she's hidden behind for so many years.

Several security guards direct two groups of people to the sides, and the line thins outside the door. Carina is already distracted talking to her visitors and signing books. I edge my way out of the line and head for the rear of the store. The door is propped open with a brick, which makes for easy access. I slide in undetected and let the door close to a locking position behind me. Now it's secure. Lazy security guards are worthless here. Finding her is easy.

The voices of all of her admirers are loud and raucous. Excitement reverberates in the air. No one is worried about an attack. They're just happy. It lets me calm down a touch.

Taking a deep breath, I count in my head until I'm no longer visibly upset. I push my way through the side of the crowd until I'm the next person in line. A few people groan, but no one says anything once they see my uniform or realize my sheer size and appearance. Add in the blood, and I might as well be a dirty video game character from *Call of Duty 3*.

"Next," Jasmine says. They're both so distracted their eyes aren't even registering the people who are next in line.

I walk up first before the person in the other group and hold out my arm to halt the woman who is supposed to meet Carina from that side. She takes a step back, eyes frightened. Perfect. This, right here, is me self-destructing.

I stop in front of her table and stare at the top of her head. She's signing a flyer of some sort, ready to give it to the next person in line. Jasmine sees me first, and her mouth opens in a small O.

"Greenleigh," I rasp.

Carina swallows and slowly tilts her face up. "Oh my god," she whispers, covering her mouth. Tears form in her eyes immediately. "Are you okay?" My attempt at cleaning myself up didn't work.

I shake my head. "I'm not okay. I haven't been okay. Not since the moment I met you," I reply. I place my hands on the table in front of me. The bloody one leaves a smear on the white tablecloth. Finally, two security guards approach, but they don't touch me.

Jasmine stands and tells them it's fine and leads them away to control the crowds.

"I can't do this right now, Smith," she whispers, tears flowing unmercifully down her perfect face.

"Why not? Because of this?" I pick up one of the books on her table and hold it in the air. "This is just fiction. Right, Greenleigh?"

Carina sobs and covers her face. "I can't."

"Fine. You don't have to. But I'm going to. I love you. I love you. I love you. You can't love someone you never had," I say, quoting her from *Never Forever*. "I disagree. Because I love you, and I never had you. Not the way I was supposed to, anyway."

She swallows, puts her hands down, but remains sitting. There are gasps from behind us, and small rumblings of conversation begin in the masses. I turn toward them. A few women shirk back, afraid of what I'm going to do. I raise the book in the air again. "I love this woman more than anything in this godforsaken world. Before the attacks even, when the world was a beautiful place, she was still the thing I loved the most. The only thing I wanted to keep. The only person I've ever loved so much that words fail to define my love," I yell.

Several women start crying. Others put their hands over their mouths as they realize the magnitude of what is happening. "Is this part of the show? Is this a skit?" someone calls out.

The smart thing to do would be to agree with this, that yes, it's a show and I'm an actor hired to portray the asshole from her novel. I'm already in too deep. I dig in my heels.

I shake my head and turn to face Carina again. "No, this isn't part of the show. This is real life. I love you, and I'm sorry I hurt you. I'm sorry I wasn't there for you when I should have been. I made a mistake. You are the only thing I want. I need you. I do," I say. I bring the book to lay it over my heart. "We are real. This book is fiction."

She stands, keeping her gaze aimed at my face. "Oh, Smith. I can't believe you're doing this right now."

"I wanted your attention," I call out.

"You got it. And the hundreds of people here." She

nods to the camera to our right. "And the millions that will see this on television."

My heart skips a beat. I didn't see the camera. I was too transfixed with her proximity. It's surreal being this close to her after all this time.

"I'm the douchebag in this book!" I shout. People cheer—shouts and hoots of praise and boos of disapproval.

Carina hangs her head. "I love you too," she whispers quietly. "You douchebag."

"Forever?" I ask.

Her chest rises and falls quickly, nervous behavior from a woman who is making one of the most important decisions of her life. Her lips pressed in a firm line, they curl up in the corner. "And always."

We stare at each other, the table separating us. I catch my breath, and she loses hers. "I need to do something then."

Carina shakes her head, laughing, her tears changing from sad to happy. "Go ahead. You have a captive audience." She leans closer, assuming I'm going to kiss her. Instead, I take the book in my hand and flip to page 452, the beginning of the end, and rip the last forty pages from the book.

With wide eyes and mouth ajar, Carina watches. I crumple them with my right fist, the one still leaking blood everywhere, and throw the pages on the floor. Then I hop over the table and take her in my arms.

"This is the ending," I whisper so only she can hear.

She blinks away a tear, and like on autopilot, her arms rise up to hook around my neck. I close my eyes, breathe her in, and relish this moment like it may be my last. She reaches up, I bring my head down, and she presses her lips against mine in a kiss that fixes everything.

I'm holding, tasting, feeling her—my home. My love. My life. "My god, this feels so good," I say, pulling away.

Her eyes are still closed. "I can't believe it feels like this. After everything."

I nod in agreement.

Carina leans away to look at me. "Are you okay?"

"I am now."

"You committed book murder," she says.

Grinning widely, I say, "You did first."

She lifts and lowers one shoulder. "You should acknowledge your fans, Smith." It's only now that I hear the applause and the loud screams.

With Carina in my arms, I turn around.

"I'm not the douchebag anymore!" I yell.

CHAPTER TWENTY-FIVE
Carina

HE'S THERE when I get home. The sight of his truck in the driveway gives me goose bumps. It's excitement, something I've only had in small doses throughout my life. Smith is sitting inside the cab with the engine running even though I'm sure he has a house key.

Emotionally, I'm exhausted. Physically, I'm drained. Both of those things take a back seat when I think about how amazing it felt to have him in my arms today. When he sees me pull in, he hops out of his truck quickly and opens the car door for me.

"Have you been here since you left the bookstore?" I ask. I finished the meet and greet, and Smith left because of the crazy commotion his declaration caused. After that spectacle, I answered so many questions I wasn't sure what was real and what was a lie. That would always be the problem.

He sighs. "I had a lot of thinking to do," he says.

I grab my handbag and a few other totes with my supplies and step out. "Uh-oh. That doesn't sound like the start of a happy story," I reply.

He kisses me. Right here in the driveway. Like we're in a bedroom naked with the lights off. It takes my breath away and steals all thoughts I had moments before. Kissing Ben never felt like this. Not even by a fraction. I chalked it up to heartbreak, but now I realize the problem was larger than that. The problem was I'd already tasted *this*.

His hands make their way into my hair, and it tingles every place he touches. My stomach is light, and I'm so turned-on, it's like no time has passed at all. That thought scares me into caution.

"You should have gone in. Poppet is all by herself," I say, pecking his mouth in a sweet kiss.

"I want *you* all by yourself," Smith replies, pulling me closer.

Truly, I can't resist. I lean into his chest and bury my face in his clean T-shirt. He's changed since the show this afternoon. A white bandage wraps the knuckles on his right hand.

"I can breathe again, Care. I can breathe." Smith tightens his grip like he fears I'll vanish into thin air.

"Let's go somewhere," I say. "The park. I haven't been able to go anywhere at night. You can abuse your handy ID to get us there, right?"

Reluctantly, Smith pulls away from our embrace. He runs the back of his knuckles down my face. It's where Roarke hit me. "Yes. Let's go. Poppet?" he asks, smiling.

We agree to go in and say hello to the cat and then leave. Poppet is sleeping on my bed but stands when I enter the room. She looks between Smith and me. "She's not used to anyone else in the house," I explain.

"Not even Ben?" Smith asks, leaning against the doorway. The way he's holding himself back is admirable. I know exactly what he wants to do and how badly he wishes he were in this room. On this bed. With me. I know because I feel the same way.

I sit on the edge of the bed, and Poppet lands in my

lap with a cute jump. I kiss her small head and stroke her fur. "No, Smith. I can't have a man in this house."

He palms his chest with his bandaged hand. "I'm a man in this house."

I roll my eyes and stand. "You pay for this house, and this is our house. It will always be our house. I called Ben on the way home," I say, clearing my throat.

Smith stands and shifts his weight to the other side. "And?"

"He called me a lying bitch. Before you get upset, I am. I told him I was over you when we started dating. I called you bad things. I also told him *Never Forever* was fiction. It is...but it's not. I lied to him."

"A bitch, though?" Smith asks, lips pressed in a firm line. He raises one brow in question.

Kissing Poppet one more time, I plop her back on the bed and brush her white hair off my dress. Walking toward Smith, I say, "My grandma always told me to do two things in person. Give bad news and apologize. Both of those probably needed to happen, and I called him instead. I broke up with him by way of a phone call on the night we were planning on having sex for the first time."

His eyes just about bulge out of his head. He runs a hand through his hair and shakes his head. "Shit, Carina. TMI. I have visions of you that are so disturbing that I could commit murder right now."

I slide my hands around his waist as he slips his hands around me. "I didn't want to, but that's usually part of moving on. He...was a good guy. His timing was unlucky, and his selection was faulty."

He kisses me on the top of the head. "We should go. Before my thoughts shift to me having sex with you instead of some dude named Ben." He thrusts his hips forward so I feel his erection. "Oh, wait. They've already rounded that corner and decided to take a detour to Blow Job Street, too."

We laugh. I kiss his neck. He groans. I melt. We make it out to his truck. Barely. He knows as well as I do that we need to talk. It's been a long time since we've had any kind of relationship, let alone a sexual one. The guards at the security checkpoint by my house know him now. They wave him on, and we're parking his truck in the empty lot just as the setting sun turns the sky a vibrant pink and red.

Smith tells me he wants to go to our tree—the one with the gangly roots that protrude through the ground like angry waves at the beach. It's a bit of a walk, but it's so silent and the night so temperate I'm happy to be outside. Especially with his hands wrapped around me.

The tree looms before us. Tall and old, leaves and roots untouched by the disaster that is our new world. I suppose I thought it would look different after all this time and after everything that has transpired since our last visit. "It's beautiful," I whisper. Smith nods in agreement and takes my hand in his. I have our park blanket tucked under my arm.

The last rays of today's light beam on the trunk, and it's a sign. Some insane, unpredictable sign that we are where we're supposed to be. Right now and forever. We sit down next to a tangled root that has several other ones fused around it and stare off in the distance. The top of the old church is visible above the treetops, almost disappearing with daytime.

"It's where it started," Smith says, leaning back on his elbows. His whole demeanor has shifted. A calmness—a fragment of peace that wasn't there any time I've seen him since our separation.

"Don't tell me it's where it ends. I don't take the Romeo and Juliet comparison literally, you know?"

He pulls me toward him. My head finds his chest—his heartbeat.

"I missed you so much, Smith," I whisper.

"Miss isn't even the correct word." He clears his throat, emotion already taking over. "I didn't feel like I belonged anywhere. Nothing made sense. I held onto an old promise because it was all I had that made sense. I lost myself more when I lost you than I did when I lost my memory. I'm sorry."

I roll on top of him, straddling his hips so I can look down and see his eyes. "Don't apologize anymore. Make me promises instead. Those mean more."

"I'd promise you anything right now. Not just because you're sitting on top of my dick either," he replies.

I smile. "Can you promise forever?" My voice shakes as I ask a question I never dared to ask of anyone else.

He sits up, a smile beaming bright on his beautiful face. Grabbing my face, he kisses me once, then again. Once more just to taste me, and I sigh in contentment. "Marry me," he orders. "Take my name and let's make babies. They'll make babies, and our love will live on forever, Carina. Marry me. Be the person you want to be. And I'll be happy to be by your side for as long as we have left on this earth."

I snort an ungodly awful noise as I'm trying to conceal my tears and emotion. Kissing the side of his cheek, the scarred one, I lean into his ear. "Only if you'll walk me down the aisle," I reply.

He leans away to look at me. "Is that a yes?"

I nod. "Of course it's a yes. I'll marry you. I'll make babies with you. I'll love you forever. You're the only thing in this world that gives me hope. The world could crumble around me...literally, but if you're with me, I'll be happy."

Smith hugs me, and the embrace turns lethal when he

kisses my ear and then my neck. I lean back to give him access to my collarbone and the front of my neck. "Are you okay right here?" he asks, his words a rush of breath and desire.

I kiss him as an answer. He lies down and takes me with him on top. "No one is outside right now. The curfew is good for something," I reply. It wouldn't have stopped me anyway.

"I want to make love to my fiancée, but I'm so excited I'm not sure what I'm about to do to you will be construed as love. You understand?" he asks, his hands unzipping my dress quickly.

I slide the dress off my shoulders to expose my lacy bra.

"You want to fuck me," I say.

He grins. "My god, yes."

Darkness conceals us, but not so much that we can't see each other clearly. I take his T-shirt off slowly so as to not harm his hand. His smile is lustful but steadfast. He can't stop smiling. Standing over him, he slides the dress and my panties off with gentle fingers. Being naked outdoors feels free. It feels naughty, the wind and air meeting places clothing is supposed to touch instead.

When his jeans and underwear are down by his ankles, I position myself between his knees and lean down, but stop right before I put him in my mouth. "This first?" I ask.

"You're trying to kill me with anticipation. Yes, yes, this moment right here is what my dreams are made of. Not so much the blow job itself, but you right there, eyes looking at me, mouth ready, my cock hard. This. Snap-shot," he says then groans. "Don't wait anymore, though."

I bite my bottom lip, and he groans some more. One hand wrapped around him, I spit as much as my dry mouth can muster and put him in my mouth. Working all the way down as far as I can, I make sure to move my tongue along the underside of his dick. He juts his hips to get more of his length down my throat. I lick as I move my hand and mouth at the same time. He likes it when I take him deep, so I focus on every other stroke deep-throating him.

He makes noises of complete bliss as I work him into a frenzy. He tosses my name into the praises every several seconds, but for the most part he's in nirvana, his hands on my head. When he tells me he's about to come, I grab his balls with my free hand and tug a little. Smith thrusts into my mouth one more time, his movement jagged and uncontrolled. Then I pull away quickly.

"What about now?" I ask. "Sex now?"

He's panting, a frustrated melody of groans and rasps. "No, your turn now. If I put my dick inside you right now, I'll come before it even starts." He spins me on my back with ease and licks my nipples. "You taste sweet. My god. This. I've missed this so much."

His warm mouth on my breasts sends tingling over every inch of my skin. I've missed this too. I've missed so much that I finally feel whole after being empty. His full, wet lips glide down my stomach. Merely lips and wet kisses turn into his wet tongue diving between my legs. There's no teasing. It's an assault of flicking and sucking furiously. It's a pleasure so unbearable that I almost forget where we are and how much time has passed.

"That. Keep doing that," I say. I arch my back, and he pushes my hips back down with strong hands. He keeps one arm draped over my stomach to control my movements. The other hand is busy rubbing my clit in small, firm circles. It's the quickest I've ever come. It's explosive and out of control. I scream out and tilt my head back as the waves hit me. One by one. Cementing the decision we just made. "I'll never not want this, Smith," I rasp. "Being with you like this is the only thing that feels right."

The truth, spoken out loud, sounds so good. Better than a million lies to make myself feel something after he left.

He sucks my clit one more time, wipes his lips off on my lower stomach, and slides up to kiss my cheek. "Promise?" he asks, lips brushing the side of my ear.

I nod. "Yes." When I kiss his mouth, I taste myself. I lick his lips, tracing the outline with the tip of my tongue. "Right now, I want this." I grab his dick between our sweaty bodies. "Inside me."

I guide him to my entrance and tease the head with my wetness. I force just the tip inside, and we both groan in pure bliss. The sensations are almost overwhelming. I want to scream and cry and come around him over and over, and it hasn't even started. "Do that again," he says, burying his face in my neck. "I want to feel that again."

"Don't move," I command. Squeezing him in my palm with a firm grip, I move my hips up and swirl them in a circle. His hard cock grazes my wet hole but doesn't enter. The next circle I make, I press a little harder. His cock goes in. Not all the way, but a little more than the time before. "Like that?"

"Just like that," he rasps.

I repeat the movement, but this time I grab his ass and push him all the way inside me.

"Fuck, yes," Smith hisses. He kisses my lips as we relish in our connection. He doesn't move at first, but we both want it so badly that I know it won't be long. His tongue dives in my mouth, and his hands fist in my hair.

"Your turn," I say.

"Permission to move?"

My core clenches in anticipation. "Please," I moan, rocking my hips.

He doesn't need any more than that. He begins thrusting into me with fury. His lips turn into teeth. He bites my bottom lip with a smile still on his mouth and absolute lust shining in his eyes. The sight is intoxicating.

"This is where I want to be, Care," he says in between kissing me. He closes his eyes as he continues his punishing thrusts. I raise my hips to meet each one stroke for stroke, the wetness and friction proving to be too much for my willpower to handle. "This is everything," he breathes, his voice ragged with desire.

I moan as a reply and tell him I'm coming and to keep the pace just where it's at. Running my hands over the sculpted planes of his back and backside, I feel his scars, the rigid indents where smooth flesh used to be. He's home.

"You're mine," I whisper. A claim I'm more than ready to accept for the rest of time. I'm his fiancée.

He dips his face into the crook of my neck as we come at the same time. Smith clutches me tightly, and I wrap my legs around his waist to keep him deep inside me. There's no one to see this moment, two naked bodies combined as one.

But I think if there were, they wouldn't second-guess what it meant. Smith is kissing my forehead and stroking my face rashly, roughly asking me if he's dreaming. I'm staring at him like he's the only man left on the face of the planet, and I can't bear to separate from him.

He eventually does pull out of me, a reluctant feat that just stirs the lust inside our hearts even more. We end up making love again, this time slower, more cautious of what it means, excited for what we've done.

We promised each other forever.

And that almost never happens.

Not in our world. Not where family turns a blind eye to abuse, or when bad men prey on insecurities and weaknesses. Not when a man loses brothers to bad men with ill intentions. No, forever is a pipe dream. We're lucky enough to have right now, and we're going to make the most of it. If luck is on our side, because we are surely owed some of that, time will grace us with the ability to love each other so much that the amount of months and years doesn't matter.

We will take the dim reality of the state of this world and color it with something spectacular.

Epilogue
CARINA

THE TREE IS DECORATED BEAUTIFULLY. I made sure it looked perfect before I went back home to get dressed for the wedding. This isn't a typical wedding, and not just because we aren't technically supposed to be having a wedding in Balboa Park, but because everything is...different. Smith's best man is married to his ex-fiancée. Megan is not only attending, she's making sure that everything runs smoothly. That includes giving us a heads-up if security shows up while we're saying our vows.

I'm not nervous because I'm getting married to Smith. I'm scared it won't be what I envisioned. The wedding day is the easy part. It's forever that proves to be difficult in marriages. That's why, combined with the attacks, we decided to have a small ceremony and reception. We've lived together for a while now and there haven't been any surprises yet. Sure, we argue about who left a centimeter of milk in the jug without tossing it and our different showering habits. I jump out of the shower soaking wet without a towel, and he has to dry off completely before he takes one step from the stall. But everything that matters in a marriage? It's been there from the word go. The love. The sex. The compromise. The push and pull of two different hearts headed in the same direction.

Smith and I have lived without each other, and it's a place we never want to return to again. I need him. He needs me. More importantly, we want each other. We choose each other every single day. The way he looks at me gives me an indescribable high. It's as if everything in the world is perfect. I need that confidence.

"I swear to God, Carina, if you don't stay on schedule, I'm going to come in there and chop your hair off!" Jasmine screeches through our bedroom door. "Smith is already at the park with the guys. They're setting up chairs, so you know we have to be there quick. Before anyone realizes what we're doing."

I laugh and pull the door open.

"Fuck. You look beautiful," she says. Her eyes widen as I spin around, the cotton maxi dress swinging around my feet.

"It's perfect, right?" I ask when I catch a glimpse of myself in the full-length mirror.

She nods. "I've been fielding PR phone calls all day. The masses are expecting some high-class wedding in the Gaslamp between their two favorite sweethearts."

Ah, the facet of my world I hadn't thought of yet today. *Never Forever* was a smashing success. The movie is filming as we speak in a production lot in Los Angeles. I stay out of the limelight as much as I can, but Jasmine dips me in it every once in a while.

For all the success of *Never Forever*, the next novel I wrote as a companion novel was received even better. I think it's because I wrote it from two points of view instead of just the heroine. I added Smith's point of view and gave it a happily ever after. His head is a more lucrative place to reside in. It's the running joke in our house.

"Poppet is in her soft cage on the bed. I have her leash and harness in the side bag. Make sure she doesn't escape. That's your only job today!" I bark at Jasmine. "No one will know to look in the park. Weddings aren't allowed there." I smile to myself. Sex isn't allowed there either, but we'll still sneak away to ravage each other under that tree where we started over.

"I still think it's weird Smith is walking you down the aisle. I mean, I get it. You're like a lone soul in the family department, but couldn't anyone else give you away to the person you're being given to?"

I shake my head and explain the Barbie story. She laughs, calls me insane, but in the end agrees that it's a sweet notion.

I look at myself one last time in the mirror. Wide, excited eyes and not a hair out of place. I'm ready for this. The happiness is almost unbearable, my stomach flipping and turning at the thought of seeing Smith in his suit—my cheeks flushed with the promise of a night full of passion-fueled lovemaking.

Jasmine prattles on and on as we drive. She talks too much when she's nervous. I fist a handkerchief in the palm of my hand as we pull into the parking lot. I see our tree from here, and a few people dressed nicely are walking around.

"Take a deep breath," Jasmine says. "This is your day." Then she squeals in excitement. It's more than my day—so much more.

Smiling, I look down at the square of fabric in my hands. It was cut from my favorite floral dress my grandmother made. The one I wore until it turned into a shirt. The dress that kept me company on the nights when no one came to save me. I get choked up for a moment but then laugh when I remember how happy it made me when she gave me this dress. It was packaged in a pretty box with a purple flower bow on top.

I let one tear fall down my face and land on the small square. And then I promise myself this is the last time I'll cry today. At least in the name of old memories.

"He said not to get a bouquet. That he was taking care of it," I explain to Jasmine when she asks if I have everything and then freaks out when she realizes the main bridal thing is missing.

Poppet meows from her bag when she hears my voice.

"Put her on the leash," I say.

Jasmine sighs, says a silent false prayer that her Louis is nowhere in sight, and does as I ask. Poppet walks alongside her just like a small dog. I beam at my trained cat.

"Groom. Twelve ow, ow, hot baby o'clock, Miss Bride," Jasmine says.

My heart picks up, and I raise my gaze slowly until I see the most entrancing sight I've ever seen. Smith waves, his face a wash of pure joy, a smile so wide and so white that I automatically break out in my own grin.

I wave back, a small gesture. I didn't want surprises on our wedding day or a revealing of the bride. Mostly because he makes me feel happy and safe, and if there's a time when a woman needs that, it's right now when nerves and emotions are running high.

Jasmine leaves, Poppet prancing next to her as she excuses herself to go make sure we're ready to begin. The few guests we have are seated, and there are probably only minutes before a pregnant Megan rushes to tell us it's time to begin. The small rolling hill hides him for a short time before I see him walking up toward me. Closer and closer that beautiful man comes, until he stops in front of me.

"Now that I've confirmed that I am indeed the luck-iest man alive, I need to know how you're doing," Smith says. "You *look* like the most gorgeous creature on the planet. How do you feel?"

I laugh. "Happy. Equally as lucky as you. Excited. Nervous excited. I want to kiss you right now," I say.

Smith bites his lip and pretends to be upset.

"We can't kiss yet, Carina. What will our guests think?"

Gently he places his hand on the side of my face. I lean into it and release a sigh of contentment.

"I don't care what they think. I need you," I whisper, eyes still closed.

Smith kisses me. A soft flutter of his lips on mine. "I don't want to ruin your makeup. You look like a work of art."

I lean into him and kiss him one more time. The response he has on me is immediate. My heart rate slows, and my nerves disappear.

He's had one hand behind his back since we met. "Are you going to give me that surprise or what?" I ask.

He clears his throat and his face goes solemn. Eyes down, he brings his hand in front of him. It's a bouquet of intricately folded paper flowers. "This is your bouquet," he says, meeting my gaze.

"They are absolutely beautiful," I say, reaching out for them. I want to look more closely. They truly are stun-ning. The petals are meticulously folded and curled, and the stems long and detailed.

He shakes his head and draws one out of the bunch and hands it to me. "There is a flower in this bunch for every one of our most cherished memories," he says, clearing his throat again. I look closer at the one he just put in my hand, and the world tilts on its axis.

"*Never Forever,*" I say, tears springing to my eyes. "Pages from *Never Forever*?"

"You're holding the first time we met," he explains. "And this one is folded from the pages of our first kiss." He extends another black-and-white bloom. I take it and put it next to the other one.

"Oh my gosh. I can't believe you did this," I say. "No one has ever done anything this special for me before in my life." The significance is so profound I'm sure no one ever will.

"No one has given me a love story," Smith replies. "Our first, *ahem,*" he says, smirking. "That one was a challenge to fold. I kept wanting to take a break to uh, take care of business."

I laugh and cover my mouth with my free hand.

"I spent about twenty hours on YouTube figuring out how to fold them perfectly. It's your bridal bouquet. I wanted to do your words justice."

I squint down at the three flowers and see words that trigger the memories. He hands me another one, and I add it to the bunch, the paper smooth against my hand and the words bleeding into my heart. "I love you," I tell him in a silent lull before he hands me the last one. He doesn't give it to me, though. He tucks it in his back pocket and extends me his bent arm.

"Let's get married first. I'm going to keep this one for good luck."

I wipe away a few more stubborn tears and take his proffered arm.

Linked, we walk down the grass-carpeted aisle up to our tree. My friend plays the violin, a sweet melody that carries on the cool air, and Poppet stands next to Jasmine. The officiant is waiting with a smile on her face and a book in her hand. We exchange very simple vows. Vows that bind us. Vows that will keep up. Vows that we will forever treasure and, most importantly, honor.

It's a short ceremony that tastes like a sweetness I never dared to dream of. It sounds like a light breeze and birds chirping. It fills me completely with a profound sense of self. When Smith leans over and kisses me after we are declared man and wife, I know without a shadow of a doubt life dealt me a certain hand so I would grasp my future tightly—cherish it fully.

We've greeted our few guests, and they have left to head to the restaurant where we will all celebrate. Smith and I steal a quick moment by the tree, holding each other close and talking about the ceremony. Moose cleans up chairs while keeping a hawk-like gaze on Megan and her clipboard-wielding hands. Smith's family, all of them, were the most happy about our union. We laugh at the fact that his nephew fell over his own two feet while heading down to his seat, and we kiss when we talk about our first kiss as a married couple.

"Let me ask you a question," Smith says.

I fold my arms across my chest in mock irritation. "I'm the one who asks the questions around these parts. Or have you already forgotten in the cloud of marital bliss?"

"Would you have married the person if a different man answered your in search of ad?" he asks, keeping his mouth in a tightly drawn line. I see the smile in his eyes, though.

I scoff. "That's offensive, but I still love you," I proclaim. I run my hand down the front of his suit and stop right at his waistband. "You're the only one I want to undress tonight." I bite my lip and cock my head to the side.

"I know." A smile appears on his face. It's a little

crooked. "I love you, too." He extends the last flower to me and sighs deeply.

"This one is our happily ever after," he says.

I shake my head. "Not in *Never Forever*." The editors wouldn't let me change that ending in a million years. It's what made it so memorable.

Smith shifts from one foot to the other. Looking over my shoulder and then meeting my gaze, he explains, "I wrote it myself."

I widen my eyes in shock and immediately look down at the typed words on the last flower, squinting to see anything that might spoil the plot. "I can't open it or I'll ruin the flower!" I say, turning it over to look at the bottom and carefully peeking in the center of the folds.

Smith laughs and takes my face in his. With his beautiful eyes boring into my own, he says, "That's the point, Care. That's the whole point."

I nod, put the flower in the bunch, and let fate weave its way into our hearts.

Always Forever,
Greenleigh Ivers

He plays to win. She refuses to be a prize.

Macs Newstead is a Navy SEAL who thrives on control, precision, and staying unattached. Combat is his comfort zone, and love? Just a liability he's never had time for. With charm as sharp as his aim, Macs lives for the mission—and nothing else.

Teala Smart built her yoga studio from the ground up, trading emotional entanglements for ambition. Fiercely independent and laser-focused, she doesn't do drama—or relationships. But when fate throws a certain cocky SEAL into her path, everything she's sworn off starts to look dangerously tempting.

What begins as a clash of wills sparks a connection neither of them can ignore. But when a mission goes sideways and secrets surface, Macs and Teala are forced to confront the one thing they've both avoided: vulnerability.

Can two lone wolves learn to fight for something other than themselves, or will the fire between them burn it all down?

AVAILABLE SEPTEMBER 2025

Why The Real
SEAL Series?

I wanted to begin a new series with my favorite types of characters, but I wanted to approach the novels a little differently. SEALs are stereotyped more frequently than they are not. Even I'm guilty of a joke or two. (I can't even type Froghog without giggling.) How many alpha, top-dog, high-and-tight-haired (even though SEALS do NOT wear this haircut), throbbing-muscled SEALs are out there? So many multiplied by infinity. Of course these reasons are some of the main reasons we love them. My characters will have those characteristics (for the most part), but they will also have a little more depth, a look into the real personas behind their main "label."

What and who is left behind in the wake of countless deployments and years of training trips? What does life look like when a SEAL sheds the tough exterior? How does that affect their lives and relationships?

In an attempt to shine an authentic light on the fictional characters I create, I came up with this new series of novels. While their stories are pulled straight out of my imagination, their qualities are genuine. A truthful look at the men we love, and sometimes love to hate. (Sorry, it's inevitable!) If you've followed my novels from the beginning, you know the type of men I like to write. I will never deviate from accuracy. I will write characters that are flawed and cringe worthy. Others will be so perfect it may raise a brow or two. Guess what? Both types exist side by side in this world and in the Teams.

I've had close contact with a REAL, live Navy SEAL, not a character in a novel. These stories (all of them) are my cathartic therapy. I share them with you in hopes you will enjoy the ride, or to merely offer another point of view you may have never considered before.

Most authors sprinkle truth into their stories. It makes relatable tales. This series is a touch different, a dash more. I hope the REAL SEAL novels capture your heart the way they thrive in mine. Macs and Teala are up next!

Thank You

Thank you to the countless people who make my stories a reality. To my beta readers who read first-draft chicken scratch, you are superheroes. Julie, for tearing every word to shreds and making me contemplate the inner workings of my character's brains. My editor, Emily, who has abilities I'm not capable of understanding. Thank you for deleting seven hundred commas in every manuscript.

My kids deserve thanks for accepting less of me to make my dreams a reality. I love you so much my heart almost explodes when I think of you.

Thank you to Critter. For everything you are and everything you are not. My every success is because I have you supporting me (near and far.) Hopefully by the time you're able to read this, we are making out instead of reading.

Rachel grew up in a small, quiet town full of loud talkers. Her words were always only loud on paper. She has been writing stories and creating characters for as long as she can remember. CRAZY GOOD and SET IN STONE, and TIME AND SPACE, three of her Navy SEAL novels are INTERNATIONAL BESTSELLERS. After living in San Diego, Virginia Beach, and then Fairfax, VA, she now resides in colorful Colorado with her badass husband, two children, her Sphynx cat, & her dog, Polly.

www.racheljrobinson.com
Rachel Robinson's Racy Readers